# VICKIE VAN HELSING

## THE FIRST BITE

A.J. GREA

Edited by R.M. Collins

Front and back cover design by A.J. Grea

Library of Congress Cataloging-in-Publication Data

Incorporated, Fiction Factory.

Vickie Van Helsing: The First Bite by A.J. Grea – 4th ed.

p.  cm.

Summary: Learning she is a descendant of the great Abraham Van Helsing, a teenage girl must fulfill her destiny and save the world from a newly resurrected Count Dracula.

ISBN-13: 978-1-968152-09-3

2      3      4      5      6      7      8      9      10

[1. Horror — Fiction.   2. Vampires — Fiction   3. Monsters — Fiction

4. Schools — Fiction]

To Robert

…who has never stopped believing.

# NAUSEA

I wish I could puke.

If I could hurl with enough force, maybe these butterflies would fly from my gut. Commencement—it sounds so important. Tonight I graduate; you'd think I'd be pumped, and in some ways, I am. Rutgers High is something I won't have to deal with any longer, right? That alone should be enough to thrill anyone. I mean, I didn't even think I'd make it to graduation. Wait, let me rephrase that—I didn't think I'd *live* to see graduation. Sounds dramatic, huh?

My name is Vickie Jenkins, or at least I thought that was my name for the first seventeen years of my plain-as-toast life. Plain? Yeah, and I liked it that way. I found it best early on to be *cool incognito*, to be the hip chick who hid herself in the background. The less attention given to me, the better. When you stand out, people tend to expect things from you, and sometimes you don't want to deliver. Not that I hate school, really—I love learning. I just don't dig the people who attend school with me. Actually, I don't dig many people in general.

Why?

Because I hate stupid people.

They have a tendency to frazzle my fragile nervous system and make me want to claw their eyes out. So, you can immediately sense that I'm a smartass, right? It's something I try to control; however, stupidity annoys me because it's not something that you can fix with a defrag on the mental operating system.

Fate didn't bless me with perfect looks, a pristine fashion sense, or undeniable charm, but it did bless me with the smarts—well, smarts and a little something extra I wasn't aware of at the time. Frankly, if I had to choose a gift, I'd choose brains. The Populars are going to learn that looks fade, but smarts last forever. *Populars*—that's what I call them: the ones who are seemingly perfect in every way. Well, let me tell you, they aren't.

So, my real name? Okay, get ready for it, because you're going to laugh. Wait for it …

*Vickie Van Helsing.*

See, you're laughing, and that's rude, dude. Yes, and I do mean the monster-hunting, holy-water-sprinkling Van Helsing. Okay, so maybe the name Van Helsing doesn't refer to the super-hot archangel Hugh Jackman badass, but it still means *warrior of the wicked*. Vampires? Monsters? Oh, yeah, they were out there, and they were all over us, but I'm hoping that I've taken care of them.

Why?

Because more than stupid people, I hate *dead* people.

You roll your eyes, and that's cool, because at first I didn't believe it either. Kyle, the creepiest of us all, didn't even believe it. Kyle Cooper? He's my best friend, the Rutgers High horror fanatic who knows everything, and I mean *everything*, there is to know about the gorrific.

Why am I telling you this? Well, supernatural things seem to *arise* at the most inopportune moments. So, you'll need to pay attention, you know, just in case you want to live to see *your* graduation night. I don't blame you for being skeptical. I've read the interviews and police statements dozens of times. I've listened to the tales repeatedly, and I still don't believe it! Those of us involved spent countless hours telling our stories to reporters and authorities who would just stare at us as if we were from another planet.

There are those who've tried to deny the facts, but I can guarantee that what I'm about to tell you is real. We only pretend as if nothing überfreaky happened, but we know the big, ugly, bloodsucking truth.

Go ask anyone about the Rutgers High Halloween Ball and they will tell you, maybe in a whisper, but they will tell you. You can even ask Mrs. Black.

Yeah, you're going to *love* her. I know I did. That's when it all started, sitting right there in her Biology class in October, listening to her drone on and on about...

"Immunity!"

Mrs. Black stood up and paraded to the empty blackboard. Through the subtle lines on her face, you could tell she was hot once and still would be a wonderful catch for your standard cougar-chaser. Personally, I thought she used to be a dude—she certainly had the balls. She scratched the word *immunity* onto the surface, and then placed the chalk back into the tray and turned to us with a dramatic pause.

"It can relate to many things, really, but in the subject of science, immunity is the ability to be resistant to infection or disease. I think most of you in here have had chicken pox."

Marshall Wilcox crowed like a rooster.

"Enough, Marshall," she said. "Well, if you've had it, you'll never get it again. That is because the body ..."

*And blah, blah, blah.* Black could have gone on forever, and she was going to, I was certain of it. You'll learn she has a tendency to do that—talk incessantly. It's her specialty, that and her ability to be an acutely passive aggressive *bi-atch.* Black's voice blended perfectly with the buzz of the UV lamps beside me, which began to lull me into a sort of trance. The plants under the lights looked like weeds. I didn't know why Black was making us grow them; I didn't know why Black did a lot of things. She made Biology an aggravation, which was bad because I love science.

"Victoria!" she yelled. Black loved putting me to the test when she could. I assure you when in her class I always tried to remain respectful, but that day I just couldn't find the tolerance. Some days, you're just not in the mood, you know?

"Yes, Mrs. Black," I replied.

"What did I just say?" she asked.

"I don't know, Mrs. Black," I lazily replied. And I didn't know. I hadn't been listening at all, and she knew it. Her voice had morphed into the old Peanuts "*wah-wah-wah-wah*" thing.

"Of course you don't, because you weren't listening," Black said, rounding her desk. "Can you answer the question?"

"Yes, if you can ask it again," I said, causing some to laugh, but I wasn't trying to be funny.

Black gave me that look she gives everyone when she thinks she's backed you into a corner. Then, she said, "If I have to ask you the question again and you get it wrong, I am giving you a zero on next week's quiz."

"And what will you do if I get it right?" I asked.

Mrs. Black thought for a moment. "If you get it right, I'll give you an A on the quiz."

I smiled. "Ask away."

"Define, in detail, passive immunity," she said.

"Which one?" I asked—you know, because there are several types.

She said, "What do you mean which one? Passive Immunity, Ms. Jenkins! Define it!"

"I need to know which type," I said.

"Zero!" Black said. "You get a zero."

Now, you know that pissed me off. At the time, studying was all I did. I didn't chase dudes or hunt monsters; I just studied. The subjects were something I knew well because they were all I had. Then, it just came out, like a pressure release.

I rattled, "Naturally acquired passive immunity occurs when a mother passes immunity onto her fetus during pregnancy. A mother's antibodies are passed to the fetus by an FcRn receptor on the placental cells."

Everyone sat quietly, unsure of what had just happened.

"Uh…what is an FcRn receptor?" Linda Burns asked from the back of the room.

"I'm glad you asked, Linda," I shot back, not taking my eyes from Black for a second. "FcRn is a neonatal molecule that is responsible for the transportation of immunoglobulin from mother to offspring during pregnancy. Now, *artificially* acquired passive immunity is a more short-term immunization process that is done by the manual transfer of antibodies, which can be administered in many ways; as human …"

"*Enough!*" yelled Mrs. Black. "Get out! Now! Go to the office!"

My face ran hot with anger. She had asked for it! What else was I supposed to have done? An office visit was the last thing my mom needed. Trouble wasn't something I found often, but I truly made it count on the occasions I located it.

With a sigh, I threw my book bag over my shoulder and picked up my purse. Though the blank stares of the other students burned me, I tried to take pride in the fact a few of them thought what I had just done was awesome. I put my junky butt (as Kyle calls it) against the handle of the door and looked back to Black.

"I better get my A," I warned before I could help myself.

"Girl, you better get out of …" she began to threaten.

As I made my way down the hall to the office, I was certain that Mr. Hillard, the principal, would be shocked to see me. He knew I had an attitude but that I tended to respect authority. However, my attitude was beginning to change, and I didn't know why. At the time, I wondered if maturity was creeping up on me, causing me to shed the shell of my youth to take on the tougher crust of adulthood. If so, apparently that meant I had to become ruthless.

The door buzzer sounded when I walked in the office, causing Mrs. May, the administrative assistant, to look up.

"Oh, Lord, Ms. Jenkins," she said with a tone of disappointment. "Did Black finally get to you?"

"Yeah, I guess," I said.

"Well," Mrs. May said, standing up. She looked to either side of the room, checking to see who was within earshot. "Don't worry about it, hon. She gets to me, too!"

We smiled at one another as Mr. Hillard stepped out from his office.

"Mavis, I need these copied if you don't mind. Mrs. Black just called me and said that Vickie Jenkins was…Oh, hello, Jenkins," Mr. Hillard said, noticing I was already there.

I stepped through and walked into his quaint office full of plants, pictures, and warmth. On his desk sat my file—my thin, little, insignificant file. Little did I know that by end of this school year, it would be much thicker!

"Have you called my mom?" was the first thing I could think of.

He said, "Well, Mrs. Black thought I should, but I thought maybe we could work this out between us first. What do you think?"

I sat quietly, and then blurted, "She tries to make me mad. She does it on purpose."

*And we know Black did.*

"You should have been listening," he said.

"I was."

*And we know I wasn't.*

"Now, Vickie," he said.

I sighed, "Well, she just went on and on and on. I know the material. I know what that stuff is all about. Why can't she just get to the point? She makes me feel like my brain is going to turn into jelly and run out of my ears!"

Mr. Hillard chuckled. He took off his glasses. "Amen to that," he said as he rubbed his tired eyes.

"She just doesn't like me," I said.

"Now, Vickie, I don't think it is personal."

"Why, does she hate everybody?" I asked.

He sat back in an impatient but understanding manner. "Vickie, let me tell you a little bit about what I've learned about life. There's a hierarchy to life that everyone has to respect. No matter how big you are, you report to somebody; you have someone to answer to. That includes me, you, and everyone else. Unfortunately, Black is one of those people in your life right now that you have to please. Now, it's not fair, but we have to take those things in stride."

"I know," I replied.

Hillard was correct in what he was saying, but it didn't make the facts (or Mrs. Black) any prettier to look at.

"You're a very smart young woman, Vickie. Black knows that. We all do. Try not to get too frustrated with her. Just think—after this year, you graduate and won't have to deal with her anymore and you can move on to dealing with other difficult people."

We laughed.

"Okay, but you haven't given me a lot to look forward to," I said.

"Well, yes, I suppose. But it gets better. I promise." Hillard reached around, opened one of the large filing drawers, and put my file back in its place. "We'll just let our little talk serve as your corrective action this time, Ms. Jenkins. Now, you get to class and try to be positive. God knows I will!"

I smiled and gathered my things in time for the bell to ring. It was on to History class and then to sweet freedom, where I could finish homework and lay around doing nothing at all for the rest of the night. As I entered the hallway, I saw Kyle coming toward me, sporting that same Frankenstein t-shirt he always wore. I was surprised it hadn't disintegrated.

I met Kyle when we were five years old, and he never grew taller. His parents had just moved from Japan then. His mother was Japanese but his father was American. Kyle had no trace of an accent but could mimic his mother's thick tongue with perfection. I loved to hear him impersonate her.

We shared a sense of style and humor, and a love for the macabre, though I didn't take it to the level he did. He worshiped monsters; it added to his charm.

"What's up, convict?" Kyle rattled.

"Bite me," I replied as we merged into traffic.

"With pleasure! Present it," he said.

I handed him my pencil. "Here you go."

"Oh, ha, ha. So, what did you do? Stab someone?" he said.

"No, Black finally pissed me off," I said.

"Finally? I thought she always pisses you off?" he said, fumbling with his iPod.

"Yeah, but this was the first time I pissed her off in return. It was great. You'd have loved it!" I said.

"I'm sure! Oh, *Zombie Vengeance* is coming on tonight. You better not miss it again! " he said.

I rolled my eyes. "Oh, I won't. Nothing like some good brain eating."

Harvey Martin from Kyle's shop class passed by and spat, "Hello, Freakboy!"

"Hey, Assman, how's it going?" Kyle shot back. "I swear, one day me and that asshole are going to be in shop and I'm going to nail his nards to the table!"

We stopped at my locker and I began fumbling with the rusty lock until it popped open. Kyle leaned back against the adjacent locker door. Then, there he was—Rod Rainfeld, the star quarterback of Rutgers High, standing in the hallway beside us surrounded by his other teammates. He was tall and dark, tightly built, and *delicious*, all the things girls wanted. I thought he had a smile that could launch a thousand marching bands. I never flipped over dudes. Normally I couldn't have cared less, but Rod was just one of those guys you couldn't ignore if you had a pulse, and that irritated me. I tried to look without looking, taking a mental photograph that I could study later. I didn't want to be obvious. I had a reputation for not needing validation from the male species (an attribute some thought *lesbianic*, but whatever). Nevertheless, I was finding myself more and more attracted to Rod, wondering what his thick hair smelled like, or what his big lips would feel like against mine. *Does he brush his teeth? Yuck!* I wondered if this was part of growing up, too.

*God, I need therapy!*

"Reach out and grab his ass," Kyle whispered. "Just reach out and take hold of it and give it a good squeeze."

"Oh, shut up!" I said.

He laughed. "Come on! Then, when he turns around to you, tell him you give him a…*B-minus,* but if he works it a little harder before the championship, you'll change it to an A."

"I don't like Rod Rainfeld," I lied.

Kyle looked at me. "Whatever, girl! You'd do him. Hell, *I'd* do him!"

"Rod!" a voice sang through the bustle of the crowd.

It was Jessica Moores, or *Jessica Whores,* as I referred to her. Unfortunately, not only did I have to put up with Jessica at school, she lived in my neighborhood, too, though not close enough to cause damage. On top of it all, she was the head cheerleader. *How cliché is that?* Oh, how precious she was with her faultless skin, blonde hair, perfect nose, and big boobs—all of which I suspected were presents from her plastic surgeon father.

"Hey there!" Rod said.

"Rod, you promised you'd wait for me after class. Where did you go?" she whined.

"Hi, Jessica," cooed Russell Cobbs, one of the linebackers.

"Shut up, Russ," she snapped.

"Sorry, Jess. I got distracted," Rod said.

"Yeah, uh-huh. Hey there, pretty Pete," Jessica said.

Peter Thorning was another member of the football team. You know—and I'm going to tell you the truth—if I were going to have a football player boyfriend besides Rod, it would have been Pete. He was cute and shy. His thick, sandy blonde hair was cut short. He had a great smile and a wonderful laugh. His plans were atypical of the standard jock: attend seminary school and become a minister—*the kind that can get married*—as he always professed to girls. I didn't think I was upstanding enough to be the wife of a minister. If you can't already tell, my sense of humor is excessively sinful. Jessica seemed to have a great time tempting him with her abundant slutiness.

"Hey, Jess," Pete replied with a blush.

"So, you going to help me plan for the Halloween Ball? I'm on the committee, you know," she said to Rod.

He said, "Yeah, I'll help. Not sure how much help I'll be, though."

"Just you being there is help enough, sweetness," she said. She turned her gaze to me, noticing I was watching. "What are you looking at, freak?"

"Oh, Jessica," I said with cool sarcasm. "Oh, please don't beat me up. I didn't mean to listen. It's just you're so…so…*loud.*"

"Yeah, yeah. You better mind your business, Jenkins!" she said.

"Oh," I said shutting my locker and walking past them nonchalantly. "I will. *I will.*"

Kyle trailed behind me with his goofy smile, stopping to look at Jessica's obscene chest. "I like your boobies," he said.

"Bite me, freak!" she shot.

"Grrruff!" he snapped at her in a dog-like fashion. Rod puffed up in defense, causing Kyle to scurry behind me.

We made our way to History, which was the only class we had together this year. Unfortunately, Russell Cobbs also attended the class—well, *when* he attended. It was taught by the wonderful Miranda Murray. To date, she is my favorite teacher, and not just because of what she ended up being to me. She and I always had this connection, even before I started taking her class. Murray had never been married, though she did have a son, one of those super-intelligent, nerdy engineer types, who lived in New York.

That day on the blackboard, she had drawn a large tree with names attached to the branches. We took our seats as the bell rang.

"Hello!" Murray shouted with her usual excitement.

"Hello!" we said.

She laughed. "So, I guess you guys are wondering what this mess of a tree is on the board. Well, today, class, we are going to learn about genealogy—spit it out, Kyle."

Kyle jumped when he realized he was still chewing his gum. He quickly spit into his hand and tore a piece of paper, folding it inside. Ms. Murray walked to him and collected it while speaking.

"*'But, Ms. Murray, what is genealogy?'* you say. Well, it is the study of families and their lineages through history. What you are looking at on the board is an accounting of Abraham Lincoln's genealogy. Lincoln was born February 12, 1809, in his family home in Sinking Spring Farm, near Hodgenville, Hardin Co., which is now Larue, Kentucky. He died April 15, 1865, and if you've been reading your assignments, you know exactly how. He was the son of Thomas Lincoln and Nancy Hanks. He married Mary Ann Todd November 4, 1842. She was the daughter of Malone Smith Todd and Eliza Ann Parker ..."

As she went through Lincoln's history in detail, she pointed to different branches on the tree to signify how they related to one another. In reality, the facts were boring. Nevertheless, Murray had a way about her that made anything and everything she talked about fascinating. For example, we watched *Gone with the Wind* in class. You'd think that would be dreary, but she dressed in a different costume from the movie each day. It was so cheesy; however, I thought her passion was awesome.

"Kyle, I bet you have an interesting lineage," said Murray.

"Uh," he replied. "Maybe."

"Do you know any of it?" she asked.

Kyle thought and thought…and thought. I saw the smoke coming out of his ears. "Oh! I know my dad met my mom while he was staying in Japan on business, and she went out with him because he could balance a pencil on his nose."

We laughed. Murray smiled. "Well, yes, that is interesting. But, you see, class, I think it is important for us all to know where we came from. There is a lot of history in each of you, tons of special things that I bet you never knew about. Wouldn't you agree, Vickie?"

"Uh…yeah, I suppose," I said, thrown by her directness. I mean, I didn't believe there was anything of particular interest about my family.

She smiled. "Of course! Why some of you may even be a descendant of Lincoln himself, or Benjamin Franklin, or…"

"Or Stalin!" added Russell from the back of the room.

"Well, maybe in *your* family," Murray said. Everyone laughed. "All right, all right…so, here's what we're going to do. Now, with the dance next week, I know better than to ask for assignments like this, but by the following Monday I want each of you to have traced your genealogy as far back as you can." She began handing out a paper with the blank tree on it, much like the one she had drawn on the blackboard. "You can use this diagram as your base, or outline it on your own if you find you have a whole lot of history."

"What if you were created in a lab by a mad scientist?" asked Kyle.

"Then I had better be able to Google 'em," she said as the bell rang. "Alright—everybody get out of my sight!"

At that moment, I had no idea that the fabric of my history had wickedness weaved into its thread count, but I was about to find out.

And so was Murray.

# VICKIE THE BEE SLAYER

Missy Lynn and her gang glared at us as we passed. They were the degenerates, the redneck hoodlums of Rutgers High. They smelled like body odor, Marlboro, and that cheap Beauty Love body spray they used to try to hide it all. I had never had dealings with them, and I was grateful. How Missy had managed to remain in school was a mystery to me, anyway. Talk about a *bi-atch!* She was two misdemeanors away from a life sentence. I loathed them, Missy especially. You didn't make eye contact with them—*ever*.

"God," said Kyle as we reached a safe distance. "I think that girl has more testosterone than me!"

I said, "I have more testosterone than you, Kyle."

The event committee members were bustling to the gymnasium, the whole lot of them, the Populars. I didn't know what made me sicker: that they were popular or that they were pretty. Actually, I preferred a small number of real friends to a large number of phony ones. The Populars were buzzing around Jessica as if she was a queen. Did Teresa really care what kind of shampoo Jessica used? Did Brenda really lose sleep over where she bought her obnoxious perfume? That would be a *hell-with-a-side-of-no*. They only wanted to bask in the sunlight Jessica pretended to be, and that was all right. I knew she had, like, eleven toes, or something.

"Just reach over and yank her hair out," muttered Kyle.

"Why do you always act like you know what I'm thinking?" I said.

He said, "Because I do. Tell me you wouldn't want to run over there and pop her big boobies like balloons right now!"

"Yeah, so what? Quit playing around in my head, loser," I said.

"But it's so lovely in there!" he cooed.

We busted through the double doors of the entrance where my mom waited for us in the car.

"Mrs. Jenkins! So nice to see you again!" Kyle said to her.

"You, too, sir!" Mom replied.

"Did you get it?" I asked.

Mom was supposed to pick up my new cell phone that day. She had managed to wash my other one, which may have been okay if she wouldn't have also dried it. Bless her heart.

"Not yet," Mom replied.

"Mom?" I sighed. "I swear. And you talk about how forgetful I am!"

"We'll get it, we'll get it. I went by the store and I couldn't find the one you had. The insurance on the phone said we had to get the same one, but I couldn't find it anywhere."

"You can get it online," Kyle added.

"Good, we can order it when we get home," Mom said. "So, how was school?"

"Good!" Kyle said.

"And Vickie?" Mom asked.

"Eh, it was all right. Not much to tell," I replied, knowing not to mention my visit with Hillard.

"You sure?" she asked again.

That was freaky. Why was she questioning again? You know how parents do, right, with the *I'm baiting your butt to catch you* thing? I wondered if she knew somehow, and that was just like her, waiting to catch me in a lie, and that would be even worse than confessing.

I sighed. "Well, I did have a run in with Mrs. Black."

"I know. She called," Mom said.

"See! I knew she would. She knew that Mr. Hillard wouldn't call you," I said, my face turning red with anger. It was just like Black to sneak around Hillard and call Mom. Hillard was wrong; it *was* personal, there was no question in my mind. Black was difficult with everyone, yes, but she was obviously after me on an individual level.

"Vickie, you know that you can't—" Mom started.

I said, "Yes, I know, Mom. But, God! She just won't let up."

"She is a big old B, Mrs. J.," added Kyle.

Mom shook her head. "Well, regardless. I know Mr. Hillard has probably lectured you already, so I'm not going to go through it again, but, Vickie, you're going to have to stay off this woman's radar. I don't care if she's a B or a C or a Y."

"What's a Y?"" Kyle asked.

"She won't let me!" I said, cutting the tail from his ignorant comment.

"Well, you mind your manners, pay attention, and stay off her radar. Don't give her any reason to come after you. Then, if she does, let me know and I will handle it." Kyle threw his hands up like Bruce Lee and made a kung fu fighting howl. Mom rolled her eyes. "Kyle, darlin', we need to talk to Judy about your sugar intake."

"Sorry, Mrs. J.," he said.

"So, let's get everyone home and get homework finished and then shop for a phone. What do we have to get done tonight?" she said.

I started fumbling through my backpack as we neared the subdivision. "Just some algebra. Oh, and Ms. Murray wants us to do a family tree." Okay, so then this weird silence entered the car. It was as if I had just dropped an F-bomb. It was obvious the wheels of her mind were turning full speed from what I just said. "Mom?"

"What?" she replied as if being shaken from a dream.

"What's the matter?" I asked.

She said, "Oh, nothing. I was wondering if we should stop and get milk."

"But we've already passed the store," I pointed out.

"Yeah, I know. I was thinking I had forgotten something. Now, what again?" she said.

"Mom? Family tree? Tell me you're not stroking out. I can't be around Dad all by myself. He'll drive me insane," I said.

"Oh, yeah, yeah. Family tree. Who's this for?" she said, trying to focus.

"History class," Kyle added. "We get to do our *geenerology*."

"*Genealogy*," I corrected. Sometimes Kyle mispronounced stuff to aggravate me.

"Well, that sounds like fun!" she said, sounding more upbeat.

Though the air in the car began to lighten, there was something odd I couldn't pinpoint about Mom's reaction. Later on, it would make perfect sense.

We pulled in front of Kyle's house, which sat at the beginning of the subdivision.

"See you later, Kyle," I said.

"Bye, hon," said Mom.

"See ya! And don't forget—*Zombie Vengeance.*"

"Yeah, yeah. Get out," I said as I waved him out of the car like a fly.

Our house was deep within the heart of the subdivision, neatly isolated from others on the cul-de-sac…thank God. The cool fall wind blew carelessly through the trees, sending leaves floating to the ground; sounds poetic, but I knew I would have the pleasure of eventually raking them. We walked in to the usual scene: Dad perched in his easy chair, watching the news and working on papers. He teaches anthropology at the local university, the one I will *not* be attending.

"John, if you are going to work on papers, can't you do it without the news on?" Mom said.

"I could, yes, Barbara. It would be illogical to say I couldn't," he replied.

"Spoken like a true Vulcan," I said.

Dad held his hand up in a true Vulcan salute. "Live long and prosper." I smiled and rolled my eyes. "And speaking of the news, you girls be careful when you're out. Vandals are running wild. According to Channel 10, over the past two weeks alone they've poured red dye in the fountains of Tyson Park, spray painted almost all of the statues on campus, and vandalized Mercy Blood Bank. What kinds of freaks steal blood?"

"Probably some cult," Mom said only half listening. "I don't know. Can you sell blood, like on the black market or something?"

"No, but I bet you can sell it on the *blood* market," he chuckled. Mom shook her head like always.

"Hey, Dad, how about you let me borrow the car to go over to Kyle's to study?"

Dad had just bought a used Mercedes that was only two years old, practically brand-new. Having a Mercedes Benz had always been one of my father's dreams. He lost his mind when someone even got close to it.

"Hehehe…you're so funny. You know the rule. Maintain a distance of twenty-five feet from the Benz at all times! I have a gun!"

Mom stopped cold, sniffing into the air. I saw Dad get nervous, that familiar look like he had done something bad, like when he left me at church when I was four years old. She walked over to him and bent down, smelling his shirt.

"John! Have you been smoking again?"

"No!" he lied.

Mom said, "You're sure? John, you smell like a cigar soaked in Brut! How much cologne did you put on to cover it up?"

I knew that Dad had never completely given up smoking, though he swore to us he had.

"I haven't been smoking, woman!" he said.

"All right, whatever. If you say so," Mom conceded.

"Um, so how was school?" he said, turning to me to change the subject.

"Well…" I began.

"It was fine," Mom interrupted. *Saved by the mouth!* "Now, did you put those steaks out to defrost like I told you to?"

"Uh."

Mom hung her head. "John! Mr. Parsons said to put them out about two hours before we cook them!"

"I'll nuke 'em! Just two minutes!" he replied, jumping out of the chair.

"Lord…I don't know what I'm going to do with that man!" Mom said to me with a wink.

Obviously, Dad didn't know that Black had called. I don't think I've really ever seen Dad angry. However, he did have a tendency to *fret*, as Mom called it. If she had told him about Black, there would have been about an hour of review and a recap of why things had occurred the way they did. Dad thrived on that kind of social assessment. Unless it was something major, Mom typically kept him in the dark, which suited me in this case.

Mom sat down on the couch and kicked her shoes to the floor.

"So, what about the tree?" I asked, more curious to see her reaction than obtaining an answer.

She rubbed her foot. "Oh…oh, that. Well, let's have dinner first and then we'll see what we can come up with. I'm sure your father's side of the family will be a chore."

This was certain to be true. Dad was the youngest of seven siblings and had a plethora of aunts and uncles. Mom, on the other hand, had a much smaller family, only a brother and a sister.

I made my way upstairs to change and get algebra out of way. Then, of course, there was the dreaded viewing of the silly zombie movie. The goofier the movie, the better it was, in Kyle's opinion. However, if I didn't watch it, I would never pass the "quiz," and knowing Kyle, there was certain to be a quiz.

I sat down at my desk, cracked my book open, and got some paper from my binder. Let me see…the problem went something like:

*The gravitational force on the moon is 0.17 of the force on Earth. This means, if you weigh 100 pounds on Earth, you would weigh 100 x 0.17 or 17 pounds on the moon. Ernest is an astronaut who will be doing a moon walk. He weighs 165 pounds and will carry a pack. His weight, including the pack, cannot exceed 34 pounds on the moon. If x represents the weight of the pack, the inequality 0.17(165 + x) ≤ 34 represents this situation. What are the possible weights of Ernest's pack?*

"Well…who cares?" I said to myself.

An insect buzzed past my ear, and I swatted at it as I sat there working on the problem: *0.17(165 + x) ≤ 34. Well, the Distributive Property would be 28.05 + 0.17x ≤ 34.*

You know, all that junk.

*Buzz!*

Once again, it flew past my ears and around my face; I could feel the flutter of its wings on my skin. *Gross! Go on, fly! Let's see, we'd have to subtract 28.05 from each side. So, that would be 28.05 + 0.17x − 28.05 ≤ 34 − 28.05…*

*Buzz!*

That was it. I had had it. I spun around to see the fly was actually a large, creepy hornet. Dude, let me tell you that I hate bees. I can't stand them. Maybe it was the nasty sting I had endured as a child. Since then, I haven't been able to sit in another room where a bee was buzzing, and there in my windowsill was a hornet, the mother of all bees. Normally, I would have simply closed my book, walked downstairs, and demanded that either Dad come up and kill it or put a *For Sale* sign in the yard. However, on that day, something strange happened.

There it was, buzzing around in the windowsill, watching me and waiting. They do that, you know: watch you. It's sinister as hell. It knew that I had locked onto it, and it sat poised, ready to strike. Fear was in my throat. I could imagine what the sting was going to feel like, the burning, the pain. Then, the fear rushed away, like flushing a toilet. I swear, I didn't even think about it. I took my crisp new number 2 pencil in my hand and with a flick of the wrist, I transformed it into a spear, sailing it through the air. It stabbed the bee directly through its abdomen, pinning it to the whitewashed windowsill. *Whap!* There it was, like a bee-kabob.

I just sat there in shock. It was as if I wasn't in control of the moment, but controlled by the moment, *instinct.* I got up, walked to the window, and reached down to pull out the pencil. It took a considerable amount of effort to get it dislodged from the wood. Obviously, I had thrown the thing hard, but it felt like I had just tossed it. There I was, holding this poor dead creature on the pencil tip, studying it. The lead had demolished its exoskeleton, allowing its icky goo to leak out. Then, to taunt me, it buzzed one final buzz.

"Ewww!" I screamed, dropping the thing to the floor and scurrying away, completely grossed out. I left the room, gagging and rubbing my shivering arms. I was getting out.

I didn't give a damn how much Ernest weighed on the moon

# Shipping and Handling

Everyone knows the fun started when Mr. Rainfeld bought Dracula. How did he buy Dracula, you ask? Who knew? The man had nearly everything else, why not a vampire? I didn't think Count Dracula had bids running on eBay either, but if you can find Elvis on there, surely you can find Dracula.

Xavier Rainfeld, Rod's weird father, was the self-proclaimed town benefactor, a legend. He was the type of dude who liked to show you he had money, and he was the type of parent my dad despised. It seemed a ton of stuff in our town bore the name Rainfeld. It was one of Xavier's requirements. He would gladly donate money toward most any cause, so long as he could get recognition. That's why Rutgers has Rainfeld Hall and Rainfeld Healthcare Center.

The auditorium was falling apart about three years ago, and it took the school board two weeks to talk him out of renaming it in exchange for his contribution for the repairs. Nevertheless, as a compromise, his portrait hangs at the doors to this day. Go by and give it a look; you'll get the willies, trust me. With the economy at the time, state funding sucked and it made the school more dependent on Xavier than they'd have hoped to be.

Not only was Xavier a *philanthropist*, but he was also a collector of the strange and unusual. Well, let's say that a different way: *junk*. Rod joked about it all the time. It was so bad that he couldn't have the guys over. There were apparently "priceless" things scattered all through the house, and Xavier couldn't take a chance on something being broken or stolen by one of Rod's football cronies.

Xavier's most coveted items were contained downstairs in a sort of basement museum he had created over time. It was equipped with sensory lighting and security cameras. You would have thought it was the Smithsonian! Rod was the only one allowed down there. Rod said he knew all of the things to avoid. It was like maneuvering through a priceless mine field.

Out of all the items that Xavier had—weapons, pottery, jewelry, Faberge eggs, coins—Rod said there were two things his father held most dear. The first was his gold pinky ring in the shape of a bat. In its chest was a deep red ruby. The second was an old book kept in a glass display case. It was tiny, about five inches by four inches, and had a leather cover with the initials *R.M.R.* on it. Rod didn't know what those things meant then, and he didn't care, but he would eventually. We all would. At the time, it was just garbage.

Overall, Rod didn't talk about Xavier much, and I found it best not to pry. I think football was all Rod had ever known. Sure, he waited for his dad to take an interest, but Xavier never did. We would watch the other parents gather at the rallies and congregate into the stands to cheer for their kids, the congratulatory pats on the back, the pride—but none of us ever saw Xavier there for Rod.

Around the time I was murdering bees, Rod was dropping Ms. Whores off at her house in our subdivision. Jessica—there was another problem. Yeah, okay, she was hot. Fine, I'll admit it. Yet, she was *only* that. I think Rod felt she was fun to be with at the time, but what about later? Rod was the football star, and Jessica was the most popular, bi-atchy girl at Rutgers, and so by social standard that meant Rod had to put up with her, at least until graduation. Appearances meant everything, especially to Xavier.

According to Rod, the day before Dracula arrived nothing was out of the ordinary. He had gone downstairs to get some chicken nuggets out of the freezer when he noticed that in the midst of Xavier's collection an empty table had been prepared. At the head of the table was a metal rod that held a large glass bowl on the end. From the bowl, a long tube extended to the floor. Rod told me that it rather reminded him of an IV tube. He was standing examining it when Xavier called down to him.

"Rod," Xavier shouted from upstairs.

Rod jumped with surprise. "God, Dad, watch it. We need to get you a bell or something!" he said as he went back up with the nuggets.

"How was school today?" Xavier asked.

Rod said, "Good. How are things with you?"

Xavier said, "Good, I suppose. Trying to finish that nasty deal with Ashton Realty for Simmons Mortuary. Those people can be so difficult. No one has used that heap in forever. That's a great deal of acreage to give away for pennies."

"But, Dad, they're wanting to build a free clinic there," Rod pointed out.

Xavier said, "And I want to build the Rainfeld Rec Center. It's for Rutgers; I thought you'd be happy. So, what about *free*? See, there is that word again. What have I told you?"

"Nothing, and I mean nothing, is free," they both said simultaneously. Rod said that the *nothing is free* mantra was Xavier's catch phrase.

"And how is Jessica?" Xavier said, changing the subject.

"She's fine," Rod said.

"Well, that's good. She told me the other day on the phone that you two were going to be collecting bottles today," Xavier said.

Rod said, "No, Dad, we're collecting cans for the dance at school."

"Sorry, cans," Xavier corrected. "Don't know why you'd need it. God knows I've sunk enough money into that place. If you didn't throw those soda cans away like you do, we'd have some to give her."

"I *recycle* them, Dad. I don't throw them away," Rod said.

"Well, whatever," Xavier said as he stood up and then added, "Oh, and by the way, I am expecting a very important antique shipment tomorrow evening. So, I'd like it if you didn't have friends over blocking the driveway tomorrow night. The truck will need to get in to the rear entrance."

"No one's coming," Rod said. No one ever came over. It wasn't worth the hassle.

Xavier said, "Good. And I have a meeting with Ashton and the school board next Wednesday at Rutgers to discuss the recreation center, so I'll be home late."

Rod said, "I'll manage."

That's the first Rod had heard about the shipment. When you think of someone getting a package, you tend to think about DVDs, cell phones, or shoes; you don't think about a delivery of the undead.

Yeah…that was the first mistake.

# The Nominees Are

The next morning I was still tripping over the bee thing. I sat there staring at my reflection in the mirror. Thanks to Kyle, I ran from zombies all night in my dreams, and there was something else. There was this voice, a voice from nowhere had entered my dream world, one I'd never heard before, and it pissed me off because I like my dream world. The whisper was calm, seductive in ways, but mostly freaky. It would interrupt my battles with the living dead, talking to me.

"*Victoria …* "it would say.

It called to me, and I woke up in the pitch dark wondering what it was and where it was hiding.  It was one of those strange things, like when you are drifting to sleep and you suddenly hear your name in perfect stereo sound as if someone is standing at your bedside talking to you.

"*Victoria…*"

I awoke after my restless night not wanting to face the day. Remember, I was going to have a quiz on that *Zombie Vengeance* BS, so I was recalling the whole movie but only in scenes—the zombies, the fighting, surviving, and again that weird voice. I was looking at my reflection without really looking at it. Then, for the first time since I was a child, I reached over and took the tube of lipstick into my hand. Yeah, I know; I was a little ashamed. Damp hair fell around my face. With my index finger, I swept the soggy locks from my skin. I opened the tube and carefully applied the shade. It was pleasantly pink and natural. I sat back and looked at myself and thought, *I could be just as pretty as Jessica and those other fakes.* The question was did I *want* to be? Did I want to conform? The answer was…*maybe.*

*Rod.*

Rod seemed to like pretty. Then again, what guy didn't?

I then picked up a very old tube of mascara, which originally belonged to Mom. It was so old that it caked on my lashes, so I blotted it as much as I could. Then, I added a bit of rouge to my cheeks. Man, I looked awful, like a clown with spiders on my eyelids. I laughed to myself and turned on the radio. I didn't know it, but Mom had stepped to the doorway just in time to see me posing for the audience in my mind. It made her smile.

I finally caught her reflection in the mirror and immediately came back to reality. Of course, she was standing there with that grin on her face.

"I'm almost ready," I muttered through my humility.

"You're pretty," Mom said sweetly.

I said, "Yeah, right. With this makeup job?"

Mom walked into the room and sat me down in front of the vanity. She took a tissue and began blotting away some of the overdone makeup.

"Yes, you are. See, if we just take away some of this," Mom said as she began toning down the colors. She worked on me for about five minutes in silence with the two of us saying everything we needed to say without an audible word. I began to wonder what Mom was like when she was my age. I wondered if she was wild and slutty, or sweet and shy, or maybe something kind of in-between. "See?" she said.

I turned around to the mirror and *I was hot!* The color was subtle, yet enhancing. Mom knew just the right angles to place the tint in order to achieve optimal appearance. She worked at a makeup counter at a department store for years.

"Well, yeah, but it's just not me, Mom," I said, getting a little embarrassed.

"Well, just wanted you to know," she said.

I smiled. "Thank you."

Mom smiled at me sweetly. "You are welcome, honey. Now, get your stuff together and let's get going. Judy is going to be here in just a bit."

That was the agreement; Judy took us, Mom picked us up. I was still running the movie through my mind—*Okay, the chick at the end lived until she got home and was eaten, which was so stupid. What was her name? Oh, no! I have to remember. I'm sure it'll be on the test!*

I began to dress. I started to wipe the makeup off my face, but then after looking at the reflection again, I decided against it. Then, I spied a pair of medium heels in the corner of my closet. *Dare I?* I got them out and tried them on. They still fit perfectly. Thinking back, I don't know where or when I'd gotten them, maybe for Easter or another formal-type holiday. Who knows? I picked out an outfit to match, including a never-before-worn dress. *A dress! Me!* I slipped it on and was surprised at how well it formed to my body. It had light, spring colors with several shades of yellow.

*Yeah. I like it. I'll do it*, I thought to myself.

I entered the kitchen to Mom's surprise.

"Well…don't you look great!" she chimed.

"I thought I would try something besides jeans," I said.

"Well, I love it!" She couldn't stop smiling.

We sat down to eat breakfast, and in a few minutes the high-pitched twittering honk from Judy's compact SUV let me know it was time to slurp down the remainder of my Count Chocula cereal (we'll laugh about the irony later).

"Woo! Look at you!" Kyle howled.

"Don't you start!" I said as I opened up the car door.

"You look nice today, Vickie," said Judy.

"Okay…did the hero live?" asked Kyle from the backseat. He always let me ride up front with Judy, not because he was sweet, but because he knew I'd slap him.

"No, and that's why it sucked," I replied.

"What do you mean, it sucked?" he said.

I said, "That's just not a good story. You have a hero that's been fighting for over an hour of a movie to come out victorious, and right when you think she did, she gets served up to a bunch of dead people. It was rank!"

"Well, it reflects real life that way. Not all endings are happy," he stated.

"No, but I don't watch movies or read fictional books for real life. I do it to *escape* real life. I want to see her whoop butt and take names!" I said.

"I agree with Vickie," said Judy in her broken accent. "I no like reality either."

"Thank you, Judy," I said.

"Oh, you ladies are crazy!" he said. "That movie rocked. When I write my own movies, they'll end realistically."

"Good, just don't expect me to watch them," I said.

"Fine! And you can't come to the Oscar party," he said.

We pulled to a stop in front of the school. The Populars were loitering around the parking area the way they always did before class. Kyle and I began to make our way through them. I have to admit, I was freaking out at my new look. I mean, I didn't have clown shoes and a rainbow wig on, but I sort of felt like I did.

"I can't believe that you wouldn't watch my movie," Kyle said.

"You have to make one first, Kyle," I said.

From the corner of my eye, I spotted Rod and Jessica standing at his car. By the look on his face, she was obviously harping to him about something of little importance. As always, I had a hard time not looking at Rod. I wondered if he would notice my look, the delicate change in my appearance. A couple of boys oogled me for the first time, but they didn't matter. I think a part of me knew it was for Rod. Somehow, a little makeup and a dress brought me from the depths of invisibility, which was a place I usually loved to stay. While Jessica ranted, Rod noticed me, and I immediately looked away. *But*—he had looked, and not just that "Hey, who's that?" look either, but that "Wow, she's kind of hot!" look.

"Hey, Vickie," Rod said.

Chills ran down my arms. The fake me became so giddy the real me slapped her! What was I supposed to say?

"Hey," was all I could manage.

Noticing our exchange, Jessica wrapped herself around Rod, signifying he belonged to her. "Hey, geek. Nice dress. Did you wear that to Sunday School?" she shot to me.

"Hello, Jessica," I replied coolly. "I was going to wear something like you have on, but I didn't want to dress so *provaca-whoritively* today."

"You only wished you looked like me," Jessica replied as we passed. I rolled my eyes with a smile. Just then, where I couldn't see, Jessica leaned her foot out into my path. I collapsed onto the pavement, books flying around me, papers scattering. I couldn't have gone down more dramatically if I were on the *Titanic*. The Populars laughed hysterically. My freshly exposed knees skinned like over-boiled potatoes. Blood stained the hem of my dress. "Whoops! You should have known better than to try heels today," Jessica said.

I didn't know what to say or do. Inside of me, there was a rage so profound that I thought I'd knock Jessica's capped teeth down her throat. It was a strange anger, something that frightened me. I could have jumped her, but a part of me thought I would really hurt her if I did, like a wild animal that couldn't be trusted. Then, there was the obvious humiliation of it all—the laughing in front of Rod, who looked at me sympathetically. The mortification sucked the wind from my livid Cover Girl sails. I was speechless for the first time where Jessica was concerned.

"You're such a mega-bitch, Jessica," Kyle said as he helped me up.

She barked, "Oh, oh…that hurts, Kyle. Why don't you go watch *Friday the 13th* and spank it, sicko?"

Surprisingly, my eyes welled with tears of anger, so I had to get away, and quick. She had gotten to me, and I didn't want her to know. As we walked away, Jessica smiled with pride at her stunt. Teresa giggled as she nauseatingly pulled on her over-chewed gum with her fingers. I saw Jessica turn to Rod and place a hand on his chest. She looked up at him smiling, but he wasn't amused.

"Sometimes I wonder why the hell I bother with you," Rod said coldly as he walked away. His words cut deeply and quickly, and I was overjoyed. The other cheerleaders stopped smiling, and so did Jessica.

The day pressed on, one of the hardest days I had to endure. All I wanted to do was get away and have a good long cry, one of those cries you have when your monthly knocks on the door. I had tried my best to get the blood and dirt stains out of that dress with cold water from the restroom. I had thought about faking some female trouble and leaving early. Hillard always became fidgety and uncomfortable at female troubles and never hesitated to cut you some slack.

The school was abuzz over the selection of nominees for what the event committee had deemed the King and Queen of Halloween. So what? I only wanted to go home. I was sick of people looking at my tattered dress and scarred legs. At least I could look forward to the rally scheduled for that afternoon. It would not only take time out of the day but would eat into my attendance of Mrs. Black's class. As you could probably guess, I definitely wasn't in the mood for Black's antics on top of the way my day had begun.

After lunch, we all gathered into the gymnasium. The cheerleading squad took the center of the floor and began their standard routine. I have to admit that I enjoyed watching them, though I would *never* admit it openly. Jessica led them as always. As she took her position, I noticed that she didn't appear to be her chipper narcissistic self. Could it have been that Rod had burned her earlier? Hmmm…that would be a *hell-to-the-yes*. The girls took their formation before the music started.

"Teresa!" yelled Jessica.

"Yes, Jess!" Teresa called back to her.

"I think it's time to…*step back!*"

Then, the music hit. *Bam!*

Okay, the Step Back was a signature move that involved the top four cheerleaders. The four of them group together in a semi-triangle with the fourth standing back as an anchor. After a synchronized routine, the two girls on either side take Jessica by the arms to steady her, and she back-flips into the air and lands on the shoulders of the girl behind her. It was always impressive, and always a showstopper. I could tell that Teresa wanted to be the center lead for the Step Back, but Jessica wouldn't have it. Jessica always had to be the center of everything. After the cheerleaders worked everyone into a frenzy, Mr. Hillard took his place at the microphone in the center of floor. The members of the event committee proudly seated themselves at the long table behind him.

Hillard said, "How impressive! Wonderful job, girls. Okay, everyone, settle down, settle down. We have some important announcements today. First, I would like to give a warm thank you to Mrs. Black and the event committee members for all of the planning they have done for next week's Halloween Ball." Everyone applauded, except for me. "And I know that you are really anxious to hear about the nominees for the King and Queen of Halloween. However, first thing's first. The pool will be closed down for two weeks to allow the water to be retreated. Mr. Hall's swim team has been advised. Many of you have asked about the band uniforms for the pep rally next Monday. Thanks to a gracious donation from Rainfeld Industries, we will be able to get new band uniforms this year and they are to arrive to us by the end of this week. Mr. Atkins will be heading up our fittings. Anything out of the normal range of sizes will be special ordered."

"Yeah, Eugene!" shouted Russ to the rather plump Eugene Phillips, who was seated at the end of bleachers.

"Bite me, Russ!" Eugene replied.

"Enough!" said Hillard. "Now, without further ado, I will read off the nominees for King and Queen of Halloween."

Jessica got up and stomped over to Mr. Hillard, handing him a sealed envelope. She sat back down next to Rod like a sulking brat. I was eating it up like yesterday's reheated pizza! The only thing I thought could have made it better would have been if Rod had said she had a *fat ass!*

Hillard opened the seal. "These nominees were recommendations directly from the event committee members and were voted on by the group. Okay, first we have the nominations for king. They are—Russell Cobbs."

Russ jumped up to applaud himself, pumping his fist in the air. God, I could have thrown up. Hillard proceeded to read each of the remaining three nominees, which included David Evans, the lead drummer in the band (thought he was kind of cute, but not really); Matt Stevens, another member of the football team (had nice arms, but his breath was always rank); and lastly, *Rod Rainfeld* (and we know what I thought about Rod). The students cheered and whistled to each of the names.

"Okay, okay," Hillard continued, trying to calm the audience. "Next for queen, we have Jessica Moores ..."

Of course, how could we not have had Jessica on the ballot? After all, it was only fitting. I sat there, glaring at her, envisioning Godzilla breaking through the roof of the gymnasium and scooping Jessica's perfect body into its jaws, taking her away, far away from me, where I would never have to look at her again. The others on the list included Teresa Haffner, Jessica's right hand, and even Paula Williams, surprisingly enough. Paula was the leader of the Glee Club and had a decent personality. I liked her well enough. Paula didn't hang around directly with Jessica and the Populars, so that made her okay in my book. Her nomination rather shocked me in a way. Nevertheless, nothing compared to the shock of the last nominee.

"And *Victoria Jenkins.*"

A strange hush fell over us all. I felt my body run hot, so hot I wondered if I had peed myself.

*What did he just say?* I thought.

"What did he just say?" asked Kyle.

"I...I don't know," I replied.

And I didn't know. I was hoping I had heard him wrong, but then I looked to the floor at Jessica, who was obviously about to rip her weave out she was so pissed, and then to Rod, who slyly smiled at me. That's when I knew it was real. I didn't know whether to be glad or mad. *How did it happen?* I made up my mind right then that I wouldn't be running against Jessica in anything no matter what. I'd had enough of pretending to be something I was not and had no plans to continue the charade.

After a final announcement, the student body dispersed for the final class of the day. Jessica marched away, leaving Rod unattended, and that was my chance. It would be my first real conversation with Rod, and I wasn't going to be too happy. The fear of speaking directly to him was offset by the diverse feelings of anger, astonishment, and nausea. I walked up to him with Kyle trailing after me, and without thought, took hold of his big, luscious arm. He spun around to me.

"What is that about?" I asked.

"What? Oh, that? Well, let's just say someone thought you deserved it," Rod replied with a smile.

"What are you talking about?" I said.

"Well, let's just say someone nominated you today, and once that person had cast their vote, the others followed along. It was beautiful."

"Listen," I said rather sharply. "I appreciate the thought, but I don't need you fighting battles for me, and I certainly don't need to be ranked up there with Jessica. So, undo it."

"Undo it?" he said.

I said, "Yeah, undo it…whatever you did. Take your personal cursor, highlight whatever you said, and press *delete!*"

"I can't undo it!" he replied. "You have just as much right to be up there as anyone else, Vickie. So you're just going to have to deal with it. Jess is my girlfriend, but sometimes she can be a pain in the ass. Believe it or not, she has her good points too, but what she did to you this morning was uncalled for, and, well, I just didn't like it."

I found it hard to believe Jessica had *any* good points, but I could really buy into the *pain-in-the-ass* part without question.

"He's right, Vickie," Kyle added. "You don't need it undone. If nothing else, it was worth it just to see her face today."

I stood there thinking. It really was nice to get Jessica's goat. It was even better to know that Rod had stuck up for me. But, why? It was in that instant that I fell in love with Rod, even though I didn't allow myself to realize it. I felt a connection to him that no one could spoil—not even Jessica. *Jessica.* Now, there was the problem. He wasn't going to leave Jessica for the plain vanilla that was yours truly. He would be stupid to do so.

"Well…thanks. Thanks, Rod," I said. "I appreciate that."

He said, "You're more than welcome, Vickie. You know, I think you really have a fair shot at winning, too. And, boy, wouldn't that piss them off?"

"Uh, good luck with that," Kyle said under his breath, to which I replied with a slight elbow in the gut.

"Thanks again, Rod," I said bashfully, so bashfully I should have giggled and skipped away swinging my pigtails.

"Anytime."

Then Kyle and I turned to make our way to Ms. Murray's class.

"Okay, you going to giggle like a little school girl now or later?" Kyle asked.

"Later," I smiled as I clutched my purse with a goofy grin plastered on my face.

"Vickie," yelled Rod from the other end of the busy hall, and I turned. "Do you have any cans at your house?"

*Cans?* Not the best pick up line, but it was a start.

# THE DARKEST SOUL

Xavier was meticulous, especially in his research. According to his journals, as the truck carrying Dracula's coffin was pulling into his driveway, I was out buying shoes. After the nomination, I hadn't quite been myself, as Mom could tell when I asked her to take me shopping after school. I had some money set aside and used about sixty bucks to buy a pair of shoes that were originally ninety. I couldn't pass them up. Could you?

The men got out of the truck where Xavier awaited them. The huge entry doors to the receiving area of the house stood open. The odd table Rod had seen was sitting right inside. The men entered the back of the truck and carried out a large wooden crate that was nearly eight feet in length and a little over four feet in width.

Xavier guided them to the table, where they sat it down. He said that's when the stone in the middle of his ring began to glow, not strong and bright, but in a low, pulsating rhythm. He hid the ring, turning the bat around to the inside of his hand, and hurried the men out, bolting the doors behind them. As he heard them begin to leave, he wheeled the crate through the curtains into the main area of the basement and began tearing it open with a crowbar like a fat kid ripping at a pack of Skittles.

There on the table, sealed tightly, was an elaborate coffin. The base coat of it was a shiny deep red, blood red, and was tipped in 24-karat gold. Gold leaf symbols were etched all over the casing, with a section of them grouped together in what appeared to be a paragraph.

At the top of the lid was a small golden hole, just big enough to insert a pencil, which led into the blackness of a place you couldn't see. Strange buttons sat at the four sides of the coffin—the top, bottom, left, and right. At the moment, he didn't know what the buttons were for. As he pressed one of them, he could hear buzzing and clicking sounds, like clockwork gears, but they soon stopped. He rolled the crystal bowl to the top of the coffin and inserted the tubing into the opening of the lid. He felt it stop when it reached its destination. A stench came from the golden opening.

He would later tell me, "If evil had a scent, that's how it would smell."

Xavier ran to the display case that had the small journal. He fumbled in his pockets for keys but couldn't find them. He ransacked his desk, but still no keys. Then, he took the crowbar in his hand and smashed the glass, snatched the journal from its cradle, and returned to the coffin. He turned to the beginning of the book and carefully moved the silk placeholder to the side. It read:

*October 13th*

*He calls to me in the darkness of the night, my master, even though I am no longer with him. If they knew of what he was, if they suspected, they would surely come and try to destroy him. He promises me life eternal, a gift unto me only. He will send his venom through my veins and make me invincible. He says I will be his salvation. He says he is charging me with his resurrection! Should the disbelievers defeat him, we, his minions, have orders to lay his remains to rest in his coffin, which is protected by dark enchantments. Master has taught me his secret tongue. I and I alone know how to read his language—the language of the dead.*

Below the journal entry were strings of strange symbols, each relating to a letter or word in the English alphabet. The random symbols were defensive charms intended to keep the coffin protected. He ran to his desk and grabbed a charcoal pencil and piece of parchment paper. He laid the paper against the first paragraph embedded into the coffin and used the charcoal to take a rubbing of a subset of the symbols. He sat at the desk and began using the journal to decipher the cryptic text. Once completed, the paragraph read:

> *The darkest soul doth lie within deathful slumber. Life's blood pure thee must attain and serve unto its wanting lips, free of impurity or sinful desire of flesh. Only then thine eyes shall see true remuneration of timeless days.*

"Pure? *A virgin?*" Xavier shouted to himself. "In this day and age? Are you serious?"

He searched the book and his research notes, trying to find clarification. He had no idea where he would find a virgin. Of course, I can tell you they exist, but they are very, very rare. He had seen the students at Rutgers and he didn't think there was an untainted one in the lot of us, and he was *almost* right. He jumped up from his desk and walked to the freezer in the back of the room, and then he dug into the bottom through the meat and frozen vegetables and pulled out a locked cooler. He entered the combination and popped it open, pulling out medical bags filled with blood.

Yeah, you guessed it. Xavier had paid a fair penny for those hoodlums to break into Mercy Blood Bank, because he knew if you were waking up Dracula, blood would certainly be involved, but the blood of a virgin?

He began searching the labels on the bags. Information was listed on each—blood type, date, zip code, patient reference number—however, there didn't seem to be a section that asked "Virgin: Y/N."

Tossing the useless bags back into the container, he walked back to the desk. He began thumbing through the book again because he was convinced that the answer was in there, hidden in the diary of *R.M. Renfield.*

# STEALING RODNEY

Murray told us she knew something had arrived that night. She could just *feel* it. She had been nauseated all day without reason. When the feeling overcame her, she was making a pot of herbal tea because it had been one of those days at Rutgers. I could sympathize because I had *those* days all the time. She had lived in the city for five years, watching, waiting, and hoping for the end, yet not wanting it to arrive. The signs led her to this place, and her research confirmed that somewhere intermingled in the student body of Rutgers was someone quite special. Of course, we didn't know that someone was *me*, though Murray had her suspicions.

She was rinsing out her teacup when she thought she saw something through the fabric of her shirt. Quickly, she reached into her blouse, pulling out a necklace made of gold. Attached to the links was a small gold amulet in the shape of a bat with a ruby in its chest, much like the ring that Xavier wore on his hand.

Murray thought she had seen the stone in the center glow for a moment and then fade back into the deep, dark red. If the stone was glowing, the time had arrived, and she was nowhere near ready. There was more to be done, and an heir to be found.

The next day, everyone could tell something was up. Murray appeared to be abnormally distracted during class. We didn't know it, but she had been awake the entire night, staring at the stone, waiting for it to glow once again for confirmation. Of course, it never did, and 6:00 a.m. came early, so everyone could feel her exhaustion. We're all prone to off days—goodness knows that I've seen many of them and quite recently. Still, Murray was usually on top of her game and always, *always in* a good mood.

"All right, class, today we are going to get our quiz out of the way," she said. We moaned. It was completely unplanned. Typically, quizzes were announced well in advance. "Guys, I know I don't *pop* these pop quizzes on you, so I am going to write a bonus question on the board, and if you answer it, I'll give you seven bonus points."

Seven points could take you from fail to pass, a very generous offer. Looking back, it was almost as if she didn't want to be bothered with us that day. The quiz was simple—not much thought had gone into its preparation. It was just long enough to keep us occupied for the duration of the period. Surprised at its simplicity, I finished a little early. I walked up to Murray's desk and laid the test face down on the upper right-hand corner.

"Vickie," she whispered.

I said, "Yeah."

She said, "You think you could stay after class for a couple of minutes? I want to catch up with you on a couple of things."

Okay, so that was odd. So, I just said, "Well, yeah, I suppose."

Murray was able to crack a smile for me in appreciation, and I returned it as I made my way back to my desk. I thought, *What in the world would Murray want to talk to me about?* With her mood, there was no telling. I thought that maybe it could've been related to my nomination for the Halloween Ball. That was the only out-of-the-norm thing going on that I was aware of at the time. I had no idea that Baron Von Bloodsucker was sleeping peacefully a few miles away from us.

*"Victoria …"*

It whispered to me again. Now I was hearing it in the daytime, like some kind of freak! I looked to my left and then my right. Kyle sat behind me, and I turned around to look at him.

"What?" I whispered.

"I didn't say anything," Kyle responded.

I said, "Funny, Dumbass."

"What?" he replied.

*"Victoria Van Hel ..."*

The bell rang, sending a charge of electricity through my nerves. I jumped like a goober, closing my book with a slam. As the class began bustling their way to freedom, I sat for a moment and then began slowly putting my things away. Kyle motioned for me to come with him, but I pointed to Murray, who was waiting for the class to disperse. Once we were nearly alone, I threw my bags over my shoulder and walked over to her.

Murray said, "Thanks, Vickie. I appreciate you staying over for a second. Sorry I haven't quite been myself today. I wanted to ask you, have you been working on your family tree assignment?"

"Well, not yet, actually. We've been kind of busy at home, and Mom and Dad really haven't had a chance to look at it," I said. "Why? Do you need it? I thought we had until—"

"No, no," she said dismissively. "I was just checking on it. I...I thought about using yours as an example is all."

Somehow, I was not so sure she was telling the truth. You know how crap has a distinct odor? Well, her explanation had that "eau de doo-doo" smell all over it.

I said, "Oh, okay. Well, I'll see if I can get something together and maybe give it to you the first of next week. I bet Dad's side will—"

She cut me off with, "Vickie, have you noticed anything strange lately? Anything at all?"

I thought, *Why, yes, Ms. Murray. I killed a wasp with a #2 pencil like some geeked-out ninja, I've been having dreams that talk to me, I feel like I've had my period every day this week, and now I am beginning to hear voices. Yes! Yes, something is very, very wrong!*

"No, nothing. Why?" I said.

She sat silently for a moment. "No reason. Vickie, I want you to know that you can come and talk to me any time about anything you like. I am a really good listener." Murray reached into her bag and handed me her card. "Call me anytime, day or night."

It was a strange statement, but pleasant, so I said, "Uh, okay. Will do."

At the time, I didn't know what to think about Murray's comments and questions. They were strange and out of place. I felt uncomfortable all of a sudden and wanted to get away, so I darted toward the door, turning to give Murray a final glance before leaving. She smiled and watched me go. Kyle was waiting in the hall.

"What was all that about?"

I said, "God, who knows? She was asking me about the genealogy project."

"What about it?" he asked.

"If I had started it," I said.

*What is it about this family tree thing?* I thought. First, there was the strange look Mom gave me when I mentioned the project, and now this? Something was going on, and I had a good idea that the answers, or at least more questions, were hiding in the depths of my DNA. Personally I was hoping DNA meant "Do Not Ask".

"Weird!" Kyle replied. We walked outside to see that Judy was there waiting on us. "I can't believe your mom is cheating today."

"She's not cheating. I told you she has to show a house this afternoon and couldn't pick us up," I said.

The whole ride home, Judy talked and talked about my nomination so much it was embarrassing. She kept thinking it was a beauty pageant. Each time she would make the statement, Kyle would correct her. We pulled up to my house just as Mom was arriving home from her showing.

As usual, Mom sat down in the recliner in the living room and kicked her shoes to the floor, rubbing her tired feet. I plopped onto the couch, unable to stop thinking about Murray's attitude. I knew she wanted to say more; she wanted to ask something other than how the assignment was going, but what? Strange things were beginning to unfold, and I was starting to believe I was in the middle of them, like a trap that was waiting to snap shut on my neck.

"So, are you excited about your nomination?" asked Mom. She was elated when I had told her the news. Mom had been prom queen her senior year in high school, a title that was a source of great pride for her.

"Yeah, I guess," I replied.

Mom said, "You guess? Why, I'd be excited!"

"It's not like I'm going to win or anything," I said.

"I think you have just has much of a chance as anyone else. Why wouldn't you?"

I said, "I'm just not *that* popular."

Mom said, "Well, I don't believe that. You're pretty, funny, and super-smart. Some people have a way of being jealous of those things, Vickie, that's all."

"Yeah," was all I could manage. I had a hard time believing people were jealous of me. "Mom, Ms. Murray asked me about my family tree assignment today."

Again, there was the air of awkwardness around her.

"Sure!" Mom said, brushing the great big, fat, purple elephant in the room aside. "When your father gets home, we'll sit down and get started." She picked up a magazine and began thumbing through it.

"Mom, why does that make you uncomfortable?" Sometimes, you just have to cut the chase.

"What?" she said.

I said, "The family tree. Do we have, like, serial killers or something in the branches?"

Mom laughed. "Lord, no. It's just a lot to remember, and I'm not so sure about your dad's side. That could be difficult. He's got all kinds of people."

"Okay. It's just that when I bring it up, you kind of zone out," I said.

"You're being silly," Mom replied.

"No, seriously ..."

*Ding-dong!*

The front doorbell rang, and I looked toward the window. There was no telling who it could be. I got up from the couch and walked to the living room window. There parked at the curb was Rod's shiny red BMW. I felt my heart jump into my throat. *Oh, my God!*

"Who is it?" Mom asked.

"Rod Rainfeld," I said. I stood there motionless, not knowing whether to run away or run to the door.

*Ding-dong!*

"Well, answer the door!" Mom whispered.

"*You* answer it!" I whispered back.

"I'm not getting it. He's here for you!"

*Knock, knock, knock.*

I took a deep breath, gathered myself, and walked to the door. I opened it with a great big goofy smile.

"Hi," Jessica said sweetly, smiling wide. Rod stood behind her. I felt my stomach turn as if I had eaten something bad. For a moment, I had actually believed Rod had come for me, but alas, before me stood my greatest, big-boobied, blonde challenge.

"Hey, Jessica," Mom said, stepping up behind me.

"Hey, Mrs. J.," Jessica said in a bubbly tone. There it was—that bubbly thing I knew I could never be. "We were just out collecting cans for the Halloween Ball, and Rod just *had* to stop by here to see if you guys had any to contribute."

"Well, I think we do," Mom said. "Let me go check."

She left me standing there at the door. I would have much rather checked for cans and left Mom making pleasant, meaningless conversation with Ms. Whores.

"So, how's the dance coming?" I asked.

Jessica didn't say anything at first. She only stood there smiling idiotically. Rod gave her a little nudge, which signaled her to mutter, "Fine. It's coming along great."

"Good." I began to think speaking to Jessica could be fun. It was obvious she didn't want to talk to me. "So, did you guys get all the decorations you needed?"

"Yes," she said.

I said, "I bet it's going to look great. Especially if you have a hand in it, Jessica."

"Oh, don't give me that!" Jessica said in a whispered tone. "You couldn't care less if ..."

"Here we go!" Mom said, arriving back at the door with a large bag of cans.

"Oh! Man, this is a lot of cans!" Jessica said, snapping back into her chipper self. "Thank you so much, Mrs. J. These will help!"

Mom said, "You are welcome, sweetie. Now, you kids be careful out there."

"We will!" Jessica replied as she began to walk from the porch.

"We will," added Rod. He turned to follow Jessica, smiling. "See ya, Vickie."

"Yeah, you, too," I said as I shut the door behind them.

Watching from the window, I could see Jessica marching from the porch, infuriated. She tossed the cans into the back of the convertible and huffed her way into the passenger's seat.

I could barely hear Rod say, "There, now that wasn't so bad, and we got a ton of cans from—"

"Oh, get in the friggin' car! I can't believe you made me come over here," Jessica replied.

Rod went silent and got into the car, but he didn't start the engine. He was beginning to get pissed—I could tell.

He turned to her, saying, "Jessica, you need to get over this thing with Vickie. Can't you let it go? I bet if you guys were to sit down and talk, you'd have a lot in common."

"Oh, my *God!* I don't have anything in common with that trash!" She crossed her arms. "You know what? I am starting to think you have a thing for her."

"What?" Rod laughed.

*Did he?*

Jessica said, "Yeah, yeah. I think you have a crush on Vickie Jenkins."

He said, "You're out of your mind."

*Well, you don't have to have a crush on me, but you don't have to act like the idea is so ridiculous,* I thought.

Watching them argue was so super fun. It was like being at a soap opera aquarium. I even cracked the window just a bit so I could hear them clearer.

Jessica kept on, "No, I'm not! I bet you'd go for her. You would! That piece of trash."

*Smack her, Rod. Smack her in the jaw!*

Rod sat there silent, infuriated. I could tell he was cooking something in his mind and I wasn't sure I was going to like it, either.

"Fine!" he spouted. He took the keys out of the ignition and got out of the car.

*Wait, what do you mean, "Fine?"*

"Wait…oh, God. He's getting out!" I said.

"He's what?" Mom asked, running to the window where she couldn't be seen.

I said, "He's getting out of the car."

Rod began to stomp toward the front porch.

"Where are you going, Rod?" shouted Jessica, but he didn't answer. "What are you doing?"

Rod rang the doorbell. Before I could even think about it, I opened the door.

"Hey," I said smiling absurdly.

"Um, hey," Rod nervously replied.

Jessica yelled, "You better get back over here!"

He said, "Vickie, listen, I want to ask you something."

"Yeah?" I said.

"Rod!" Jessica yelled.

"Um, well…the thing is …"

"Yeah," I said.

It was very cute to watch him behave so anxiously. I watched Mom stand back, hands clasped at her mouth, hoping and smiling.

I said, "Well …"

"Dammit, Rod!" Jessica screamed out as she got out of the car.

Rod said, "Would you like to go with me to the Halloween Ball?"

"That's it!" Jessica said, slamming the car door.

"Um, what about Jessica?" I asked.

"Screw you, Rod!" Jessica said as she began marching down the street.

"Oh, she'll be fine," he said.

*Obviously!*

"My daddy was right! You're a spoiled rich punk!" Jessica called, still walking.

"Well, sure!" I said. "That is, if you're sure she doesn't mind."

"Asshole!" Jessica yelled.

"She's okay with it," Rod said with a huge smile. It lit him up, like a spotlight. "So, I'm going to run, okay? I'll pick you up here…at six?"

"Dumbass!" Jessica yelled.

"Sure!" I said with a smile.

"Great! It's a date, then," he grinned.

"It's a date," I said with my face burning.

Dad pulled into the driveway, arriving home from the university. He got out of the car and saw Jessica stomping down the street. As he threw his satchel over his shoulder, he called to her. "Hey, Jessica," he said pleasantly, the same cheerful way he talked to everyone.

"Oh, shut the hell up!" she snapped at him.

"That's marvelous, Jess! Have a good evening," Dad replied as he made his way to the door, not even hearing what she had said to him. He could be oblivious that way sometimes.

"Hello, Mr. Rainfeld!" Dad said to Rod as he stepped up on the porch.

"Hey there, Mr. Jenkins. Well, Vickie, I'll see you then," Rod said, his face now flush with the presence of my dad.

"Okay. Take care," I said.

I simply couldn't stop smiling. It was the silliest I have ever felt in my entire life. Rod walked away with a wave and got into the car. I stood at the door and watched him drive away, passing Jessica, who gave him a familiar gesture with her middle finger. Then, I shut the door and turned to Mom. I thought her face would slide clean off her skull from smiling. We stood there, silent, grinning at each other like idiots while Dad looked at us completely confused, wondering what was going on.

"Uh, what?" Dad whispered to us.

*Ahhh!*

We began screaming at the top of our lungs and ran toward one another, locking into a rocking embrace. I think Dad nearly jumped out of his skin.

"I can't believe it!" I yelled.

"What? What?" Dad urged.

I said, "I'm going on a date with Rod Rainfeld!"

"Outstanding! He's loaded. *His* dad can pay for the wedding," Dad added, dropping his bags to the floor.

# The Nervous Mister Winks

For the next few days, nothing mattered. I was flying so high from the thought of the date with Rod that I had little time to think about anything else, even the strange events that had been consuming me before. The voices had been silent, which suited me just fine. My parents had sat down with me and mapped out our genealogy that weekend to the best of their recollection. Better yet, they acted normal about the process. Dad had a buttload of branches, just as we knew he would. At the time, I still didn't know why Murray expressed interest in my chart, and I no longer cared.

Kyle was so incredibly sick of hearing about Rod he could have slipped into a coma. I couldn't blame him, really; I had never acted that way before. Never had I been so elated at the thought of a dude. As a child, boys had given me appalling infestations of cooties on several occasions, so I stayed away from them at all cost. With the exception of Kyle, I shunned the male species.

When the alarm buzzed Monday morning, I leapt from bed like Snow White. Mom was surprised that I wasn't dancing and singing like a lovesick character in a musical. I hadn't ventured into the wild world of Cover Girl and heels again, but I was definitely perking up my appearance. Jessica had little to say to me and didn't even look in my direction, which was simply full of awesome, if I must say. The word in the halls was that Jessica and Rod were officially over. Jess was no longer hanging around football practice, barking orders at Rod, and he was smiling a great deal more because of it, especially at me. So, was I in the stands at practice like a whooped puppy? No, not quite. Even though I was overjoyed at the thought of Rod, *he* couldn't know that. That's one important thing: never let them know you want them!

Walking nonchalantly by the gym, I peeped inside, hoping to catch a covert glimpse of my prince possibly playing basketball or something,—you know…*sweaty*. However, the main thing that struck me was the huge collection of cans that rested in several large containers in the corner, and the committee still wasn't finished with the drive. All had to be accounted for by Wednesday when the recycling company would arrive to pay out. The money was going to be taken to finish out the decorations and the food for the ball that Friday— *the date with Rod Rainfeld.*

Jessica passed me on the way to Murray's class without saying a single word. Against better judgment, I started to say something nice, but thought better of it. That would have been just a bit overboard, and though I can be catty, I pride myself on not being an outright ass. In fact, I rather felt sorry for Jess. There was even a part of me that wanted to apologize, but I would quickly snuff out the desire each time it arose. Listen, I am nice, but not *that* nice.

"I still don't know why you're handing in your tree today," Kyle said from behind me.

"Well, apparently Murray wanted it," I said.

Kyle said, "Yeah, so you can devote all of your time worshiping Rod the God."

"Down, Kyle. Play pretty," I said.

"Play pretty," he mocked.

We entered the classroom to see Murray nowhere around. At her desk sat Mr. Winks.

*Oh, man—not Winks!*

Winks was the token substitute teacher—jack of all subjects, master of none. He was Rutgers last-ditch effort should a teacher be a no-show. He stuttered nervously all the time. Once, at a rally, someone popped a balloon and sent him into fits. He nearly had to be sedated. His anxiety was so serious that we dared not tease him in fear of encouraging a stroke. I walked to the desk, where he sat engrossed over the lessons for the afternoon.

"Mr. Winks?" I said politely.

"Oh!" Winks replied with a start. "I didn't see you there."

"Sorry! Sorry, Mr. Winks." *Jesus! This man needs some herbal tea or something!* I thought. "I was going to hand this in to Ms. Murray today. Can I give it to you?"

"Sure! Sure. No problem. She's just feeling a bit under the weather. I'll make sure she gets it this evening," he said as his trembling hand reached for the paper.

The good news: I managed to sit through the class without my heart stopping from boredom. The *bad* news: through my daydreams of Rod, the fantasies, and what-ifs, that strange, gnawing feeling surfaced once again. Where was Murray? Just what was her deal?

*"Victoria …"*

There was the voice again! Thinking it simply had to be Kyle, I turned around to him to find that he was also trying his best not to fall asleep. Then, I heard the voice plainly in both ears. It was more than just a faint whisper; it was audible and clear.

*"Victoria Van Helsing …"*

*Van who? Dammit. Who is that?* I looked again to Kyle, who was now asleep and drooling. Rolling my eyes, I began to turn my head toward Winks when something in my peripheral vision caught my eye. I snapped around. There, to my right, was a something—a creature, a monster! Our noses were nearly touching. It was a hideous thing with the darkest blackness for eyes. Its jaws were open, coming for me, with drool dripping from rows of bloodstained fangs. Its hand reached for my hair, taking hold of a lock of it. On its long, bony finger was a small golden ring with a red stone in the center. An involuntary scream burst from my lungs, piercing the air. My arms flailed at the thing, trying to escape, but I was trapped in my desk. Kyle grabbed me.

Then, as quickly as it appeared, it was gone, and there, resting on the floor were the strands of my hair…and the unconscious Mr. Winks, of course.

# VLAD

The evening we were preparing for the pep rally, Xavier was still looking for a solution to his big, dead problem. According to his journals and research notes, he had studied the coffin's symbols and text until his head was about to pop like a zit, and there was still no definitive solution to his problem. The only thing that would bring his buddy to life was blood, pure and simple, and not just any blood, but the blood of a *virgin!* Nevermind finding one, how would he get their blood if he did?

I came to realize Xavier never fancied himself a killer. He certainly wouldn't have been able to walk up and pop a cap in some unsuspecting virgin. Sure, what he was trying to do was evil, but I believe his motives were noble. Angela, his wife and Rod's mother, suffered horribly from cancer. I can't imagine how awful it was to watch her fade away. Her sickness and the injustice of losing her finally took him over. When something like that happens, it's the *why me's* and the *not fair's* that finally drive you nuts, trust me. Therefore, he devised a plan: find Dracula's remains, bring him back to life, and for that service be rewarded with immortality for both him and his only son. Well, without a virgin that was over, right?

Maybe virginity was a virtue that existed at one time, but not in the world of internet, Bluetooth, and cell phone pornography. Sin was ready and waiting at the touch of a finger, and everyone was at the party, if only for a little while. It was enough to drive you insane and, as we would discover, madness was built into Xavier's genes.

All other symbols in the diary and on the coffin led nowhere. Nothing he tried, physical or metaphysical, would break the coffin's seal. There were no secret spells in his research or Renfield's diary, no hidden clues, no direction. It was useless.

*Ding-dong!*

He gathered himself and made his way up the stairs. He opened the front door, ready to yell, when something caught him by surprise. She was about five feet tall, dark-haired, and smiling from ear to ear. It was Teresa Haffner on her humble little can quest.

Reluctantly, Xavier went and retrieved some leftover cans from the kitchen recycle bin and handed them to her to make her go away. However, before she skipped away, she said the most curious thing.

"Thank you, Mr. Rainfeld. Hey, have you seen Rod?" she asked.

"No, no. I think he may be with Jessica," he replied, simply wanting her to leave.

Teresa added, "Oh, they broke up. Didn't he tell you?"

Xavier looked at her. "No, Rod hasn't mentioned it to me yet. I haven't had a chance to speak to him. Uh, what happened?"

She said, "Well, apparently he wants to date Vickie Jenkins or something. Jessica is pretty p-o'ed."

He said, "Well, you know, it doesn't surprise me."

She said, "It doesn't?"

"No. You know, I was never really fond of Jessica."

This was, of course, a lie.

"You know what?" Teresa said in a whisper. "I wouldn't tell her this, but I'm not too fond of her either. I always thought Rod could do better than her, and especially better than Vickie Jenkins!"

(We'll ignore that comment for now, thank you.)

I don't think Xavier knew where he wanted to go with their conversation, really. Maybe he was trying to find out if she at least knew a virgin. Well, frankly, anyone could have looked at Teresa and known she neither knew one nor was one. Still, it was obviously a chance he was willing to take.

"Yeah, see? In my opinion, Rod has always needed someone more," he said.

"More what?" Teresa asked.

"I don't know. Someone nicer, someone more innocent, more *pure*. Do you know anyone like that?" Xavier asked.

Teresa said, "Well, yeah! I'm nice—a lot nicer than Jessica."

"Innocent?" he continued.

She said, "Mr. Rainfeld. Apparently, you don't know Jessica. She lies all the time. As a matter of fact, she cheated on Rod several times…with *Russ Cobbs!*"

Xavier said, "Are you serious?"

"Oh, yeah! I mean, if Rod was my guy, Mr. Rainfeld, I would *never* ever cheat on him."

"Really? And what about pure, Teresa?" Xavier said. "Are you *pure*? Rod needs someone…*pure*. Someone untainted."

Yeah, I know. Creepy, right?

That's when Teresa cocked her eyebrow, snapped her head at him, and said, "Hold up, you asking me if I've done the *nasty*?"

Rod had just pulled into the driveway and was surprised to see Teresa standing on his front porch talking to Xavier. He was even more shocked when she slapped the piss out of him.

"Hi, Rod," she snapped as she stomped past him to her car.

Xavier came running down the steps yelling, "Wait! Wait! That's not what I meant!"

"Boy, you got one dirty old man for a dad. He's sick!" Teresa said as she marched toward her car. Then, she turned on her heel to Rod and with a smile said, "Call me!"

Xavier rushed after her, holding his freshly slapped face.

"Uh, Dad, is there something I should know about?" Rod said.

"Yes, yes, there is. Your father is a putz," Xavier said.

"Yeah, so what else is new? Seriously," Rod said.

"Oh, it's nothing. We were just talking and she took something I said out of context." He walked past Rod, nearing the steps. "And why did I have to hear from her about you dumping Jessica? Why didn't you tell me?"

Rod told me the question caught him off-guard, because the two of them didn't really talk about things like *feelings*.

"Well, Dad, I just didn't think you'd have time to listen," Rod said.

Xavier said, "Well, you should have told me, anyway. And what about this Vickie girl? Jenkins? Do you think she would really be a good match for you, son?"

"Uh, well, I don't know. I was kind of wanting to talk to you about it," Rod replied.

I believe Xavier wanted to think about something else besides coffins, blood, and virgins, because to Rod's amazement, he replied, "Well, come on in. I have work to do. You can talk to me while I do it."

Astounded, Rod followed him inside and down to the basement. With all the lights on, Rod could see that the collection had expanded. Of course, he couldn't figure out the coffin setup in the back of the room, but there was so little of the collection that ever made any sense.

"So," Xavier began. "This Vickie girl."

"Yeah," Rod said as Xavier fumbled through papers. "Well, you see, I think she's great. Now, I know you don't think she comes from the right type of family."

Xavier said, "You got that right. At least her father is a professor. Her mother, bless her soul, couldn't sell her way out of a paper bag."

"She sold you this house," Rod said.

"This house sold itself. There was nothing she had to do," Xavier said.

"Anyway," Rod continued, "Jessica's just too full of herself. She thinks she's perfect and everyone else is trash. And her dad's an ass."

Xavier said, "Well, I can't fault you there. Howard is as bright as a bag of wet hair. And language, please."

"Sorry. I just couldn't see me spending my life with her, you know?" Rod said, looking down. "You know, like you and mom."

Xavier stopped for a moment. "Son, you don't need to be thinking about who you're going to marry at your age. I swear. You know I loved your mother, but her dreamy, wishy-washy attitude rubbed off on you."

"Still. I get nervous because..." Rod began.

"Because?" Xavier said.

Rod said, "Well, because I don't have a lot of...*experience*."

"What are you talking about?" Xavier said, shuffling through his papers. "You have tons of experience. You have football to fall back on, if nothing else, and—"

Rod sighed. "No, Dad. I mean, *experience*. With girls."

Xavier froze.

Yes, you heard it here first: the super-fine star of the football team—a virgin.

Top that!

Xavier said, "What do mean, with girls?"

"God, Dad. Come on. Work with me a little!" Rod said as his face filled with blood. I don't think he had ever thought of uttering that secret to a soul, at least not at that point. Let alone to Xavier.

Xavier asked, "You mean, you're a *virgin*?"

Rod said, "Well, yeah."

"Oh!" Xavier said, clapping his hands together. "This is just too sweet!"

Rod said, "Dad!"

Xavier put his hand out, calming him down. He wasn't making fun of Rod, of course. It was only that the answer to his conundrum was sitting right beside him and was his own flesh and blood.

"No, no, no. Nothing bad. That is totally fine. It is great, actually. You don't know how great!" Xavier said.

"Dad, listen. I haven't told—" Rod began.

"What about Jessica? Didn't you…you know…with Jessica?" Xavier interrupted.

"No," Rod replied.

"Why not? I mean, not that you should be doing things like that, but …"

"Well, she always said she wanted to wait until she was married."

Xavier laughed. "Yeah, okay."

"What's that supposed to mean?" Rod said

"I mean you better talk to Russell," Xavier said. "But regardless, son, there is no shame in being a virgin. You can't be embarrassed of the fact that you have a sense of integrity about you. Why, if your mother was alive, she would be so thrilled to hear this! I had naturally assumed that with all of the male camaraderie that comes with football, someone would have pressured you into it by now."

Xavier positioned himself behind Rod and slowly reached to a display stand, taking a large clay vase from it.

"So, you don't think it's stupid?" Rod said, oblivious to what was about to happen.

He raised the vase high into the air above Rod's head.

"No, son, I'm proud!"

And…*wham!*

Rod hit the ground like a ton of bricks. Yes, Xavier had just knocked his own son out cold. To cover his tracks, he quickly took a large African mask from the wall and put it on the ground next to where Rod had been sitting to make it appear as if the mask had fallen from the wall and struck him.

Next order of business: blood. He ran over and snatched up a small ritual spear, got the crystal bowl from the coffin, and made his way back to Rod. He knelt down and picked up Rod's arm. Yeah, it was cruel, but far less cruel than killing someone, especially his own son. With a quick slice, the deep red blood began to pour from Rod's arm and into the bowl. He had to work fast before Rod regained consciousness. After he felt enough blood had collected into the bowl, he used a makeshift bandage to seal up Rod's wound.

Then, working quickly, he ran to the coffin. He placed the bowl of blood in his holster, reattached the tubing, and fed it into the golden hole of the casket. The fresh blood flowed through the tube. There was barely enough to do the job, but this was the only chance he had. The ring on his hand began to glow brightly. He waited, but there was no movement or sign of life from inside the casket.

Then, once again, the ruby in the center of the bat faded into darkness. Xavier's heart sank. At first, he thought Rod lied to him about the virgin stuff. Of course, there was also the chance that he didn't get enough of Rod's blood.

"What am I doing?" Rod heard him say as he began to awaken.

Rod moaned and Xavier ran to him and knelt down.

"Man!" Rod uttered. "What just happened?"

"Uh…that mask fell off the wall from behind you. Knocked you out cold and cut…see, that's why I don't let people down here!" Xavier lied.

"What?" Rod replied, rubbing his head. "*You* asked me down here!"

"Well, yeah, but…"

*Boom!*

The seal of the casket broke free, sending bellows of smoke pouring to the ground. They could hear a machine gun-like sound of the unlatching locks rattling from inside. With a crack, the lid popped ajar.

Rod yelled, "What the hell? Dad, what is it?"

"Go! Get upstairs!" Xavier said.

"What?" Rod yelled.

They saw fingers slowly creep from inside the casket and take hold of the lid. The digits were long and gray, tipped with yellowish claws. The bones cracked as they tightened their grip. Xavier and Rod stood there in shock, bracing themselves. The thing inside the casket opened the lid and a foul odor entered the room. It was a scent we eventually came to recognize. It slowly sat upright, popping and cracking like an old door. Then, it turned its head to them, opened its black, lifeless eyes…and *smiled.*

As it stood, dust puffed from its elegant nineteenth-century style clothing. It wore a long coat and a roll collar vest over a shirt made of muslin. It jumped to the floor, never taking its eyes from them. Then, it reached into the casket, pulled out a silver-tipped cane, and, after gathering itself, began to walk toward them. Xavier moved in front of Rod.

"So!" said the thing. "Here we are. The year?"

"Wh-what?" Rod said.

"*The year?*" it shouted as its face grimaced. "I want the year!"

"Two thousand ten!" replied Xavier.

"Goodness me!" laughed the creature. "That would be…my, my…well over one hundred years." It quickly slid across the floor and smelled Rod's wound, taking in his scent with deep breaths, like a dog. "Renfield! The lineage lives on! Shocking. I always thought your bloodline was far too ignorant to survive, yet here you are. Here *we* are. And where, pray tell, are we?"

Xavier said, "Georgia, the United States."

"America! Land of the free," it mocked.

"Dad …" Rod began.

"Dad!" cheered the beast. "Oh, this is your son! Wonderful!"

"Who are you?" Rod asked.

"Who am I? Didn't Daddy tell you?" Rod didn't reply. "Well?"

"No, he…he didn't," answered Rod.

It said, "I, dear boy, am prince of Wallachia, son of the dragon, *Dracul.* Or, as others have known me, *Dracula.*"

Rod looked at the creature blankly for a moment, not quite knowing what to say. "A vampire?"

Vladimir laughed. "Yes, yes. You have the capacity to learn. I enjoy that." He began to circle the men, watching them. "I must say, I do appreciate that you have allowed me to enter once again into this world that I hold so dear. So much livestock! I can only imagine how many humans are on this miserable planet in this age. Much to do, much to do. But …" Vladimir sat down in the chair in front of them and elegantly crossed his legs, holding his cane in both hands. "First thing must be first. Blood. I need it. I certainly can't go on looking like this, now can I? Next, I will need whiskey. The best." Then, within an instant, Vladimir had Rod firmly by the neck. He breathed him in, as if he smelled a fresh flower. "*Your* blood. I can smell it. It is pure. Your offering was most gracious."

"Offering?" Rod muttered. "Dad, what did you do?"

"Let him go! Take me!" Xavier said.

Vladimir snapped his head around to Xavier. "Why would I take your tainted, wicked life when the boy's is so much sweeter, so much more powerful. What does it matter to the likes of you? Obviously, you *gave* him to me. It was his blood that brought me back from the limbo where I was imprisoned."

"Dad?" said Rod. Naturally, he couldn't believe it. His own father had attacked him. How sucky was that?

Xavier said, "Rodney, listen …"

Vladimir laughed. "Boy, I may not kill you yet. I may turn you, make you my first in the new century. Wouldn't that be fun?" He opened his large jaws, which appeared to unhinge like a snake.

"No!" Xavier shouted. He picked up the ritual spear from the floor and shoved it deep into Vladimir's back causing him to scream out in pain and drop Rod to the floor.

Xavier yelled, "Rodney, run! Get out!"

Rod began to run toward the steps. Vladimir pulled the spear from his wound and flung it at Xavier, stabbing him in his shoulder. Xavier wailed and dropped to the floor. Vladimir leapt into the air and effortlessly transformed into a bat-like thing with massive leathery wings. The creature soared toward Rod as he stumbled out of the door and slammed it behind him. It beat furiously against the door, growling and hissing like a rabid cat. That's when the doorbell rang.

Rod bolted toward the foyer.

*Crash!*

The bat burst through the basement door, ripping it to splinters. It flew after Rod, who could feel the wind from its wings on his back. He flung open the front door to see Russ, who had arrived to pick him up for the rally.

Russ turned around with that ignorant grin on his face. "Hey man, you ready? What is going on in—"

"Get down!" screamed Rod.

Rod ducked, trying to grab Russ and drag him to the ground, but it was too late. Drac snatched Russ and hoisted him into the air as he screamed into the night. The thing bit into him as he continued to yell, and then dropped him and flew away into the dark. Rod ran to him.

"Oh, my God! Russ! Russ, are you okay, man?" Rod said.

Russ held his spurting neck, shaking as shock was taking over his body. In only seconds, the venom had him. It does that—quick, like fire. He screamed in agony, his body quaking. Rod backed up, not knowing what was happening. Little did he know that Russ was no longer Russ; he was something else, something hideous. He was a vampire, his bat-like features pronounced, his black eyes glaring at Rod as his nostrils flared, smelling Rod's virgin blood. Russ roared and charged at Rod who took him by his varsity jacket and flipped him over, stunning him.

Rod ran to the patio and pulled an umbrella from the table, turning just in time to dodge Russ's attack. He took the umbrella and drove the point deep into Russ's stomach, pushing it through to the other side of this body. Black blood poured from the wound. Russ squealed at him in a high-pitched tone, like an eagle or some kind of bird. His long fangs snapped like an alligator. Rod fought with him, wrestling him over to the edge of the drop-off beside the house. He kicked Russ's knee, breaking it, and with a heave, he sent him flying over the railing to the landing below.

Xavier was running toward him from the house. "Rodney!"

He couldn't look at Xavier. With tears in his eyes, Rod began running as fast as his legs could carry him. I don't think he knew where he was going or what he was going to do. I mean, whose mind could process stuff like that? His father had betrayed him, he had fought the real-life Dracula, and then he killed a guy who he believed to be one of his best friends. That kind of stuff can ruin someone's day. What other choice did he have but to run away, far away, into the night?

Though I didn't know it at the time, my own revelations were creeping up on me, too. And they were going to hurt like hell.

# Discovery

While Rod was fighting Dracula that night, I was shaving my legs. Shut up—first shoes, now this—I get it. Murray was at home going through the assignments that Winks had delivered to her from that day. She had finished her evening shower. She said she woke up that morning not able to face the day; she just needed a mental health day. I totally get mental health days. I think they should be mandatory. After having absolutely no sleep, she needed a break.

She still couldn't let herself believe that the amulet had roused. She had seen the thing ever since she was a little girl and it had never even glistened, not even a sparkle. She had tossed it into her jewelry box before her shower to make herself stop obsessively looking at it. She was beginning to think she had imagined it all.

She picked up the folder that Winks had left. Inside there were homework assignments she had to grade before morning. Thumbing through the papers, she saw Russ Cobbs had mistakenly submitted his doodle page that portrayed a frightened Mr. Winks next to an overinflated balloon. She smiled and shook her head, not knowing it was the last thing he would ever hand in to her.

Destiny had called to Murray years before. It had taken her by the hand and led her to my town, though she wasn't certain of its motivation. It had taken years, but she had finally narrowed it down to me, although she didn't know why. She told me that there was just something about me, a feeling she always got when I was around. That's why the whole genealogy project had come to mind in the first place. It was her way of testing us, a way of knowing without asking. Winks had told her of my outburst in class that day, the scream that caused him to faint like a possum. She thought that maybe I could be feeling something as well, though she knew at the time I wouldn't understand it.

At that moment, she spied my tree amidst the plethora of papers. Murray yanked it from the folder. If the answer existed, she was certain it was there. She turned on the light next to her and put on her reading glasses.

Murray carefully went down each of my branches. *Jenkins, Halsworth, Stuffle, Peterson*…but, no Van Helsing. She went through the listing again, hoping she had missed it, but it simply wasn't there. She took off her glasses and tossed them to the side in disgust. If she was wrong about me, she couldn't trust her instincts. I wasn't the only one who had a secret in my blood; Murray had her own hidden agenda. The ancestry of Mina Murray was not as powerful as the Van Helsing line, but still vital and significant. If Murray couldn't find the Van Helsing heir, then all was going to be lost. If there was evil brewing, a Van Helsing was the only one who could stop it.

She took a deep breath and got up from the desk, walking to the bedroom to put the necklace back on, but she wasn't going to obsess over it. She had to get some sleep. With the exception of bath time, the amulet was always with her. As she walked up to her dresser and reached down to open the small wooden drawer, she could see the light, the red glow seeping from the edges of the wood. She immediately jerked open the drawer. The amulet shined so brightly it lit the whole room.

"You have to be a Murray," Vladimir said from the door. Miranda spun around. "You look just like her, my Mina, just as beautiful."

There he stood. With some fresh blood, new flesh had managed to form on his old bones. He leaned against the door, facing her bedroom with his arms folded, his long digits drumming his bicep.

"Who…" she began.

Vladimir said, "Oh, don't try that with me. If you have that," he pointed to the amulet, "then you know who I am." In the blink of an eye, he was holding her by the neck. He took her arm and opened the skin near her wrist with his claws. Warm blood dripped from the cut. He leaned down and smelled it. "Ah, yes. I can smell her in your veins, so sweet, so kind. I loved that about her, you know. I crossed oceans of time to find her. My, my—I'm reuniting with all of my old friends."

"Leave me alone!" Murray yelled.

"You know," he said, "I learned a new word tonight. *Dude.* I'm not quite sure what it means. Does it mean *monster*?" He let go of her and began walking around the room. "I only know the young man I just ate kept saying, *'Dude, this is so whack.'* It's like another language you people speak. *Dude* and *whack.*"

"How did you get here?" Miranda asked, trying to buy time, thinking of a way to escape. Oprah could have been standing in her room and she wouldn't have been more surprised. She had been ready for him…*eventually*, but his arrival that evening was a little unexpected, of course. Just beside the door in her nightstand was a kit of protection she had made years before: holy water, a crucifix, and a wooden dagger—if she could just get to it. To do so meant she had to get past him, and that was easier said than done.

"How did I get here? Well, now I can't tell you that, my dear. I can't give away all my little secrets," Vladimir said.

Murray began easing her way toward her nightstand. "Why are you here? What do you plan to do?"

Vladimir laughed. "What do you think I plan to do? What I've always planned, my dear. I will spread my disease to everyone in the land, and eventually the world. My minions will then bow down to me, and I will be king."

"And what then? What happens when there are no more humans to eat?"

"Oh, but there will always be humans. Have you ever researched the human reproduction rate? It's astounding. Maybe I'll farm you, herd you like cattle or turkeys!"

Miranda inched closer to the nightstand. "It sounds like you've thought everything through."

"Well, yes. I've had a lot of time, I guess you could say." Instantaneously, he was in front of her, blocking her from the drawer that held her weapons. "Listen to me, woman," he growled, eyes blazing. "You cannot defeat me with your meager armaments."

He reached into the nightstand, grabbed the kit, and threw it across the room. Yeah, that wasn't cool. There was no escape. He tightened his grip on her as he opened his jaws, leaning into her slowly, targeting the exact area on her neck where he would attack. It was faster at the neck; she was thankful for that.

Then, miles away, I did something stupid that caught his attention. As I was completing the final upward stroke with Dad's mega razor, I sliced right into my ankle. Okay, so it had been a while since I had shaved. With the possibility of a new boyfriend on the horizon, I had to do something. What I didn't know was that Drac caught my scent from miles away, the unmistakable aroma of Van Helsing DNA that seeped from my veins into the bathtub.

"*Van Helsing …*" he whispered into Murray's ear.

As mysteriously as he had arrived, Dracula vanished into a cloud of smoke without another word. She fell to the bed, catching her breath. At that moment, she knew the bloodline did exist. It was there. It was *now*.

And the battle was about to begin…right after I found a Band-Aid.

# Truth Sucks

"**D**ammit!" I shouted, blotting the blood from my ankle with a tissue. "That's going to be pretty!"

"What are you yelling about?" Mom called.

"I cut myself!" I said.

"Good Lord! Is it bad?"

"No," I replied.

"Well, then get a Band-Aid and shut up!"

You had to love her sympathy.

I rolled my eyes. The bleeding had finally stopped, but the accident had left a nasty gash in my leg that I hoped would heal before the dance. I didn't have a clue how the Populars did it, how they took so much time to look a certain way. It was a needless bother to me. Undoubtedly, there were some people, like Rod, who were naturally pretty. I suspected he didn't have to do a thing to look the way he did. Guys seldom do. Why does it have to be girls that have to go through the torture? It isn't fair.

Being careful of the wound, I dried off my legs and brushed my teeth. I walked into my room and flopped onto the bed with a sigh. The flash of that creature, the thing I had seen in history class, kept repeating in my mind. When I'd see it, I'd close my eyes tight and breathe until it passed. I had fallen asleep in class—that was it. That's what Kyle thought. Nevertheless, it was so real. I mean, I could even feel its breath on my chin and smell that it was in desperate need of a Tic-Tac. Still, I thought it was something my mind had cooked up.

That Winks had passed out cold during the outburst was a perk. At least his dramatics took some of the focus from my freak-out, which I later attributed to the bug-on-my-leg defense. Kyle was the only one I had actually told of what I had seen…or imagined.

The doorbell rang, causing me to spring to life. I sat straight up thinking, *Oh, my God, it has to be Rod!* I heard Mom answer the door. She seemed pleasantly surprised. I jumped from the bed and flung open the closet. I looked horrific. My hair had dried on its own, and you know that is an outright hairdo no-no. To top it all off, I had toothpaste on my chin. I took one look at myself in the mirror and thought, *Oh, I'm a hot mess!* Rod couldn't see me in such a state, at least not that early in the game. After twenty-five years of marriage, I'd sit in my underwear scratching my butt along with him, but not at that point.

"Vickie," Mom called. "There is someone down here to see you."

"Dammit," I whispered. I ran to the vanity and frantically brushed my hair, putting it back in a slick ponytail. I then put on a little lipstick (not too much), a little powder for shine, my best jeans, and my brand new shoes. I ran from my room to the top of the steps, but *not* down them. You never want to seem too eager. I took a deep breath and then casually descended. I rounded the railing with a welcoming smile and looked right into Miranda Murray's eyes.

"Uh, Ms. Murray? What are you doing here?" I asked in surprise.

Murray sat on the loveseat across from Mom, looking highly uncomfortable, as if she had a cork lodged in her butt. Dad was sitting in his recliner.

Murray said, "Hi, Vickie. Um, I wanted to talk to you about something."

"Okay, what?" I said, stepping behind the chair.

She looked down. "Oh, Mr. Winks came by and gave me your genealogy assignment this evening, and, and I had a couple of questions about it."

*What? That's not even remotely a good explanation,* I thought.

"And you couldn't wait until tomorrow?" I asked.

"Well, I wanted to present it to the class tomorrow morning, and I was out this way, so I decided to stop by," she clarified.

I said, "Okay…well, I'm pretty useless in that area, I'm afraid. If you want to know the particulars, the people you need to talk to are sitting in front of you. I barely remember who *they* are most of the time, let alone my other family members."

I rounded the chair and plopped down. Apparently, my history teacher's cheese was sliding off her cracker. It happens to the best of us.

"Sure!" said Mom. "We can help, can't we John? John!"

"Oh…oh, yeah, yeah," Dad said, being roused from his newspaper.

Murray looked at them uncomfortably. It was apparent she had intended for it to be a private conversation, but what did I know of my ancestry? I hardly saw any of my family besides the few who lived in the area.

"Well, okay, I guess. Now, don't take this the wrong way, but I'm not certain your tree is exactly…*accurate*," Murray said timidly.

Mom immediately tensed up. "What do you mean, *accurate?*"

Murray put her hand up. "Please, I don't mean to be disrespectful. It's just that I have some very, very important work to do, and I was thinking that Vickie's ancestry was the key to a few answers I need. But if this tree is fact, then Vickie isn't the one I'm seeking."

"Answers you need for what?" I asked, beginning to grow impatient.

Murray's nerves were on edge. I literally thought she was going to be sick. She would start a sentence, like, ten times. It was as if her mouth was falling down the stairs.

"Vickie," Murray finally said, "have you ever heard of a person named Abraham Van Helsing?"

"That is enough, Ms. Murray!" shot Mom.

"Please, I …" Miranda said.

I leaned in. "Yeah, yeah. I've heard of him. He's that monster hunter guy. The one in the movies and comic books and stuff."

"Ms. Murray, I need to ask you to leave," Mom said.

I had never seen Mom so upset. She had already acted strange when I had mentioned the assignment; now for her to be this upset piqued my curiosity. I had to uncover what it was all about.

I said, "Mom, chill out. It's not that big of a deal."

"Barbara, sit down," Dad said loudly.

Murray pleaded, "Mrs. Jenkins, I swear I don't mean any disrespect."

"What is it?" I said.

Murray looked to Mom and said, "It's started again, and if I'm wrong about your daughter then I may not have time to look anywhere else. There's no time left."

"What?" I said again, feeling as if they didn't see me.

"This is not the place for this discussion!" Mom yelled.

"Barbara!" Dad said.

*"Someone needs to tell me what is happening!"* I screamed as I stood up. It was one of those screams where you didn't quite intend for it to be as loud or intense as it turned out to be.

Everyone fell quiet. Mom sat down. We all remained silent for a few seconds, feeling anything that we said could and would be used against us in a court of the insane.

Murray looked up at me. "Come on, sit back down." I took a seat. "Vickie, I don't really know how to say this, so you're going to have to work with me. I'd like to think that you and I have known each other long enough for you to know that I would never mislead you. You're going to think I'm crazy, but Abraham Van Helsing…he was a real person."

I looked at her sarcastically. "Really? Well, so what?" I didn't care if the dead geezer had lived at one time. What did it matter to me?

"He was a doctor from the Netherlands who lived in the latter part of the nineteenth century. He was a master of medicine and taught medical practices throughout Europe," she went on.

"So," was all I could manage.

Murray leaned toward me. "In 1861, a strange virus began spreading through London. A doctor named John Seward, a former student of Van Helsing's, had a friend named Lucy Westenra who became infected by the disease. Though he tried, Seward couldn't figure out what was killing her. So he called on Van Helsing to evaluate her condition."

"Okay, hold on a minute," I began. All of it started to sound a little too familiar.

Murray kept going. "And she died from it, but, she didn't really die, she…*changed.*"

"Changed?" I asked.

"Yes, *changed,* and after her death, children in London began disappearing. The papers suspected a woman was involved in their disappearances," Murray said. "Van Helsing believed it was Lucy who was responsible, because she wasn't dead, not completely. One night, he pulled together a group of men, and they found her there, deep in the grounds of the cemetery, alive. Lucy had been the victim of Count Dracula, a *vampire.*"

Now, what do you say to something like that?

Exactly ... "Uh, say what?"

"Dracula had traveled to London in search of Mina Murray, *my* great-great-great-grandmother. He believed her to be the reincarnation of his wife from centuries before. Vladimir and his army nearly killed them all. But Van Helsing and his team cornered and killed Vladimir, or at least thought they had."

That's a terrible amount of information to receive in only a few seconds. I sat there trying to absorb what was just told to me. Then, my defensive smartass mechanism activated.

I said, "So, you're telling me that this Van Helsing guy was real, and not only that, but vampires are real, including *the* Count Dracula?"

After a second of uncertainty, she said, "Well, yes."

"Okay, even if you're not crazy, and I'm not sure you aren't, what does any of this have to do with me?" I asked.

Dad got up from his chair and walked to the window, gazing into the darkness. Murray knelt down and took my hand into hers. "Listen, Vickie," she said wholeheartedly, "I'm not certain, but if my research is correct, I think that Abraham Van Helsing was your great-great-great-grandfather. Dracula has been awakened in our time, and I believe that *you* are the only one who's going to be able to stop him."

I looked deep into Murray's eyes…and then laughed my ass off. "You're insane, woman! Wait a minute, wait a minute. You are telling me the story of Dracula is true? With the blood and the bats and coffins and stakes?"

"Yes, Vickie. What I am telling you is the truth. He came to see me tonight," she replied.

I scoffed, "Oh, my God! Who? Dracula?"

"Yes," she said.

I couldn't deny Murray's sincerity. I knew then that if her story wasn't true, she obviously believed it to be. Furthermore, I realized that if what she was saying *was* true, it immediately turned my parents into liars. I stopped smiling, looked at them, and said, "Mom? Dad? What do you have to say about this garbage?"

Mom didn't say a word. I could see the tears welling in her eyes. Dad was the first to speak.

"Michael and Claudia Van Helsing," he said looking out of the window. "God, I haven't said those names in a lifetime. You know, Claudia introduced your mom and me while we were all in college together in Tennessee. It used to piss Mike off when I made fun of his last name. I would ask him why he never changed it, and he would say because he loved it."

"Dad, what are you talking about?" I said. I felt cold and numb, as if I had just been dipped into ice water.

"At the end of our junior year, there was this man, the janitor at Ayer's Hall at the university," he continued. "He was so strange. He stalked us for weeks. It was obvious to me that the guy was watching them…watching *you*. I told them—I told them to watch out for that guy, but Mike would just laugh at me. You were only three months old when it happened. They were driving back to Knoxville one night. It was raining; God, it was raining so hard that night. There was a wreck involving another car. The police called it an accident, but I didn't buy that for a minute."

"What are you telling me?" was all I could manage. There was nothing else to say. I could feel the hinges of my world coming apart; the foundation of my life began to crack.

"The driver of the other car was that creepy janitor, the same one who was always around us. No one survived." Dad turned to me. "Except you."

At that point, my eyes were not able to hold back the tears. I looked to Mom, waiting on her to deny it, waiting on her to dismiss the whole thing, but she didn't.

"Mom?" I said.

"It's true," Mom said, beginning to cry. "Claudia saved you, honey. She must have known someone was after you, that you were being chased, because she climbed into the back seat and used her body to protect you. The police were amazed someone could survive a wreck that terrible, a baby at that. They found you, safe and dry, in Claudia's arms. So we, your godparents, took you, and we packed away your past upstairs in the attic." She wiped her eyes. "I'm sorry, honey. We wanted to tell you so many times."

It was one of those moments where I didn't necessarily want to be angry. I really didn't, especially with Mom crying, but I just couldn't help it.

"You're lying!" I shouted.

"Vickie, wait," Murray pleaded.

"And you! You shut up. This is all your fault!" I said, pointing at her.

I rushed from the living room and up the steps to the attic door. I yanked the small stairs down and ran up into the darkness, not knowing what I was looking for or where it would be. I stomped through the blackness and fumbled for the light cord. With a click, the nearly spent 60-watt bulb began to flicker

70

with light. There was junk everywhere. I began frantically searching for something: facts, truth. In reality, I had no clue.

Finally, I saw that hanging on a large, old mirror was a bow, a real bow. I had held one once back in summer camp, but it was nothing like this. It was crafted with amazing artistry. I felt drawn to it and I didn't know why, like a moth to flame, as if I was supposed to touch it. It was one of those funky compound bows, the ones with the series of levering systems, cables, and pulleys. It looked like it would be very hard to draw. I took it, held it in firing position, and pulled the shooting string. To my surprise, it extended for me with ease. On the other side of the mirror was a quiver with a bolt of wooden arrows inside. Reaching into it, I took one to check it out. It looked as if it had been hand-carved. I heard Murray stepping into the attic.

"It was Abraham's," she said. "He was famous for it, actually. I think it may be history's first compound bow. He made it himself. I don't think the compound bow came out until the sixties."

I didn't reply. I was kind of hypnotized by it. It felt so natural in my hands as if it had always been there. As I leaned forward to put the arrow back, my foot kicked against something. In front of me was a chest covered by an old cloth. Dust flew from the tattered sheet as I slung it to the side. The scent of "old" was everywhere. Inside of the chest were tons of old newspapers and college books. I opened one and on the inside cover was the handwritten name *Claudia Van Helsing*. These were my parents' things. There were even pictures of them. I looked so much like my real mother it was almost freaky. Buried within the things I saw what looked like a certificate closed within the pages of an old book. Anxiety crept into my throat when I saw it was a birth certificate. It read:

This certifies that: <u>Victoria Lee Van Helsing</u>
Sex: <u>Female</u>
Was born to: <u>Claudia Anne Van Helsing</u> and <u>Michael Wayne Van Helsing</u> on <u>Monday</u> at <u>2013</u> hours, this <u>17th</u> day of <u>July</u> 19 <u>93</u> at <u>St. Mary's Hospital, 2503 Waverly Street, Knoxville, TN 37999</u>

A single tear splattered on the page, slapping me with the realization that I was crying. Apparently, it was all true, at least the part about my folks. At the time, the notion of Dracula was too much for me to conceive. Mom finally stepped into the attic, too, and handed Murray a tissue, which she gave to me.

They stood there silently, allowing me to have my time. I could have sat there on my knees the whole night and they would have stayed right there. When I opened up the small cloth-covered book my birth certificate had been kept in, I realized what I was holding was actually Abraham's diary. I began thumbing through the journal and found an entry that began with the name Lucy Westenra, the name Murray had mentioned earlier.

I began to read.

# OCTOBER PART ONE

October 1

Poor Lucy Westenra. As my carriage approached the gates, I could see the crimson moonlight shining upon Seward, who had gathered with the others at the cemetery gate. He paced back and forth in the night. His hand was clutching a worn, damp copy of what appeared to be the London Times. I myself had read the same copy bearing the headline "Mystery Lady Steals Children." Well, she was no mystery to me. I have no doubt they think me insane. Seward had loved her once, as did the Texan, Quincy. I am certain they never anticipated they would eventually hunt her alongside her fiancé, Arthur, the man who won her heart.

Through the mist, my carriage approached and pulled to an unbalanced halt before them. As I exited, the fog rolled around me, covering my body like a blanket. The stench of the dead night air penetrated my lungs.

"Are we ready?" I asked Seward rather directly.

"I do not know. This does not make sense," Seward timidly replied.

"Wicked things rarely do, Seward," I said.

I retrieved my large case and dropped it to the ground. I bent down, popped the latch open, and began presenting the weapons to them. I provided them with the most substantial items. Each received corked vials of holy water with cloves of garlic submerged in them, an assortment of crucifixes, and hand-carved stakes. Though I am experimenting with numerous other types of weapons, this night was not the time for trials. Too much was at risk.

My bow was all I required. Though I knew it would arouse their suspicions, I bent down to the satchel and retrieved the syringe full of my dark concoction. I rolled my sleeve and injected myself. The pain was strong.

"Oh, great! We're being led by an addict!" yelled Quincy.

"What do we do with these things?" said Arthur, impatiently examining the items I had distributed.

"I need only men of faith. I do not care what kind of faith you have or to whom you pray, so long as you pray. If you do not, then leave now," I replied, ignoring Arthur's question. "The items you have won't be of any use in saving your life if you don't have faith. The vials? Holy water laced with garlic. If it touches their skin it will burn like acid. The crucifix you hold is your shield. They cannot bear to look at it when held by a person with faith. The stakes you have are your sword. Drive them deeply into the heart. Be accurate."

"I don't need this mess," said Quincy in his thick Southern drawl. "I have my own protection." He proudly displayed his useless rifle.

"I fear that your bullets will be of no use, my good man. They will not protect you from them," I replied.

"And who in the blazes are they?" shouted Quincy.

"Yes, what are we doing here?" Arthur demanded through his imminent tears. "Lucy is dead!"

"No," I said to him. "Your fiancé is not dead, sir. She was a victim of something immensely evil. Now, she walks in death among the living, stealing the life's blood from the children she finds easy prey. However, I hope tonight we can finally lay dear Lucy to rest, alongside our fears."

Seward stepped to me. "What do you want us to do?"

"I want you to lead me to her grave," I answered.

Two of the men opened the large iron gate, and the metal reverberated with a fearsome groan. Then, grudgingly, we entered with my lead. We crept through the darkness like rats in a sewer, trying to remain invisible to things we could not see. As we walked along, a woodland creature suddenly scuffled in the high unkempt grass of the cemetery grounds. They all froze.

"You will have to be braver than that, gentlemen. There is more waiting for you than mere rabbits," I said.

They found their wits within their shame and continued to follow me into the night. Finally, after what seemed like an eternity, we happened upon Lucy's grave deep in the heart of the cemetery. I reached into my satchel and retrieved torches and a canister of oil. Once lit, we could see that the grave stood wide open. In the darkness, the pit seemed to extend into a bottomless ravine. I took a torch and dropped it into the hole. After a moment, we heard it hit solid ground. The light from the flame allowed us to see that the drop was not far. I was, of course, the first to go. Soon, the others followed me. Once we were all together again, we proceeded.

The tunnel was freshly dug and quite narrow. We were in a passageway leading somewhere, a place to which none of us wanted to venture. It happened quickly. The noise came from behind us, the screaming of Jacob, the young man in his twenties. I saw it only for a moment. Jacob held the cross to it, and as the half-human/half-beast turned away in pain, its eyes shined a bright red. It appeared to be partly human and partly bat, yet all evil. It moaned at first, but then began to chuckle. It turned around to the timid, defenseless Jacob, who held the cross with conviction, but without faith. It vanished into the depths of the tunnel, taking Jacob's crucifix, and his head. The wicked laugh of a woman then echoed through the soil along with the cries of a child.

"Oh, ye of little faith," I muttered. "Come. If you have not done so, I suggest you find a God to whom you can pray," I said. I had no time or patience to be consoling to them. They needed a leader, not a father.

The tunnel led to the opening of an earthy cavern. The crying of the child became louder, more distinct. Through the torchlight, we could see Lucy's elegant casket displayed prominently in the middle of the area. Surrounding it were several other coffins of modest make and design. The lids to the vacant coffins were displaced. Guardedly, we entered completely and stood together at the entryway. I noticed several other openings dug into the walls. I could only assume that those passageways led to multiple areas of the graveyard.

There, in the corner of the room, bound to the ground by a chain, was the child, a boy four years of age. He did not appear to be injured. John immediately moved to his rescue. I thought better of it.

"Stop!" I said, grabbing his collar.

He said, "Someone has to release him. He is a child!"

"He is bait!" I said. "What you are looking at is not a child but a trap."

I saw the shadows and armed my bow.

"What is it?" Arthur asked, nerves eating at his flesh.

"You would do good to arm yourselves now," I warned.

The rustling of fabric cut into the air. Fading into the torchlight was the figure of a woman dressed in white.

"Hello, gentlemen," she said in a raspy, seductive tone. "I was just about to have dinner. Would you care to join me? He is quite small, though. There may not be enough for everyone."

"Lucy?" said Arthur.

"Arthur! My love . . ."

She stepped into the fullness of the light, presenting her revolting appearance. She was still dressed in her burials, the tattered white dress now stained with soil and blood. Her long hair was matted and tangled, and her once pink flesh was now gray and peeling like rotting fruit, pungent and sour. Her hands were long bony digits tipped with sharp talon-like claws. She began to walk toward Arthur with her arms stretched out.

"Lucy?" Arthur said again.

"Yes, come to me, my love. I have missed you so," she moaned.

She began to walk toward us. The cock of a rifle sounded with a crack as Quincy stepped forward. He raised the barrel, aiming at her head. She smiled.

"Lucy," Quincy commanded. "Stop where you are."

She laughed and looked to me. "Did you not teach them anything?"

She lunged like lightning toward Quincy, who fired, peeling back a large section of her skull and sending her backward to the ground.

"Now, that's how you get it done!" Quincy stated proudly.

Others in the group smiled in a congratulatory manner. Then, the body began to stir. She raised, black blood seeping onto her shoulders. With her left hand, she repositioned her skull and smiled. Her wound began to heal in front of our eyes.

"That... was... rude," she said.

I called for the men to fight as creatures descended on us. They came from everywhere, through the soft soil of the walls, from underneath us, through the various tunnels. My arrows sailed through the air, and each time one hit its target, the creature would burst into flames and burn into ashes of nothingness. The men used their weapons as effectively as they knew how. I had no time to be proud.

John ran to the child and released him, hiding him near the far wall of the cavern. One of the creatures challenged him. It pounced upon him, snapping and clawing. He withdrew his crucifix and showed it to the thing, causing the beast to wail in agony before he impaled it with a stake. As I turned around, I saw one of the men get bitten, and within seconds, he converted into one of them. I saw the virus spreading through the group like evil. Once bitten, you had no time to react, you only became.

Arthur ran after Lucy, cornering her. She turned to him, seductive and alluring. She suddenly appeared as she did in life, young and fair, full of desire.

"Arthur," she called. "What... what are you doing? What is the matter with you?"

"Lucy?" he asked.

She stepped toward him.

"Arthur, what is going on? Get me out of here!"

"Lucy," Arthur replied dreamily, arms outstretched, waiting for her.

She stepped to him, her cheeks damp with tears.

With a ferocious scream, she flung her head backward. Her massive jaws gaped open, preparing for the kill. It was then that Arthur realized that one of my arrows had found its way to Lucy's black and rotting heart. It protruded from her chest like a maypole. She burst into flames, knocking the stunned Arthur to the ground.

"Thank me later!" I yelled to him.

We were prevailing, though most of the group was either dead or transformed. The remaining creatures began to scatter into the confines of the tunnels. Only a handful of us remained, including John, Arthur, Quincy, and of course, myself.

Then, I saw the familiar fog began to flow into the room. The remaining beasts ran at the sight of it.

"Take the child and leave. Leave now!" I told John.

He dared not argue. Though they were unsure of my motivations, they left quickly. I watched as the figure moved in its smoky form along the ground. The fog began to take shape in front of me, slowly and surely. It was now the outline of a man. It bowed to me, and upon returning upright, said, "Good evening, Abraham."

"Good evening, Count," I replied.

It had been a while since I had seen him in such bright light. He was very tall, much taller than I. The blackness of his eyes glowed with a royal red hue. His mouth was lined with razor-sharp teeth and his cold, pale flesh was etched with small capillaries hidden just beneath the surface. He closed Lucy's casket with his large hand armed with claws. Sitting on the lid, he crossed his legs and looked up to me.

"I have to admit, you did good. I was impressed," Vladimir said. "You have always been very impressive with that bow, Abraham."

"Why, thank you," I replied.

"Here, take a seat," he said.

He motioned toward a casket, which slid effortlessly across the soil to me, and I sat.

"So, how have you been?" I asked.

"Good, I suppose. I grow weary of all of this, Abraham. I can't help it."

"You have never been satisfied," I said.

"That is true. It is a weakness of mine... discontentment," he admitted. "You would not happen to have some with you, would you?"

"Certainly," I said.

I reached into my coat pocket, retrieved my flask, and passed it to Vladimir, who unscrewed the lid. I noticed that familiar ring on his finger, the golden bat with the glowing stone, much like the stone of the amulet he gave to young Mina.

"Um, I can trust you have not blessed this," he stated.

"Of course not—I do not think the Lord blesses whiskey, Vladimir," I replied.

"Good." He took a long drink from the container and closed his eyes. "I have always respected the fact that the two of us can sit and talk like this, this momentary truce. You must realize you are the only one who understands me, Abraham."

"I know, Vlad. Sometimes I feel the same way about you. Pity that one of us will have to die eventually," I said.

"Yes, that is a shame." He took another drink from the flask. "Whiskey is one of the finest inventions I have seen come to pass in my long years. Oh, and I am sorry to hear of your son's passing. I had so wanted to give him my gift—your beautiful wife as well."

"Thank you," I said. "Yes, I do miss William so. As far as Louise goes, if you are going to take her, take her fast. Do not leave her wandering around to bother me for eternity. You can at least rid me of that nuisance."

"Well, knowing she causes you such distress gives me some kind of pleasure," Vladimir said with a smirk.

Though the two of us were understood enemies, we sat together in silence for a moment. It was pleasant, though it shames me to say so. After a while, I grew tense. I could not help but pull the syringe from my coat pocket. Again, I rolled up my sleeve and plunged the needle into my arm, pumping the concoction through my veins.

*"Abraham," he said. "It pains me to see you like this. These poisons are no good to you. A man of your intellect must know this."*

*I said, "I know, but it is a shameful and necessary evil."*

*"It is strange how you humans deal with despair. Sad," he said.*

*I took a deep breath, gathered myself, and said, "Well, shall we?"*

*He finished off the last of the whiskey and said, "Let's…"*

I closed Abraham's journal and held it in my hand, bewildered. What world was I in? There were so many questions my mind didn't have the will to ask. They swam in my brain. Murray and Mom remained silent. I put my hand on the lid of the trunk and slammed it shut, causing Mom to jump.

"I've got to get out of here," I said.

"Vickie, listen," Murray said.

"No! No more," I said. "I need to get out!"

"But, Vickie…he's waiting. He's out there—trust me. He was at my house tonight, just two hours ago. He knows you're alive and he will be looking for you," Murray said.

I was infuriated. "Who? Who will be looking for me? Dracula? Ms. Murray, with all due respect, I think you're crazy as hell. All of you! I think you're all crazy!"

I ran past them, nearly tumbling down the steps of the attic, still holding tight to the diary. No one was getting hold of that thing. In my mind, it was the only link to the madness, and it had to go. The first part of my plan was to destroy the journal, and the second part was to be alone—and I knew of just the place where I could do both. I just didn't know that something was there waiting for me.

# The Creep Catalog

While my past was coming back to *bite* me, Rod was on his way to the one person he knew could help him, someone who would understand vampires, monsters, and other creepy creatures. Who? Kyle Cooper, of course!

Kyle sat alone on the couch, wrapped in the safety of his blanket, with the glow of the television his only light. Judy was working late, and his father was at the lodge with his medical buddies. That meant Kyle was home alone with popcorn, darkness, and *Halloween H20* on the coveted hi-def seventy-two-inch LCD in the living room. He sat there, anxious, fearful. Jamie Lee was just about to see Myers for the first time face-to-face through the window of the door. She was going to get the kids inside just in time to escape him. Kyle knew this because he had seen it over a thousand times.

In his lap, Kyle held a large bowl of popcorn. The movie was at that part where the kids finally get in the door and Jamie Lee shuts it just as Myers presses his white, empty face against the glass. Captivated by it, Jamie Lee freezes, remembering when Myers had stalked her and trapped her inside the small closet of the bedroom. Then she comes to her senses. She wrestles for the gun hidden in her jeans pocket, and then …

*Bam, bam, bam, bam!*

"*Son of a b…*," screamed Kyle, throwing the bowl of popcorn to the floor.

*Bam, bam, bam, bam!*

Kyle crept from the couch, keeping his blanket with him. He was definitely not expecting anyone and with a knock like that, whoever it was didn't have good news. He slowly walked toward the door, wondering what could come of his opening it.

*Bam, bam!*

"Who the hell is it?" Kyle yelled.

"Kyle…Kyle, open the door!" said the voice.

Kyle couldn't believe what he was hearing. He opened the door to see a very out-of-breath Rod Rainfeld standing there, dripping sweat.

"Dude! What the hell?" Kyle said.

"Kyle," Rod heaved. "You…you've got to help me, man. You're the…you're the only one I know who can."

"Dude, are you like running from the cops? Because if you are my mom will, like, totally go into a Japanese conniption and no one goes Kamikaze like my mom." He moved out of the way and let Rod into the foyer. "Rod, seriously, what's up? Here, sit down."

Rod fell to his knees on the floor, catching his breath. "You're never going to believe it. I mean, *I don't believe it!*"

"What? What?" Kyle urged.

Rod took a few thick gulps of air and rattled, "Kyle, my dad bought a coffin that had Dracula in it. He came to life and he just killed Russ."

Kyle looked at him like he was an idiot. "What a minute, dude." He took his finger and wiggled his ear canal. "Okay, say that again, because if I heard you right you said Count Dracula just ate Russ Cobbs."

"It's true!" Rod huffed.

Kyle busted into laughter. "Oh, dude! You are good. What's this all about? Does the football team need you to punk a nerd or something? Do you think I'm pissed 'cause you're wanting to date Vickie, 'cause dude, that's all right, I don't—"

Rod jumped from the floor and grabbed Kyle by the shoulders. He looked deep into his eyes.

"Dammit! I am telling you! This Dracula thing is loose. He is out there! I'm not playing with you! I mean, he turned into a friggin' bat and everything, man!" Rod sunk back to the floor. "And…and he just. I mean, Russ was at the door.

We were going to the rally tonight. I…I tried to pull him down, but the thing got him. It just swooped down, got him, and flew outside. Then it did something to him. I don't know. After it did, he…he wasn't Russ anymore. He was something else. And he came at me. There was nothing else I could do. I stabbed him…knocked him into the ravine by the house."

Kyle could see that Rod was obviously telling the truth, or what Rod believed was the truth. In reality, Kyle didn't like Rod back then; I knew that. But he didn't enjoy seeing anyone fall to pieces, not even Rod Rainfeld.

"Come on, Rod. Come with me." Kyle helped Rod up, and together they walked up the steps to Kyle's bedroom at the far end of the hallway. They stopped at the door, and Kyle said. "Now dude, no one has ever—*ever* been in here, and I don't want to hear any crap about it. No laughing, no telling the school, nothing! Right?"

"Yeah, man, whatever you say," Rod said.

Then Kyle opened the door to his legendary monster museum of a bedroom, a geek paradise. There was anything and everything related to science fiction, comic books, and horror films in the room: masks, comics, action figures, collectibles, posters, special effects makeup—you name it, it was there.

Kyle said, "Welcome! This is my domicile, my career, my life's work. Can you *feel* the power?"

Rod looked around, amazed. "Oh…I can feel it."

"Now! First thing's first. Dracula, you say?" Kyle said.

"Yeah," Rod replied.

Kyle walked in. "Okay, tell me everything you remember."

Rod followed. "Well, it's no secret that my dad is a collector. He travels all the time and comes back with all kinds of crap. The other night, Dad had this thing delivered, this coffin."

Kyle said, "And you didn't find this messed up?"

Rod replied, "Well, no. He's got all kinds of junk like that. He's one of those weirdos who collects all kinds of stupid crap." Kyle looked at him, taking offense. "Oh, sorry, man. Not crap like this. I mean, stuff like…Anyway, the coffin was strange, with all kinds of writing on it. We were downstairs talking and then, all of a sudden, it opened and this thing rose out of it and said its name was Dracula. Then it tried to eat me."

Of course, Rod decided to leave the details of his father's intentions out of the conversation, at least for the time being. Kyle plopped down at his PC. He started a program that could only be called …

"*The Creep Catalog* welcomes you! All right, good enough. Let's get started. This, my good man, is a database I've built with every piece of information on every single monster, killer, psychopath, alien, and degenerate ever imagined. It cross-references by origin, strength, and weakness. Because that's how I roll."

Rod was wowed. He pulled up a chair next to Kyle and said, "You've got a lot of free time, man."

"And this is what happens when you never see naked chicks! Anyway, moving on." Kyle typed in the name *Dracula*. The database began searching the archives. "It will search the hard drive as well as the internet for any information you need." In seconds, tons of pictures and information loaded onto the desktop. "Alrighty, then. This coffin you were talking about, what did it look like exactly?"

Rod thought for a second and said, "Well, it was long, really long. It looked like it was red, like a deep red, with a bunch of weird symbols on it."

"Like this?" Kyle asked. There on the screen was a sketch of the exact coffin Xavier had on display in the basement.

"Yeah! That's it!" Rod said.

"What you are looking at is Dracula's final resting place," Kyle said as the image moved around the screen to give a 360-degree view. "See all of these symbols? These are spells, protections to keep people from opening it. There's supposed to be some secret way to get it to open, but who knows?"

"Well, I know it was opened when that thing came out of it!" Rod said.

"Yes, and that would be due to…this." The image focused in on the paragraph that Xavier had deciphered using R.M. Renfield's journal entries. "And you would think we'd be out of luck since we don't know what any of these symbols mean, right? But …"

Kyle punched a couple of keys on the keyboard. Suddenly, the program began deciphering the text.

"And it reads: *The darkest soul doth lie within deathful slumber. Life's blood pure thee must attain and serve unto its wanting lips, free of impurity or sinful desire of flesh. Only then thine eyes shall see true remuneration of timeless days.* Translation? You need the blood of a virgin to wake up Dracula. So, my first question is how was someone able to find a virgin in the twenty-first century?"

Rod didn't answer; he knew exactly how.

"Oh, don't look at me, dude," Kyle exclaimed. "I'm a nerd, not a virgin. Misty Winnart—eighth grade band camp. Boo-ya! So, you say that your dad didn't do anything to the coffin before Dracula popped out of it?"

"No, no…not that I saw," Rod lied.

"Hmmm. Then, someone would have had to do it. Maybe before it was delivered? Anyway, I would imagine whoever it was took the blood and put it here."  Kyle pointed to the hole in the lid. "This opening must be how the blood gets to Dracula without disturbing the seal of the coffin."

"Okay, so what about Dracula?" Rod asked.

Kyle smiled and began typing. "Dracula. Count Dracula, a.k.a. Vlad III Dracul; Vlad III Dracula, Prince of Wallachia; Vlad the Impaler; Bloodsucker Dude Extraordinaire. The main part of his reign was from about 1456–62. History says that he killed about a hundred thousand European civilians in his time. Apparently, he was a hard guy to please. He would put them on these big sharp poles, like a shish kabob, so that's where he got the name the Impaler. Legend has it that he eventually went against the church and insulted God, which wasn't cool. So, God cursed him and turned him into a creature that can't live on food or water alone, but must have human blood. His curse was to live forever, alone in torment. And voilà—the birth of the vampire."

Rod said, "Yeah, yeah, I know about vampires. I go to the movies."

Kyle pulled up a host of photos. "Oh, you can't go by what you've seen in the movies, dude. Forget all of that *glittering*, handsome vampire stuff. It's no good. Vampires don't look like you or me. They are ugly and they *stay* ugly, and when they morph, they only go from ugly to *uglier*. And you can also forget about this, '*Oh, I vill bite you vunce, zen twice, and zen a third time, and poof—you are a sexy vampire, my love.*' There is venom in a vampire bite, venom they can release at will. *But!* Not everyone can handle it. Some have a bad reaction: they drop dead or go nuts. Vampires can bite you to eat you or to you change you. And once the venom hits you, it's just like a snakebite. How quickly you vamp out depends on where you're bitten. That's why they usually go for the neck, right next to the brain. One bite there and *wham!* In five seconds you *suck*, just like the rest of them!"

Rod said, "What about Russ? When Russ changed, he really didn't look like Dracula. He was more gory looking."

"Well, vampires are social creatures, like bees, and they have a hierarchy. You have three different types." Kyle began pulling up photos. There was a pic of a zombie-looking creature, somewhat batty in appearance, just as Russ had looked. "You have your standard *Grunts*. They are just your typical crazed killer. They can't infect anyone and they don't have any real power…well, besides being crazy strong." Another photo crossed the screen. This vampire looked more human, more like Dracula. "Say hello to your *Contaminator*. These guys share many of the same attributes as Dracula, but not all of them. They're not as powerful, but they can infect others, and some can shape-shift."

"Yeah," Rod said. "So, what about the bat thing?"

"Good question. It's said that part of Vlad's curse was to 'feed on blood in the seclusion of darkness as all wicked things do.' Dracula as well as some other Contaminators can turn into that bat thing. No two are alike. However, Dracula can go beyond that. He can turn into just about anything creepy: spiders, snakes, rats, bats. If it can gross you out, he can probably pull it off. Another cool thing he can do is morph into a fog-like mist and get through, like, the bottom of doors or keyholes. It's part of his magic and only he can do it."

Rod said, "What about the third kind of vampire?"

"The last kind is a Host, the king, the head honcho. That, of course, is the Count. He can create another Host, one that is just as powerful as he is. But only he can create one."

"How do you kill them? Is it the same as the movies?" Rod asked.

Kyle said, "Yeah, mostly. You know your basics: sunlight, wooden stakes through the heart, garlic, holy water, crucifixes, all that good stuff. What you don't know is why; the *why* is the most important part. See, those things are pure and unpolluted. Garlic is a natural antibiotic. Sunlight is the purest of all light. Wood is organic and uncontaminated. Crucifixes and holy water— enough said."

"God, how did my dad get wrapped up in this mess?" Rod said to himself more than to Kyle.

"Who knows, man? Maybe your dad didn't know what was in it. Maybe he saw it on Amazon.com and said, 'Hey, I want to plant posies in that.' We'll have to ask your dad."

Asking Xavier really wasn't an option at the moment.

Rod said, "How did Dracula end up locked in that thing?"

"Well, Dracula was defeated back in the day, but he wasn't dead, of course. And since his body was defenseless, he had to protect it. It was sealed in this coffin thing where he would wait on one of his cronies to come along and bring him back to life," Kyle explained.

Then, Rod remembered the name Dracula had called them. "Dracula mentioned the name Renfield. Who's Renfield?"

"Man, don't you ever watch movies? R.M. Renfield," Kyle said, calling his picture and history to the screen. "He was a solicitor and legal agent in the nineteenth century who was sent to Dracula in Transylvania to assist with his estates. God only knows what Dracula did to him while he was there, but it drove him insane. I mean *looney tooney* nuts. He became a devout follower of Dracula, worshipping him, waiting for Dracula to give him eternal life. He was locked up in an asylum for, like, eating bugs, and spiders, and junk because he wanted to absorb their life force or something. Who knows? Finally, he betrayed Dracula and Dracula offed him."

Rod looked at the screen. He later said he could see his father in the eyes of Renfield. I think that's when he knew that there was no doubt about it: they were related. He said at that moment he started to tell Kyle the truth, but how would he tell someone a truth that he didn't believe?

"So, you say Dracula was defeated?" Rod said.

"Ah, my hero!" Kyle pulled Abraham's file. "This dude here, Abraham Van Helsing. He was, like, wicked cool. He was the supreme monster ass-kicker back in the day.  Van Helsing was a doctor who knew all about the vampire stuff. Dracula had come to London in search of this chick named Mina who he believed was the reincarnation of his dead wife, his true love. Dracula began infecting people, trying to build an army. When Van Helsing and his peeps tracked Dracula down and saved Mina, they killed him, or so they thought." Kyle turned and faced Rod. "Dude, if what you're telling me is true—and I'm not saying you're lying—but if it's true, Bram Stoker knew his stuff."

Rod needed to be alone for a moment. He excused himself and went into the bathroom, locking the door behind him. I'm sure the fact that any of it could be real was too incredible for him to imagine. I was thinking the exact same thing, huddled safely in my childhood hiding place just a few blocks away, unaware that something was with me.

# The Rank Vampire

oor Xavier. I think up to this point I might have painted him as an ass. He wasn't completely evil, really. After Rod had run away into the dark, Xavier sat on the floor in the basement among all of his shattered artifacts, aimlessly scribbling in one of his journals. His mind was in pieces wondering if Rod was still alive, or now dead at the hands of the demon Xavier had helped revive.

"I would suggest you stop blubbering like a child and finish what you have started," said Vladimir from the shadows.

Xavier spun to see a much healthier looking vampire before him. "No, I've had enough of the thought of you. Either go away or kill me, just get it over with. You've taken enough from me."

Vladimir rolled his eyes. "Well, how dramatic. I've taken nothing from you…yet."

Xavier turned to him. "My son? Rod?"

"Oh, yes, yes—alive and well. He's a slippery thing, like a mouse. He is alive and well, um…um. Say, I don't have the pleasure of knowing your name," Vladimir said.

"Xavier."

"Xavier! Lovely. Well, listen Xavier," Vladimir said as he walked toward him. "I've done absolutely nothing to your boy. I assure you. His friend at the door? He was not so lucky. Neither was the young gentleman in the alleyway, nor the woman selling her body on the sidewalk, but your boy is perfectly fine."

Xavier said, "How do I know that?"

"Okay." Vladimir plopped down in the chair in front of Xavier. "Let's get one thing clear between us, Xavier. I mean what I say. Honesty is my code of honor. I am a fiend of my word; a slave to it, you might say. In the thousands of years I have been here, I've *never* lied. Not once. And I don't expect to be lied to, either. That is what got your ancestor into trouble. He was less than truthful with me. He betrayed my trust, and that is one thing I do not tolerate. I always deliver exactly what I promise in the precise manner I promise it, and I expect the same. So, if I have told you that your son has not died by my hand, or my command, you can believe it."

"Thank you," Xavier said.

"Oh, don't thank me!" laughed Vladimir. "I needed him, you see. He is my bargaining chip…for *you*, Xavier. I will promise you here and now that I will not harm, nor allow harm to come to your son if you promise me that you will do exactly as I command to the very detail. If you do that for me, I will guarantee that your son will not die by me, my kind, my intention, or my invention. Do we have a deal?"

"Yes, yes. You have my word," Xavier replied.

"Splendid! Oh, I just love it when things work out. Now, my first request: please hand me my ring or I shall pry it from your bloody digit." Xavier looked down at the ring and handed it to Vladimir. "Now, I thirst. Hand me your arm."

Naturally, Xavier asked, "Are you going to change me?"

Vladimir giggled and said, "No, my dear man. I just need a little refreshment is all, and it has been so long since I've tasted a Renfield." Reluctantly, Xavier rolled up his sleeve and offered himself to Vladimir. He gently bit into his flesh and eagerly sucked the fresh blood. Then, he leaned away and dabbed the remaining blood from his lower lip with a kerchief from his pocket. "Next, do you have any whiskey?"

Xavier thought it was a weird request of a vampire, but said, "Um, yes. I believe so."

Finally, Vladimir said, "Good, and do you have someone who washes garments? I smell like hell and am in need of a bath."

"Well, I have a shower," Xavier said.

"Come again?" Vladimir said.

Xavier repeated, "A shower."

"And what is a *shower*? Like rain?" Vladimir asked.

After some convincing, Xavier coerced Vladimir to get in the shower. It was one of those really cool ones that had multiple heads with an auto temperature setting, you know? He tried not to pay attention to the fact that Vladimir was naked; his smell was bad enough.

"This is body wash," Xavier said.

"Body wash," Vladimir confirmed.

"This is a loofa. You put the body wash, or soap, into the loofa sponge and use it to wash your body. This here is the handle that turns on the water. These buttons here adjust the temperature," Xavier said.

Vladimir looked at him suspiciously. "Xavier, do you know what I said about being honest? If this is a trap, should you fail it would be most unpleasant for you and your son."

Xavier huffed and rolled his eyes. "Now listen, the water pressure is a little hard, but there are massaging heads." Xavier leaned over and turned on the water. Vladimir jumped with fright. He was nervous at first, but then after a moment he seemed to get into it. "See? Now, what about these other shower heads? You want them on?"

"Yes, please!" Vladimir said. Xavier turned them on. "Oh, Xavier! How wonderful this is! How do you refrain from staying in here forever?"

Xavier said, "You get used to it. Here, here's some music. Enjoy. I'll be in the study."

Xavier turned on the shower radio. He could see that Vladimir immediately found it magical to hear music coming from the box in the "water room." Of course, from Xavier's notes the "wonderful music" was *Electric Avenue* by Eddy Grant.

Hardly Mozart.

Drac stayed in the shower, drinking whiskey and singing at the top of his lungs, until all of the hot water had disappeared, which, with the water supply of the home, took around three hours. Then, he strolled out of the bathroom wearing Xavier's robe, playfully twirling his towel and singing.

"That was wonderful! Thank you, Xavier," Vladimir said.

"Yeah, you're welcome," Xavier said flatly.

"Now, don't be that way, Xavier. This doesn't have to be *all* bad. You'll find that I am a right cheerful ghoul most of the time—well, as long as things are going my way, of course. When they aren't, I can be a *real son of a bitch!*" He laughed hysterically and downed the last of the whiskey, though he was hardly drunk.

"Don't you think you've had enough?" Xavier asked.

Vladimir said, "Oh, it's only for taste, my good man. I cannot become intoxicated. I so wish I could. I miss those days. I can eat food and drink, but it never soothes my hunger or quenches my thirst. Eh, what are you to do?"

"So, what now?" Xavier asked.

"Ah! Yes. Now, I need to get some recruits, you know. I have to build a brand-new base. There is a Van Helsing alive. I smelled the scent, I know it, but I lost the trail before I could locate them. If I know my old adversary, his kin is my only threat. So, I will need your assistance. I can tell by your lavish surroundings that you are an influential man. I will need a modest gathering of people whom I can convert. I will need at least twenty to start. Yes, yes, twenty should nearly do it to begin. Do you know where and how we can do this?"

Xavier knew exactly where: the school board meeting that was less than two days away. "There's a meeting that I'll be having in a few days. It should include all of the people you need."

"Wonderful!" Vladimir stood and threw the towel over his shoulder. "Are my garments ready?"

Xavier said, "Yeah, they're in the other room."

As Vladimir left the room, he said, "Good! I simply love this era! Oh! And one more thing: do you know what the word *dude* means? No one seems to be able to tell me."

Xavier rolled his eyes again and changed the channel.

# MY VERY FIRST MONSTER

There I was in the park, the place I used to love as a little girl. Stupid now that I think back, especially if Vladimir was searching for me, but I didn't really believe that at the time. The water rustled below me. I began to think back on the days when I was a little girl, before the strangeness, before madness had contaminated my reality. With a tight grip on Van Helsing's journal, I stretched my arm out directly over the stream below. All I had to do was let it go, let it drop into the dark water, and it would all be over…or would it? Would ridding myself of the journal change the truth? Not quite. The vampire element of the story was the ridiculous part of the equation. I couldn't wrap my mind around vampires. They did *not* exist. I didn't care what *Twilight* said.

So, I pulled the diary back to me and looked at it in light of the street lamps and moonlight. It was so very old. I rubbed the skin of the cover and felt the cool leather. It was rough in places, but mostly soft, like a blanket. Then, I opened the diary to a random page and began to read.

*December 25*

*It has been so wonderful finally to be in America with my wife and son, and in time for the holiday. Dracula is no more, yet I find myself questioning his defeat. Is it truly possible to kill that which does not live? I hug my William all the time, much to his aggravation. Should any danger have befallen him, I do not know how I would have continued my life. My fair Louise—truthfully, she is my light. Without her, I could not exist. I am so glad to be with them now, safe and secure, blessed to be together.*

*Through my studies and experiments, I seem to have instilled an imprint of my knowledge into my blood. Even now, William displays awareness and techniques that I possess, though he has not been trained in my ways. He seems to be inherently conscious of dark things that cower at the sight of sunlight. I only hope that I pass my abilities to my relations so that they too may have the knowledge, ability, and courage to fight the evils they cannot see. I pray for you, my children, and my children's children. I pray you always know what I know and do as I do. Should Dracula ever return, he will come for us. He will seek the name Van Helsing and will smell the scent of our lineage pumping in our veins. He will never stop.*

*Regardless, tonight I rest within the love of my family and friends. Merry Christmas . . .*

That explained a lot. Van Helsing couldn't let on that his family was alive unless he wanted to put them in danger, and I was beginning to feel the same way about Mom and Dad. I flipped back a few pages.

*November 5*

*Dear Mina still sleeps in the protection of the Holy Circle I created for her safety. Though she remains infected by the vampiritic virus, I have managed to keep her sickness at bay with my techniques. Though it is uncomfortable to her, I provide injections of the holiest of water, pure, laced with the smallest amount of garlic, unpolluted silver nitrate, and other uncommon ingredients. It burns in her veins, but keeps the virus from taking her completely.*

Moments ago, as she rested, I ventured to the castle alone to stop those who were hunting us. With the help of my blacksmith hammer, I broke the old door from its rusty hinges. It took me only a moment to find the chapel where the three lay in deathful slumber, the wicked three, who had tempted poor Mina and killed our horses. They knew my treatments were attempts to cure her of her illness and wished to infect her further, turning my hopes to ash. As I neared the first coffin, the beast awoke. My garlic did her in. She lay melted onto the floor while I ventured to the next. She was not in her tomb, but hanging above the rooftop, waiting to fall upon me unknowingly. My wondrous bow had an arrow that silenced her screams. My bow that has seen so much battle has developed a taste for it, a life of its own. The last beast nearly took me. She spun into her changeling self, the winged bat creature that, while not as great as Dracula's form, was still threatening. It scratched my flesh, bringing blood. After her disposal, I poured my concoction on the wound as a precautionary antiseptic.

The dramatic fashion in which some vampires choose to leave this earth eludes me. Some of them simply fade into dust while others explode into fire, yet all leave quickly and with haste once their time is over. The soldiers, the evil henchmen that hunt, are the worst. Their bat-like faces screech at you and pierce your ears. They cannot infect. I've often wondered if they know this and are upset by it, jealous of those vampires who are able to do so.

Vladimir will know I have blessed his castle and will be none too pleased with me. As promised, I did not set it afire. It contains memories of his bride long since passed, the same visions that pulled his evil heart unto Mina. Some may find it impractical, yet he and I share respect, a respect that should exist between adversaries. I learned of his honor early in our battles, and it was that honor that allowed me time to save my wife and son. Though, as with any enemy, you never fully trust. It was for that reason I developed false stories of their fates, the death of my son, the insanity of my wife, all for my life and love.

Though he and I share respect, we also share the desire to rid the world of the other. We are to each other both a greatest friend and a worst enemy. Truthfully, once Vlad is no more, I will miss his presence in many ways. It has given me nightmares and worries, *yet it has also given me purpose. What shall I do when the adventure is over, either by his death... or mine?*

Closing the journal, I took a deep breath and let the cool night air fill my lungs. The anger I had felt toward Mom and Dad began to fade. I realized that if my "godparents" knew the tales of Van Helsing, then their love for me caused them to hide the facts. In reality, they had been wonderful parents; I couldn't have wished for better. I mean, I could have had Xavier! So, why be angry with them? They did their best with what they had. If the shoe had been tied to the other foot, I'm sure I probably would have done the same thing: hide the bizarre truth and raise the child like any other normal little girl. There was only one problem: I was beginning to learn that I was anything but normal.

A rustle of wind in the trees shook me. I looked into the night sky and decided that it was best to go back home and try to wrap some sense of sanity around it all. I had to apologize to Mom and Dad for showing my ass; then, I had to figure out how I was going to deal with Murray.

I took hold of the railing and pulled myself up, but I didn't pitch the journal. I knew better. After I placed it in my pocket, I reached for my cell phone to call home. Yeah, Mom had finally ordered the new one, thank God. When I flipped open the phone, I saw that I had six missed calls. They were all from home, of course. However, I also had a text message. It was from Kyle.

## Hey...UR BF is @ my house saying vampires R after him. Cld U get over here like NOW?

*Rod? Oh hell, you have to be kidding me!* I stuffed my phone back into my pocket. Kyle's house was only a few blocks away from the park. For Rod to go to Kyle meant something was definitely up.

*Vampires.*

What was I going to do with vampires?

Jogging from the bridge and making my way out of the trees to the main walkway, I noticed something in the distance. It was a Rutgers High varsity jacket, number 37, Russ Cobbs. Now, at that time I didn't know how freaky Russ was—well, aside from the typical. So, I did a really, really stupid thing.

"Russ!" I yelled. "Russ, hey wait. Have you talked to Rod?"

I should've just covered myself in barbecue sauce and rang a dinner bell. He stopped. His stance was peculiar, drunken, as if he was hurt or something. He staggered for a moment. Then, a strange feeling caused me to stop where I was standing. At first, I thought he was drunk off his ass, which wouldn't have shocked me. Then the feeling was something more, something threatening, a feeling that I needed to prepare myself for something bad that was about to happen. Without thinking, I took a deep breath and slowly placed my left foot behind me, as if I was about to be tackled on the Rutgers field. Then, I bent down and held my arms open and ready. *What in the hell am I doing?* I thought. It was like I wasn't in control of my body.

Russ trembled and slowly turned to me. That's when I could see his black eyes and gray flesh. My fists clinched together. *No, don't run. It wants you to run.* Then Russ let out this piercing screech and began running toward me with full force, like a diesel truck.

You know what? I wasn't afraid.

*This is it…this is a vampire. Murray was right.*

*Bring it.*

He was about five feet in front me before I kicked into the air, using his shoulders as a springboard. I jumped over him and safely to the ground, like I was a friggin' gymnast. It was ability, innate and instinctive, and it took me over. I thought it best to let it do its thing and not interfere. Russ ran several more feet before realizing what had happened.

"Russell Cobbs! Hey, you prick. Over here. I've been waiting on this for a long time," I shot.

He stopped and snapped his head around to me. This time, he crawled at me like a funky spider thing. He jumped at me. I hugged him tightly, turning to the left, and throwing him to the ground with a thud. He yelped. Immediately, he was up again. I held my arms in this kind of martial arts stance, a skill I had never seen outside of the movie *Kill Bill*. I tried not to think about it because I was doing fairly well without letting my mind get in the way. He stepped to me, and we began exchanging blows and blocks in quick succession. Left, right, block, hit to the jaw. Upon contact with my fist, I could feel the rough cold flesh of the thing that used to be the annoying Russ Cobbs. I knocked him backward into the bushes and stood there, ready to continue, but it didn't leap out of the hedges.

So, I stood there for what seemed to be an eternity, but what actually could have only been seconds. *Where did you go?* I didn't notice him softly drop from the tree behind me to the ground. He made no noise, like some ninja on rice paper, yet I knew he was there. Just as he opened his jaws and was getting ready to pounce, I spun toward him with a roundhouse kick that could have shattered steel, racking his mouth like a set of pool balls. He fell to the ground and leapt at me again, throwing me full force into the tree trunk behind me.

Yeah, that hurt like a bitch.

It knocked the wind from my lungs, causing me to gasp for air. While I was catching my breath, he charged me. I had to think fast. In an instant, he was against me, his claws at my throat. I held him by his neck with a strength I had never known. Then, I reached up and pulled a branch from the tree he had me pinned against and kicked his right leg out from under him.

As he fell to the ground, I jumped into the air and came down hard. I plunged the sharp branch into his chest, causing him to burst with a loud *bang* into a colossal cloud of damp demon dust. It was as if I had popped some big, gory balloon. As the dust began to settle, I realized I was kneeling on the ground with the branch stabbed into the grass beneath me, covered in icky dead vampire muck. Russ had exploded into nothingness.

I had won.

At that moment, a couple walked through the trees along the sidewalk all kissy-kissy. They looked at me like I was a psycho. Of course, they had missed the battle that had occurred only seconds before they got there. They only saw a teenage girl on the ground, covered in dust, stabbing the ground with a tree branch like a lunatic.

Well, I did the only thing that came to mind. I waved pleasantly, dust flying from my sleeve, and said, "Hey, there! How's it going?" There was no reply from the couple. Then, they walked away…*quickly*. I just waved again.

"Uh, have a good night!"

# COME TOGETHER

Kyle met me at the door, with Rod trailing behind.

"Dang, girl, what happened to you? You stink!" Kyle rattled.

"It's true," I said, catching my breath.

"What? That you stink?" Kyle said, bewildered.

He had texted me to rid himself of Rod. Sure, Kyle had entertained him. It was monsters, it was what he did, but at the time, Kyle didn't really believe it.

I said, "Trust me, it's true. I just killed Russ in the park, well, what *used to be* Russ, I think."

"What?" Kyle repeated.

"If you say *what* one more time, you're next!" I said.

"Okay. Huh?" he replied.

"First! Get…this…junk off of me!" I said. "Rod, how are you?"

"Um, good considering, I think," Rod replied.

Kyle fetched me a wet towel and led me to the bathroom. I cleaned myself up as best I could. Russ's rank odor was embedded into my clothes, but at least my new shoes were okay. I walked down the hall and into the museum. Kyle flopped into his desk chair and I sat on the bed with Rod.

"Wait!" Kyle said. I stood up. Kyle took my towel and placed it on the bed. "Don't get that junk on my comforter. Mom will have a cow."

I rolled my eyes. "All right. Now, what is going on? What happened?" I said to Rod.

Rod went through the story, recounting the events that led him to Kyle's and Russ to his grave, leaving out some details, of course.

"And that's all I can remember. God, I think I'm losing my mind!" Rod said.

Kyle jumped in, saying, "So wait a minute, wait a minute. Guys, I still can't get my head around this. Vampires are *really* real? I mean, really, really, real?"

He needed proof. Okay. I reached into my back pocket and presented Van Helsing's journal.

"Yeah. You tell me."

"What is this?" Kyle asked.

"A journal. It belonged to Abraham Van Helsing," I said.

Kyle looked at the book and then to me. "You serious?"

"Yeah."

"Wicked!" he said, and he began thumbing through the pages. "Oh, wild. Oh, man, it's all here. All the stories, the vampires. Look, look here…here are the symbols that are on the coffin. Where did you get this?"

"My attic," I replied. "He's…he was my great-great-great-grandfather."

Rod and Kyle stopped and looked at me like I had slapped them.

"What?" asked Rod. "Your parents are Van Helsings?"

I said, "No. My parents are my godparents. Listen, it's real messed up. I'm adopted. I'm adopted and I was attacked by a vampire in the park. It's been a really bad day, guys. Work with me, okay?"

Kyle took me by the hand and got down on one knee. "You…you are my hero."

I swear I could have kicked him in the teeth. "Oh, get up!" I said.

Kyle took his seat. "But wait, wait. Van Helsing didn't have any living kids. His wife had a nervous breakdown after his only son was killed."

"Not according to that diary. It's all there," I said. "Murray came to the house tonight and *outed* me. That's why she was having everyone do the family tree assignment; she was searching for the Van Helsing bloodline. According to her and that journal, he has a living ancestor and I am it."

"But, why Murray? Why does she care?" Rod asked.

"She's the descendant of Mina Murray," I replied.

"What the fu—oh…my…*God!*" said Kyle, jumping up. "The chick Dracula was in love with? This is just too wild!"

I noticed that Rod was uncomfortable. He wouldn't look me in the eye. I think it was because he was afraid I would realize the truth. He was Renfield, the missing link to the historical puzzle. Dracula was alive, Russ was dead, and it was all his father's fault.

I scooted closer to him. "Rod, listen, I'm sorry. I'm sorry about Russ, really I am."

Rod stood up, saying, "It's all my fault."

"No, it's not. How does this have anything to do with you?" I asked.

"My father brought that thing here. If it wasn't for him, Russ would still be alive and none of this would be happening," he replied.

Kyle leaned in. "Rod, your dad probably didn't have a clue about what was inside of that coffin. Like you said earlier, he just collects stuff. Hell, that coffin is sweet. If I had that kind of money, it would be sitting over there beside my statue of the mummy!"

"Right. Rod, this isn't your fault," I said. "No one could have planned on something like this happening. I mean, I've looked directly at one of them and I still don't believe it."

"I'm sorry," Rod said.

I believe what his heart meant was that he was sorry for not telling the truth. He probably took the consolation we provided and used it to bandage the guilt he was feeling because of his homicidal father and dysfunctional lineage.

I walked over to him. "Rod, we don't care. Really. It's going to be all right. I promise. *We* promise."

"No, man. We don't care. Stay with us. My parents won't be home until late. Let's just hang here for a while and figure out what we are going to do," Kyle said.

Rod looked at me, still unsure, his big blue eyes focusing on mine.

"Yeah, it's okay. Come on," I assured.

He followed me back and sat on the bed next to me. He put his large hand on mine. I took comfort in him, even though I'm sure I smelled like road kill.

"Vickie," he said sweetly.

"Yeah," I said.

"You smell like a fart," he said with a smirk.

"Amen, brother!" Kyle added.

"Okay!" I smiled. "Fine. Now what's next? We have to be a step ahead of Dracula if we want to beat him."

"Do we go to the police?" Rod asked.

"Oh, please. When is the last time you watched a horror movie?" Kyle said. "You *never* go to the police over the supernatural. They just laugh in your face and throw you in jail with some guy named Bubba who braids your hair. No police!"

"So, what do you suggest?" Rod said.

"Murray. I say we go to Murray and lay it out, see what she says," I suggested. "She's been after this stuff for years apparently. She knows some bits and pieces we need to know. We're going to have to do this together."

"Agreed," Kyle said.

With that, we gathered our things and left. Kyle was kind enough to lend me a tacky jogging suit of his so that I could rid myself of my funk-nasty clothing. We were not getting into Kyle's truck with me smelling the way I did. I would've hurled.

There was no time to think. We had entered into a world where little was understood and much had to be learned. Our lives depended on it. I kept my hand behind the passenger's seat, holding onto Rod's as we drove on. I could feel his fear and wanted to fix it; I wanted to make it go away as if he was a little kid and I was his protector. We drove into the darkness together and hoped to remain that way: *together*.

…And *alive* wouldn't hurt either!

# THE WRITER NAMED BRAM

By the time we arrived, I believe Murray had turned on every light in the house, as if she was guiding ships into shore or something. She knew there would be no sleep that night; we all knew that.

I could see her through the window, staring off into the distance, wondering. She was holding tightly to her *kit*, her weapons, her salvation. She had a crucifix draped around her neck alongside Mina's amulet, which barely shined—just bright enough to notice. It was her alarm. So much garlic had been draped around the entryways and windows you could smell it outside.

"Ms. Murray?" I called from the other side of the door as I knocked.

"Vickie?" she called back.

Kyle said, "Let us in. We need to talk to you."

Murray looked through the peephole in her door. She kept looking at us, checking us for *vampiness*. We appeared to be in good health, at least physically—frightened, but human. She flipped the lock and opened the door.

She said, "Come in, quick."

We entered.

"Uh, nasty! God, it smells like an Italian died in here!" Kyle said.

Murray locked the door behind us. "Yes, sorry about that. But you don't know how effective garlic is against them. Please, have a seat."

Rod and I sat next to each other on the loveseat, and Kyle flopped into the adjacent chair. Murray offered us something to drink, which we readily accepted. We took turns filling her in on the parts of the story she did not yet know. As we sat talking, Murray held Van Helsing's journal in her hands. I watched her face—it was as if we were handing her missing pieces to a puzzle she had been working on forever.

Finally, she said, "With your fight in the park, I think it's safe to say he's already started turning others. I thought it would take him a little longer than that."

Kyle said, "Okay, how is she a Van Helsing? Are you sure? She don't seem that hot to me. I've always believed Van Helsing had no descendants and died a lonely old geezer."

"Lies, all lies to throw Vladimir off the trail. Abraham knew that Vlad would attack his family. So, he made up his son's death and his wife's insanity and sent them to America."

"Alright, so how did all this come to you, Ms. Murray?" I asked.

"Well, it started about ten years ago, I think. My son was about eleven at the time. I began having these dreams, these wild lucid dreams about vampires in the nineteenth century. I didn't know why. I thought I was going nuts. Every night it was the same thing, over and over. I kept seeing my last name written everywhere and hearing these voices. The dreams started leading me to research my genealogy. It was then that I found out who I truly am."

"That necklace," I said, pointing to it. "Van Helsing's diary talks about a necklace and a ring."

"Yes, my mother gave it to me. It's been in our family for generations. Of course, when my mother gave it to me, I just thought it was a tacky necklace. Vladimir has something just like it, a ring he wears. He had given this necklace to Mina so they could remain connected, so they could each know when the other was close. I thought I saw it glow the same night you say Xavier's shipment arrived but I wasn't sure. The closer he is, the brighter it glows. After I found out about the Murray name, I began researching vampires. That led, of course, to Bram Stoker's novel from 1897. I discovered the importance of the necklace, my name, and the Van Helsing bloodline."

"Yeah, see, that's where I get all messed up. I mean, how did a novel lead to all of this?" I asked.

Murray said, "No, it's the other way around, Vickie. Bram Stoker was a writer and worked for Lyceum Theatre in London. He was looking for inspiration for stories, folklore, tall tales. Stoker would travel the country, attending auctions and visiting small markets. He was looking for the strange and unusual, something that could be his muse, I guess. In the winter of 1896, Stoker attended a small estate auction in London. The things that were being sold belonged to a man named Jacob Holmwood, who was the son of Lucy Westenra's old fiancé, Arthur."

"Lucy…the vampire who was kidnapping children," I stated.

"Exactly," she replied. "In the auction were a set of diaries, phonograph records, and newspaper clippings from what was being called the Carfax Abbey Affair. The locals believed it was all a hoax, just a group of people trying to get famous. In the set there were accountings from Jonathan Harker, Dr. John Seward, Lucy Westenra, Mina Murray, R.M Renfield, and, of course, entries from a Dr. Abraham Van Helsing," she said.

Kyle laughed. "Dang, that's a lot of diaries. I'm glad we have the internet now."

"Well, yes. Today we have blogs. Handwritten diaries were all people really had back in that time," she confirmed. "Stoker took the diaries and studied them. He fell in love with the subject matter and began to draft what would be his greatest novel."

"Didn't the people involved wonder how he got their journals?" I asked.

"Please…information didn't travel like it does today. Everyone was gone. Most were dead. Those who survived didn't want to remember. Some had changed their names. Van Helsing had moved to America before Stoker began writing his novel. By the time it had gained popularity, Abraham was dead." Murray got up, walked to her book chest, and pulled down a large hardback version of *Dracula*. "See," she said, handing it to me. "If you really look at it, Stoker retained the journal format. He added the romanticized version of what a vampire was for effect and created his own story. Of course, he left out the part where it was, well, *real.*"

"That's an important part," Rod said.

"So, what do we need to do?" I asked.

Murray said, "Well, it appears that all of the ancestors are coming together to have one final battle, one great war to end it all. I mean, we have Murray, Van Helsing, Dracula…"

"Yeah, all we need is a Renfield sitting around eating bugs and we've got it made," Kyle said.

"Ewww! Gross, you idiot," I said.

I noticed Rod look away shamefully when Kyle mentioned Renfield, but I didn't make the connection, not then.

Kyle said, "So, what do we do now? Wait to become vampire burgers?"

"No, we have to think ahead," Murray said. "Dracula's plan has always been to populate the earth with vampires and keep us as food, like livestock. He will be looking to build up a small army. He can't do it alone."

"And what about Vickie?" Rod asked. "What is her role in this stuff?"

Murray said, "That's our wild card. Now, he knows the Van Helsing blood lives, but what he doesn't know is *who* carries it. We have to keep that a secret for as long as possible. So, Vickie, you have to be very, very careful about accidents. If you hurt yourself and bleed, he'll be able to smell it for miles. What happened earlier? You must have cut your finger or something. When he was here, he smelled you."

"I cut myself shaving."

"Had it been that long? God!" Kyle said.

"Piss off!" I said.

Murray said, "See, it's accidents like that which can get us into trouble. So, no more razors. Learn to wax. Dracula doesn't need to be aware of your abilities."

I said, "And what of my abilities? Are you going to, like, train me or something? Is there someone that can show me what to do?"

Murray laughed. "Well, I'm afraid I'm not a *Watcher*, Vickie. Frankly, if I've done my homework, I think your DNA will teach you everything you need to know. You only have to follow its advice."

And apparently, Murray had a point. Instinct seemed to be the key. From my run-in with Russ, it seemed as long I just let my instinct lead me, I would do all right, at least for the time being.

"Rod, what are you going to do?" I asked.

Murray looked at him. "Rod, since his coffin is at your house, I wouldn't recommend you go back. He won't stay there forever. He'll need to find somewhere else to call a base, somewhere more secluded and dark, but we don't want to take any chances. Have you been able to get hold of your father? Is he all right?"

"Yes," Rod lied. "He's with friends."

"What about me?" Kyle said. "What do I get to do?"

"Oh, honey. Right now, you're the entertainment, and that's a good thing! You'll finally have a chance to put all of that useless monster knowledge to good use." Murray smiled.

"Right," Kyle said, content with that fact.

"For now, I suggest we go on like nothing is happening," she said. "People who find out will either think we're crazy or be in danger. We'll need to stay aware and keep our eyes open for any signs. Rod, are you meeting up with your dad? Do you have a place to stay?"

"Uh …" Rod replied.

"You can stay with me, man. No problem," Kyle said.

Murray turned to me. "And, Vickie, would your parents mind if you stayed with me? We have to keep them safe until this is over, and as long as you're there, they're in danger. I have this place locked down. There's no way a vampire is getting beyond that door. We have to keep you and your parents protected."

"They shouldn't mind," I said.

Murray got up. "Okay, boys. I'll take Vickie by her house to get some things. You guys get to Kyle's and settle in, but before you go, let me give you this." Murray went away and gathered the basics: a rosary, a crucifix, garlic steeped in vials of holy water, a small bundle of stakes. She stepped back into the living room with the box of essentials she had made for the boys and handed them an oil. "This is blessed garlic oil. Rub it around your doorframes and windows to keep them out. A little goes a long way. It's not much, but this should get you through. So, now let's get some rest. We're going to need it."

We said good night to the guys and started to my house. We drove along the dark streets saying nothing. What else was there to say?

"So, how were Mom and Dad?" I asked, trying to make conversation.

"Well, after you left I think they were a little in shock. Worried about you, of course. I don't know if your mom is going to speak to me ever again."

"Oh, she'll get over it. She's probably over it now," I said.

"Good," she replied. "Listen, Vickie, I would have never … If I had known…I mean, I just thought that maybe something was hidden in the tree. I didn't know that you were …"

I stopped her. "It's okay. I'm glad it's out in the open. My parents are still my parents. Mom and Dad raised me, you know? They are what matters."

"Good, good," Murray said, relieved.

We drove on for a moment more in silence, wondering what was in store for us next. What were we to talk about—vampires, ghouls, bats?

"So, tell me about Rodney," Murray said.

I smiled. "Can't we just talk about dead people, Ms. Murray?"

"You can call me Miranda. Seriously, when did all of that happen? I thought he was dating Jessica Perfecto?"

I said, "Well, yeah, he was. I mean, I wouldn't say we are necessarily dating yet. He just asked me to the ball. It's not a marriage proposal."

Murray said, "No. I know that. Come on, though. I was watching the way you were looking at Mr. Rod tonight. I think it's definitely love."

I laughed. "No…it's not love."

I didn't know quite what love was at that moment.

"Oh, yes," Murray laughed.

I smiled and said, "Well, who knows? We'll see."

It felt nice to laugh, to be comfortable enough to relax and let the fear float away like leaves in the breeze. After the hugging was over, we briefed Mom and Dad, who had no issues with my staying with Murray for a few days. They didn't quite know what to think of Dracula or vampires, but my safety, as well as their own, was essential.

I stood upstairs packing my bag when they walked into my room.

"Hey," I said, trying to sound as normal as possible.

"Hey, kiddo," Dad said.

I continued to pack my things while the three of us said nothing.

"Listen, Vickie, about your parents," Mom began.

I knew that was coming. "Mom," I interrupted. "Look. I'm sorry for the way I acted. I don't know what any of this means or why it's happening. To be honest, I'm still not sure I believe it. But the one thing I do know is that you guys are my parents. I love you guys."

"We love you too, honey," Dad said as he brushed my bangs from my eyes.

I added, "And I can't let anything happen to you. If this stuff is real, I have to face it alone. I can't lose you guys too, you know?"

The three of us hugged tightly. Mom sobbed quietly in typical mother mode. They watched us drive away, not knowing if it would be the last time we would see each other. Both Murray and I had school the next day and an entire afternoon of smiling and pretending that everything was normal.

Would life ever be *normal* again?

# DETENTION

Jessica had been in a good mood all day, even though I now had her man and had been nominated alongside her for the queen thing. Weird? Oh yeah. Really, though, Jessica was the last thing on my mind. She had been rattling about the Halloween Ball decorations all day long.

The gym looked pretty awesome. The committee had put the can money to good use. The decorations were super spooky. It looked like a gigantic old haunted house with basketball hoops. They had draped black material over the windows. Large candelabras were at every corner, the fake kind with lights and air that blows pieces of red material making it appear to be flames. The stage was decked out with coffins placed in a semicircle around the podiums, where undoubtedly the king and queen of Halloween would be standing. Personally, I could've done without the coffins. Voting was to take place in seventh period that day, and I was thinking of voting for myself. *Why not?*

I had spent every free moment that day sneaking and reading Abraham's diary, learning the events of 1861. It was all so amazing. I walked into Mrs. Black's class and took a seat. The bell rang as I placed my book bag to the side, slipping the diary in the front pocket. Black appeared to be in rare form. The chip on her shoulder was larger than usual.

She continued the discussions on immunity, in which I was not going to take part. Nope, I'd had enough of that. I needed to stay under the radar, just as Mom had said. If I spoke, Black would lock on target and start something. I really wasn't in the mood for that since I was dealing with my dysfunctional family issues. I sometimes wondered what had happened in Black's life to make her the dictator she had become. I listened as she tore into another student in her distinctive passive-aggressive manner. Poor Amy Charles—it was her turn that day. I could see Amy didn't know how to respond. *Don't do it, girl. It'll only make it worse. Just act like she's right and leave it alone,* I thought.

"So, you don't know the four humors?" Black said to Amy.

Amy sat fidgeting. "Um…uh …"

Black said, "Okay, let me give you a hint. Between the era of Hippocrates and the nineteenth century, people said diseases were caused by the imbalance of four humors, or four substances that made up a human body. What were they, Ms. Charles?"

"I…I don't know. Blood?" Amy said.

"Yes, very good, Ms. Charles," said Black tauntingly. "Let that little brain keep working. What was another?"

"Uh …" Amy pondered.

It was enough to make me sick. *Just let it go, woman. She doesn't know. Come on, Amy. Bile—yellow and black. There's two right there.*

"Amazing. You guys listen to nothing I say," Black said. Alan Reed raised his hand. "No, Mr. Reed, let's let Ms. Charles answer." Amy went to reach for her book, causing Black to shout, "Don't touch it! Now, tell me the other humors."

Amy was beginning to get upset. "Uh…stomach acid?"

"Close, but no. Come on, Ms. Charles. We can sit here all period if you like." Black rounded her desk and sat down, waiting for Amy to answer.

*Dammit! This is crazy! Phlegm. Come on, Amy, there's an easy one. You have allergies all year long!* I knew that since Amy was humiliated, her mind wasn't working. She was frozen like a deer in headlights. If you've been paying attention, you probably know I couldn't hold my tongue any longer.

"Blood, phlegm, black bile, and yellow bile," I rattled before I could even think about what I was saying. I couldn't take it anymore.

"See!" exploded Black. "I knew you couldn't keep your mouth shut! It's impossible for you, isn't it, Ms. Jenkins?"

"Obviously no more impossible than it is for you."

Yeah, that's what I said. It was on.

A collective "*Oooh*" was heard throughout the class. Black got up from her desk and said, "What did you say to me?"

I said, "I think you heard me, Mrs. Black. I *know* there's nothing wrong with your ears. Your mouth? Now that's a different story."

She said, "Why must you be so insubordinate?"

"Why must you be such a bitch?"

*Gasp!*

Yeah, maybe that was a little much, but I was on a roll. Inside me something grew…the rage, the need to fight…and I was ready and willing to do so. Neither Black nor anyone else knew the things I'd learned in the past twenty-four hours. You have to admit, learning you're adopted and that Dracula is after you is a lot to take!

Black smiled. She didn't explode like most thought she would. She walked around to her desk and got a stack of papers from her drawer. She walked to my desk and plopped them down. They were the voting papers for the dance.

"You see this, Ms. Jenkins? I bet this makes you proud, doesn't it. Thinking you're finally *popular*, like you belong, you finally fit in. Well, you *don't*." I stared back at her. I could feel my eyes burn with tears of rage. If I could have staked any monster at that moment, it would've been Black. "You're just an afterthought in life, Ms. Jenkins. You'll always be passed by; you'll always be dismissed. This piece of paper doesn't make you stand out. It doesn't even make you noticeable. You'll grow old and you'll look back and realize you never made a difference."

"Like you?" I said with all the hatred I could muster.

"*I have just*—" Black began.

"Mrs. Black," said Mr. Hillard. "I think that is just about enough from you on that subject."

Hillard had come into the classroom to deliver the updated flyers for the dance just in time to hear Black's speech, or at least enough of it. I didn't know when he had entered. I hadn't even noticed his presence, but I was glad he had arrived.

Black grew nervous. "Mr. Hillard, you should've heard what Vickie was saying to—"

"Honestly, I really don't care to know. Vickie?" I looked to Hillard. "Please go to my office and wait for me there. Mrs. Black, please come with me. Class, stay here. I will send Mrs. May down to sit with you until the bell. Don't forget to cast your votes, now."

I sat outside of the office while Mr. Hillard yelled at Mrs. Black. I don't think I had ever seen him so infuriated. Though I couldn't hear the words he was yelling, I used his rantings like a warm blanket, snuggling into them. Black stomped out of the office without even looking at me. Hillard stepped out as well.

"Vickie, come on," he said. I followed him inside and shut the door. I took the seat in front of his desk. "I'd like to begin by saying that you aren't going to be troubled by Mrs. Black anymore. I am taking you out of her class and putting you in with Mr. Mason for the rest of the year."

I smiled. That *rocked*.

"She said you called her a bitch, Vickie."

That, alas, *didn't* rock. It was shocking to hear him say the word.

I started, "Yeah, I mean …"

"That disappoints me." His tone was hard and overflowing with displeasure. "Vickie, that's unacceptable, and I would have never thought you would do that in a classroom."

"I know, but you heard what she was saying to me," I tried to explain.

Hillard said, "Yes, but you can't curse someone and expect them not to retaliate. Now, Mrs. Black has been reprimanded. But I'm afraid I'm going to have to keep you in detention after school, Vickie, at least for today."

"But …"

I couldn't remain after school. I had to get back with Murray and the guys and figure out what our next step was.

"I don't want to hear it, Vickie. Now, I'm going to call your mom and let her know to pick you up tonight around six," he said.

I said, "Mr. Hillard, listen, please don't call my mom. We kind of had a fight last night and it was sort of my fault. Disappointing you is enough. I can't handle disappointing her, too."

I couldn't take the chance on having Mom at the school. It would not only upset her, but it would call attention to her. In a world where I didn't know whom I could trust, that couldn't happen.

Mr. Hillard thought for a moment. "Vickie, I don't know why I do things like this for you. Fine, okay, you win. As long as you promise me that I'll never hear of behavior from you like that again."

"Deal," I said.

He added, "I assure you, Vickie. I'm not going to tolerate it. Go on. Go to Mr. Parks for the remainder of the day."

"But what about history class?" I asked.

"We'll get your work from Ms. Murray. Now go. And Vickie, just so we're clear—the next time I hear of an outburst like that, not only will I call Barbara, I'll be forced to suspend you. Understand? We don't curse teachers," he said.

I sat there wounded but knowing what Hillard was saying was correct. "I'm sorry, Mr. Hillard." And I was, though I didn't regret it. Black deserved every bit of what I said.

"I know, Vickie, and that's why I know you're better than that. Now, run along and I'll check on you later."

I managed to find Kyle and fill him in before Murray's class. Murray texted and said she would come and get me that evening so we could meet up with Kyle and Rod to begin planning our next steps.

Mr. Parks had already heard about the events in Biology and made me give him the full details. Contrary to Mr. Hillard, Parks thought it was the funniest thing he had ever heard. He made me tell him the whole story…*twice*.

At five fifty, Parks let me go. It was already growing dark outside, one of the negatives of autumn. I quickly made my way down the hallway. Murray was to meet me at the side entrance of the school where it was easy to loop around in the circle driveway and pick up students. As I rounded the corner next to the auditorium, I ran headfirst into someone coming the opposite way. The impact caused an explosion of papers and books that scattered everywhere!

"Oh! Oh, man…sorry about that," I said as I started to gather my stuff. It was then I noticed that the person I had bumped into was none other than Xavier Rainfeld. "Oh! Uh, Mr. Rainfeld. How…how are you doing tonight?"

I then noticed that he looked strange, disconnected. It made me feel sick to my stomach, like after the tenth ride on the Tilt-A-Whirl.

"Fine," he said distantly. "Do I know you?"

I said, "Oh…oh, no. We've never really met, but I know you, of course. My name is Vickie." I stuck out my hand to shake his, trying to appear as unaware of his funkiness as possible.

"And how do you know who I am?" he said, not taking my hand.

*What do you mean? Everyone knows you, idiot. You picture is right over there!*

I pointed to his portrait next to the auditorium. "Everyone knows you, Mr. Renfield."

*Oh, no! Where did that come from? Rainfeld, not Renfield!*

"What did you just call me?" Xavier muttered.

"Mr. Rainfeld," I said, trying to act as if he had misheard me.

He said, "No, I think you said…Renfield."

His eyes were sort of glazy white, his irises dimmed and hazy. I didn't know what to say. I had no other lies to pitch. He looked around us for others, as if he wanted to make certain no one would see. Then, I saw it—the bite on his neck. At that moment, I knew that he was no friend.

"Xavier!" said someone pleasantly. It was Mrs. May. "My, how are you? You are here awfully early."

"Yes, I know. It's a bad habit of mine. I am doing wonderful," he replied to her, snapping into a cheerful state.

Mrs. May said, "Well, I was just about to leave, but I think we've got you set up in here for the meeting. The others haven't arrived yet, but Mr. Willis said he would be here by seven thirty. Vickie, what are you still doing here?"

I said, "Oh, I was just about leave. I had to stay over." I got my junk and started toward the side entrance, *quickly*. "Nice to see you, Mr. Rainfeld. Bye, Mrs. May!"

*What the bajeebus was that about? What was he doing at the school?* I thought. Truthfully, I didn't care. I just wanted to get away from him. He gave me the willies, that creepy crawly kind of feeling. Even though he had been bitten, Xavier obviously wasn't a vampire. He looked nothing like Russ. Worse, he looked downright disturbing, like a hollow shell of who he once had been.

*Zombified.*

# WEAPONS OF WONDERMENT

Needless to say, I was completely tripping out. I took the next corner without even realizing that I was going the long way to the side entrance. It was the quickest way out of Xavier's line of sight. I didn't know where I was headed; I only knew that I had to get away from him. I felt threatened, like I was in danger. It was a feeling so intense that I kept glancing over my shoulder to make certain he wasn't eerily floating behind me like in the movies.

I could see Murray's headlights outside, and my pace quickened. Again, I looked behind me—nothing. My calves began to burn; I was near a full run, walking as quickly as my legs would carry me. Grabbing the handle of the door, I turned once more to look behind me.

There he was, standing motionless about a hundred feet from me, staring intently. I had no idea how he had gotten to where he was in the hallway without me noticing him before that moment. It was definitely one of those *Friday the 13th* moments, where no matter how fast you run or how slow they straggle behind, they still manage to catch you. His arms just hung at his sides. There was no smile, no expression, just blank nothingness in his gaze. I couldn't move. He slowly raised his hand and gave me this creepy little wave, like he was saying, *Hello, little girl, want a piece of candy?* He smiled and I could see his stained, rotting teeth.

That did it! I bolted from the door, ran to Murray's car, and jumped in.

"Go, go!" I said.

"What? What's the matter?" Murray asked.

"Just go!"

Murray threw the car into drive and squealed out of the parking lot. She drove as fast as she could, and by the time we had arrived at her house, the boys were sitting in Kyle's truck in the driveway. We whipped in beside them.

Once inside, Murray locked the door behind us. I didn't know who was more frightened—her or me! I began peeping through the windows, making sure we hadn't been followed.

"Uh, are you going to tell us what the frick is up?" Kyle said, plopping down in the chair.

"What is it?" Rod asked.

"Your dad," I replied.

Rod tensed. "What?"

"Xavier. I was leaving detention tonight and I ran right into him in front of the auditorium."

"What was he doing at the school at night?" Kyle asked.

"Wait, wait. It's no big deal. Dad put together a school board meeting last week," Rod replied. "He said it was tonight."

"Well, that explains why he was there, Vickie," Murray said.

Still, there was more. I knew it. "Yeah, but you guys should have seen him. You should have looked at his face."

"Was he vamped out?" Kyle asked.

"No, I don't think so. That would have been obvious. He didn't look that way," I replied.

"Then what?" Rod asked.

I walked away from the windows and sat down beside Rod. "I don't know. He just looked, odd, like he was out of it."

"He could have just been tired, Vickie. He hasn't been able to go home," Murray said.

"No, it was different than that. I've seen Kyle after a weekend-long PlayStation fest and it wasn't tired," I replied. "He was, I don't know, *absent,* like he was…*dead.* Mrs. May walked up to us and started talking to him, and I just bolted. When I got to the door, I looked back and he was there. Out of nowhere, he was standing in the hallway, watching me. He just smiled that creepy kind of smile."

Kyle said, "Xavier always smiles creepy, just like in that picture at the auditorium."

"No!" I said, standing. "You guys aren't listening to me. I'm telling you. Something about him wasn't right. I mean, I feel it in my gut."

I began to notice how uncomfortable Rod was becoming. I knew that Vladimir had done something to Xavier, but he didn't *change* him like he had changed Russ; he made him something worse, something not quite alive.

"Okay, okay," Murray said, trying to calm me down. "Rod, did you see Dracula do anything to your father?"

Rod looked at us. "Uh…not that I saw. It all happened so fast."

"Where did Xavier go after it happened? Who was he staying with?" I asked suspiciously. "Maybe Dracula found him."

"I…I don't know. Maybe he went to his friend Carl's house. He didn't say." Rod's lie was beginning to burn inside him. As his deceit began to smolder, it seeped from his pores like smoke. I could almost see it.

"I thought you talked to him on the phone after it happened?" Murray asked.

Rod said, "I did. I…I called him from the bathroom that night, at Kyle's house."

"Have you talked to him since?" I asked.

Rod said, "No, not yet."

Murray looked at him oddly. "You mean, this tragic thing happened and you haven't talked to your dad since that night? You guys haven't met anywhere or anything?"

Rod didn't answer. We sat there waiting on his response.

"Fine," he said. He got up from beside me and started pacing the room. "It…it was Dad. He did it. He brought Dracula back."

"What?" Kyle said. "Dude, why would your dad have wanted to do that?"

"*Renfield.*" Murray knowingly looked up at Rod. "You're a Renfield. aren't you, Rod?" Rod didn't answer. "That brings it full circle. The cast is all here."

Rod looked into my eyes. I actually thought I saw his heart sink into his chest as if it were bound by chains and cinderblocks.

"It happened that night. Dad brought him back," he began. "We were just talking one minute and then everything went black." He showed us the scar on his arm. "When I woke up, my arm was bleeding. At first, he tried to play it off.

I believe he thought my blood wasn't going to work. He made up some stupid-ass story about a mask falling off the wall and knocking me out. I was groggy. My head felt like it was going to split open, so I wasn't thinking straight. He was helping me off the floor when those locks, dozens of them, starting unlatching in the coffin. God, they were so loud. Then the coffin lid opened and it rose out of it. It could actually *smell* my blood. It called us Renfield then. I didn't know what it meant. I really didn't care. I thought I was hallucinating, you know, from the whack to the head. It wanted more of my blood, and Dad…he wouldn't let it at me. He stabbed it in the back, and I ran. That's when Russ rang the doorbell."

"Why did you lie, Rod?" was all I could say.

"Okay, what would have made you guys run faster—the fact that my own father brought back Dracula and used *me* to do it, or knowing that we were Renfields? You would have thrown me out into the street! I *needed* you guys. I didn't have anyone else. I didn't know how I would face anyone at school if they knew." Rod's eyes glossed.

Okay, I'm a sucker for muscle-bound dude with a sensitive side. What can I say?

"Dude," Kyle said. "Wait a minute—that means you're a *virgin*?"

I said, "Shut up, Kyle!"

I got up and walked over to Rod. I stood there for a moment, looking at him. I think he was waiting on me to scream at him or slap his face. However, I got it. I understood and could clearly see the guilt that stabbed at him. Rod was right. What else was he supposed to have done? His entire world had changed in a matter of minutes, just like ours. I smiled.

I took him by the hand. "Rod, listen, it's okay."

"She's right, Rodney," Murray added. "It's not your fault."

"But, I'm a Renfield," he said as his bottom lip slightly quivered. I stood on my tiptoes and hugged him. He buried his face into my hair.

Murray walked over and placed a hand on his shoulder. "Rodney, there's something you don't know about R.M. Renfield. If it wasn't for him, Dracula would have won a long time ago. It was with his help that Van Helsing was able to defeat him the first time."

"Don't worry about it, man," Kyle added. "I kind of lied about band camp." Rod giggled. "And don't worry about the jerks at school. With any luck, Dracula will eat the board members and school will be cancelled for the rest of the year."

"No doubt," Rod laughed.

Then, Murray looked to Kyle. "What did you just say?"

Kyle said, "Uh, I just said I lied about doing it at band camp, lady. Fine, rub it in!"

"No, no, about the school board," Murray clarified.

"I said hopefully Dracula will eat the school board members and …"

"Oh, my God!" Murray said. "That's it!"

I stepped back. "The school board. Xavier's taking Dracula to the school board meeting."

"Building his army," Murray said.

They had to be stopped. I wasn't crazy about most of the members of the school board, but we couldn't let them be killed. "We've got to go!"

"Come with me, guys!" Murray said.

She took us to a huge walk-in closet in the spare room and threw open the doors. Inside, it was overflowing from front to back with stakes, crucifixes, and supernatural weapons of all kinds. She began handing them to us and piling them into large duffle bags.

"Okay…where did you get this stuff?" Kyle asked.

"My son is an engineer. He makes most of it and sends it to me from New York. I guess you can tell we've been expecting this for a while. Here, take this," she said, handing Kyle this weird-looking long stake.

Kyle said, "What is this?"

"It's a Coldseeker. It's like a heat-seeking missile, but the opposite. It hones in on the coldness of the heart. A vampire's body temperature doesn't reach above fifty-five degrees."

Kyle said, "Dude! That's cold!"

Murray rolled her eyes. "Press this button when you're ready to use it. Once you throw it, it will separate into multiple stakes. One of these will give you five rounds."

I saw a metal ball about the size of a basketball. "And what is that?"

"Well, it's called Divine Light," Murray said as she sat it on the floor. She tapped the button on the top with her foot, but it didn't respond. It just sat there like a trashcan.

"Seems like a *divine waste* to me," I said.

"Yeah, I haven't quite figured it out. Charlie didn't say much about it. He's always making new things, and some of the things he's sent…well, let's just say he tries," Murray said. Then, she freaked out when she noticed Kyle playing with a little round cylinder that looked like a whistle.

"What?" Kyle said as she yanked it from his hand.

"Kyle! You need to watch out with some of this stuff. This thing is a Squealer. Vampires have extremely sensitive hearing, like a bat. This thing is like a dog whistle on steroids. It'll drive them nuts," Murray said.

"Yeah, Kyle, why don't you just climb up on the roof and ring a dinner bell?" I said.

Then, she reached into the closet and handed me a large cross with a chain on the end. The chain reminded me of a rosary with beads along the links.

"I think you'll be able to handle this, Vickie, or at least I hope so," she said. "This is a Morningstar. Press these buttons here."

The buttons were along the base of the cross, and when I pressed them, blades ejected from all around it.

"Oh…wow," I said.

"You swing it by the chain. If the metal cuts their skin, it'll burn them like fire. *Be careful* with it. Your mother will have my ass if you lose an eye," Murray said.

Then, she showed us bags filled with a white powder.

"This is Holy Powder. It's made from blessed salt water that is dehydrated to the point where only the salt is left. Then, you can take a coffee grinder or mortar and pestle and grind it into a fine powder. You can use it all sorts of ways. You can even pack it into bullets like gunpowder. It's a little more potent than the holy water, so a little goes a long way. Don't waste it."

She handed Rod a small bag of beads. They were silver and a little smaller than golf balls.

She said, "These are Flares. Press them on either side to activate them. Once they go off, they emit a burst of UV light that can take out a small group of vampires if you can catch them off-guard." Rod began fumbling with one. Murray stepped in. "No, you have to …"

*Flash!*

And we were blinded for about thirty seconds.

"Woah!" Kyle said, rubbing his eyes.

Murray held her burning eyes and said, "Yes, dear, you want to be sure to close your eyes when you let one of these babies loose. You can't fight vampires if you're blind."

Kyle reached into the closet and pulled out a set of hand swords in the shape of crosses. They were awesome.

"Wow," he said. "What are these called?"

Murray looked at him like he was an idiot and said, "Uh, knives."

"*Knives*," Kyle mocked, sticking out his tongue.

We finished packing up as much of the arsenal as we could and ran from the front door toward Kyle's truck. I held tight to Rod's hand.

"Woo hoo! I get to see a live vampire!" Kyle said as he pulled out his keys.

Murray and Kyle tossed the weapons into his truck bed and locked it down. Suddenly, Rod let go of my hand and stopped right where he was.

"What? Come on! We have to go," I said.

"I…I can't, Vickie," he said.

"What? Why?" I said.

He said, "My dad is going to be there. I can't trust it."

I rolled my eyes. "I trust you, Rod! It's fine. I'm not worried about you."

"Yeah, but I am. I can't trust *me*, Vickie. I'm a Renfield. I'm just a weak link," Rod said as he backed away from me.

He had to come with us. I didn't know if I could go without him. If he was with me, at least I would know where he was; I'd know he was safe.

"Wait. You're being stupid!" I pleaded.

Then, he ran to me, grabbed me tightly, and kissed me. You know, I kissed Bucky Thornwell in the hall in fifth grade and thought that was the coolest thing ever, but this? Oh, this was a whole other kind of kiss, let me tell you. It was so intense, I felt my legs weaken. I could smell his peppermint gum and taste the sweetness of it on my lips. He towered over me as I went all gooey in his arms, just like Scarlett O'Hara, *I declare*.

"Be careful, Vickie," he said, looking deep into my eyes. Then, he began to run away.

"Rod! Rod! Wait!" I yelled.

"Vickie, come on. We can't waste time. We have to go now!" Murray called. "I'm driving," she said to Kyle, taking his keys.

"No, no, no…now wait a minute," Kyle tried.

It was too late. Murray was already in the driver's seat. I jumped in as Murray threw the truck into reverse and ripped out of the driveway. As we sped away, I touched my lips, still feeling Rod's against mine, smelling his gum, his lips. I looked back and watched him disappear into the cover of shadows, not knowing if I'd live to be kissed that way again.

# SCHOOL BOARD BUFFET

Some of us were fortunate enough to watch the security recordings from what is now secretly referred to as the *School Board Buffet* before the video files disappeared. But, trust me, it was something that would have caused anyone to hurl.

It was no secret that Xavier didn't care for the members of the school board or the representatives from Ashton Realty, and that was great for him since he was going to have them killed. The board wasn't pleased about a meeting outside of business hours. It didn't matter—little did they know it would be their last meeting.

As we were packing the weapons into Kyle's truck, Mr. Deason from the board was barking, "So, when would we break ground on the new center?"

Deason positioned his pudgy body in the narrow seat amidst the lot of them: the entire board, and members of Ashton Realty. Ms. Harris, the board's secretary, sat in the front row near the doors, taking the minutes of the meeting in a leather-bound notebook. There appeared to be over twenty-seven people lining the seats that evening, more than enough for a meal.

"We would be able to break ground in the spring of next year," Xavier replied from the podium. "We've finalized the deal for the mortuary and the land it's on with Ashton Realty today. So, we should be ready to begin."

"So, why wait until spring?" Deason asked.

"Well, we wouldn't want to start now with the cold temperatures approaching," said Thom Ashton. "The foundation will be best worked in the spring.

You could see Xavier begin to drift while Deason and Ashton babbled on. He didn't seem to have much control over himself. Whatever Vladimir had done to him was causing his brain to twist in on itself, splitting him into two halves. There apparently was the part that was the ordinary Xavier, but another part was insane and was eating away any normalcy that remained.

"Mr. Rainfeld, are you listening to me?" Deason said.

Xavier shook. "Yes, sorry about that. Come again?"

"I said, while we appreciate your generosity, as we always do, the board is beginning to feel…well, indebted to you, Mr. Rainfeld."

"Oh?" Xavier replied.

"Yes, we mean no disrespect, of course," Deason added. "However, we've received enough funding from the state to cover the building of the center. So, we would like to use the mortuary and its land, except we would like to *buy* it from you instead. This way, we can plan independently of Rainfeld, Inc. and not tie up your resources."

"Oh, I see," Xavier said as he looked over to Ashton.

"Don't look at me, Rainfeld; that old heap is all yours. The contract is final," Ashton said.

"Mr. Rainfeld," Deason began.

"So…you don't want to *name* it after me, is that right?" Xavier asked.

The members looked at one another as if someone had farted in the middle of a eulogy.

"Mr. Rainfeld," said Mrs. Dover, a broad stick of a woman with a trashcan face. "Please try to understand. We've been given funds that we have to use before the year is over or we lose the money. We will gladly give you what the land is worth. It's of no use to you."

"So, you're still going to name it *Renfield* Recreation Center, correct?" Xavier said without noticing his blunder.

"Pardon?" Mrs. Dover asked. "Who is Renfield?"

"Sorry," Xavier corrected. "I mean Rainfeld. That's my name."

"Yes, we know your name, Mr. Rainfeld. Are you feeling okay?" asked the short and *portly* Mrs. Portland.

Xavier stood there looking at them for a moment growing noticeably upset. "I don't know how I feel anymore," he softly muttered.

"Uh, do we need to reschedule?" Mrs. Dover asked.

"No, no," Xavier said, regaining his composure. "Tonight is fine. So, let's get back to the name thing. You're still going to use my name, correct? I mean, it is my land."

Mr. Deason said, "Land that we would buy from you."

"So then the answer is no," Xavier said.

"We thought of calling it Rutgers Recreation Center. You know, so that it is clearly connected to the school," Mr. Deason said.

"Ah!" Xavier replied sarcastically. "Well, why don't I just keep the land, let you stick your money up your asses, build my own building there, and call it anything I like?"

"Now, listen here!" said Mr. Williams, the head of the board. "First of all, Simmons Mortuary hasn't been used in over ten years. It's useless to you. You just bought it a few days ago! Nevertheless, it's in the best location for school functions. Now, we didn't need to get out tonight. I was already pissed off that you scheduled something like this outside of normal business hours, dragging us to the school at all hours of the night. However, we accommodated you, as we *always* do, Xavier. Now, for you to sit here and talk to us in this manner is inexcusable."

The members of Ashton Realty got up and began to gather their things. Ms. Harris stopped her note taking and closed her pad preparing to follow them.

Xavier laughed. "Sure, you *accommodated* me, Chester. It was fine to please me when you needed something from me, wasn't it? When you needed the gymnasium floors redone, or when this auditorium needed rebuilding. That was all fine! You were hanging pictures of me all over town; but now that the state has found a few bucks to give you, you toss me out, right?"

Ms. Harris reached for the door handle.

Xavier screeched, *"Don't touch that door!"*

The door pulled from Ms. Harris' hand and slammed shut on its own. She stopped in her tracks and turned to Xavier. There was a fearsome feral look on his face, like a rabid dog about to attack. Taking the clip-on microphone from his shirt and tossing it aside, he began to stroll across the stage.

"You think you're getting out of here?" Xavier laughed. "You're not going anywhere. As a matter of fact, you won't be going anywhere—*ever again!*"

One by one, the sharp sound of the bolting of locks came from all sides of the room. The others piled against the doors, trying to push them open, but they wouldn't budge. Ms. Lawson pulled something from her purse that looked like a cell phone, and as she did, Xavier leapt from the stage at her. He took it and smashed it on the ground.

Mr. Williams pleaded, "Xavier! Please! Control yourself!"

Xavier laughed and stood upright. Then, he straightened his shirt and slicked back his hair.

Calmly, Xavier said, "You must forgive me, Chester. I've not been myself lately."

"I…I understand, Xavier," Williams said with a controlled fear. "Now, please unlock the doors. We'll leave tonight and sleep on it. Then, in the morning, we'll discuss this further. Maybe we can come to an agreement on the name. I could call you and we could have lunch over at—"

"Oh, but wait, wait, wait, wait," Xavier said with a crazy giddiness. "I have someone I want you to meet first, please. Oh, pretty, pretty, please."

Then, Xavier seemed to notice something moving, an insect scurrying across the floor. With a smack, he snatched the bulky creature and gobbled it up. Mrs. Dover grew ill.

Deason looked at him in disgust. "Oh, Xavier…what is happening to you?"

"Nothing," Xavier replied. "Should I have shared? I'm sure there's another running around in here somewhere." He ran back up to the podium. "Please, please, take a seat, take a seat." No one moved. "*Sit down!*" he shouted.

They slowly walked over to the seats as a peculiar fog began to flow from under the doors and pool around their feet.

"What's happening!" yelled Ashton. "Fire! There's a fire!"

Xavier laughed and hit the lights, casting a sinister red glow on them all.

"Now, I wish to welcome to the stage someone very, very famous! I bet you didn't think we would have a celebrity guest, did you?"

The fog ventured up the steps and began puddling on the stage.

"You've heard of him, you've read about him, you've watched inaccurate depictions of him," Xavier continued as the fog began to stand upright. "Welcome to the stage…the one…the only …"

Then, the fog opened its eyes.

After that, the videos cut to snow.

# ROUND ONE

It was difficult to concentrate, and focus is essential when you're about to fight a buttload of vampires, you know. Not only was the guy of my dreams running around with monsters on the loose, I was possibly about to fight a horde of them. I was a little preoccupied. I held tightly to the backpack full of the cool junk that Murray had handed out. I wasn't so sure about the Morningstar, though. As a kid, I was notorious for being a loose cannon with a baton. Add razor blades to one and let me give it a twirl and you've got yourself a massacre.

I looked in the rearview mirror and noticed that Kyle's level of enthusiasm had dropped significantly now that the gravity of the situation was setting in.

I said, "Kyle, you don't have to go in."

He said nothing.

"Kyle?"

"Yeah, yeah. I'm good. No problem," he rattled.

I watched him as he examined the items in his bag, holding his crucifixes, investigating the stakes—he looked as if he was going to heave. It was so cute!

"Kyle," I said with the same soft tone Mom used with me as a child. "I'll be with you. I'll protect you. Promise."

Kyle looked at my face. I didn't want him to see one ounce of fear in my eyes; I wanted my confidence to console him. Maybe it would console me, too.

The voice in my head kept saying I had already fought a monster in the park and won, and that was without the armory we had with us.

"You better, woman!" Kyle replied with a more confident smile.

"We're going to be fine, Kyle," Murray said.

A surplus of cars littered the teacher's lot at Rutgers. Light shined through the frosted windows of the auditorium, letting us know someone was home. We got out of the truck and stood there, listening, watching. We could faintly hear voices, but no screams or cries for help—you know, no horror movie crap.

Murray said, "Thank God, we're not too late."

*Oh, whoopee!* I thought.

Being stealthily silent, we made our way to the main entrance of the school and walked inside, pausing at the second set of auditorium doors. We gave each other one of those looks before opening the doors, one of those *here we go* looks. I took a deep breath, letting the cool air of the hallway fill my lungs, and I could smell stale chalk from decades gone by.

"Ready?" Murray said as she placed her hand on the door.

We were as ready as we were ever going to be. Murray slowly opened the doors to the sound of Xavier talking about…

"Now, as we've seen, the land here is a little unleveled, so the foundation will have to be built high to start. The ground is naturally damp. We'll have to remain aware of that as we plan. Here we see Simmons Mortuary, which will be your new home," Xavier said in a professional manner.

His back was to the audience. I watched them sitting there, listening to what he said, nodding their heads in agreement with his overview. As I began to wonder if we could have been wrong about the Drac-attack, embarrassment began to take hold of me. I took Kyle by the arm, and Murray followed us to the back of the auditorium, trying to remain out of sight.

"What's going on?" Murray said quietly.

"I don't know. A meeting?" I said.

"It all sounds fine to me," Kyle said. "Maybe nothing is going down. Sooo, let's get outta here!"

"No," I said. "Something's not right, guys." I looked up to the ceiling and noticed that all of the new security cameras were broken. "Guys…get ready," I said.

"And to the tasty morsels in the back of the room, would you like to join or die?" Xavier said without even looking in our direction. At first, I wondered if I had heard him right. Then, he turned to us with an appearance that was fantastically freakish. He looked so much worse than when I had seen him in the hallway earlier.

"Um, should I say, 'Oh, hell,' now, or later?" I muttered.

Murray leaned in. "I think now is as good a time as any, sweetie."

"Everyone!" Xavier exclaimed, pointing to us. "*Get 'em!*"

They snapped their heads to us and snarled as if they were demons raised from the nether realm of hell. It happened in a flash—they rushed us quickly and viciously as the three of us armed ourselves.

I needed that instinct to kick in, and it did without effort. Amazing. Without forethought, I sent a stake zooming through the air. It flew like a bullet through the entire length of the auditorium, spiking one of the gruesome board members.

*Poof!* It erupted into a sticky dust.

Murray and Kyle watched in amazement as I jumped into the air like a weightless badass and ran atop the backs of the seats of the room with the grace of a ballet dancer. I reached into my pack and armed myself with two long daggers. Then I ran between two of the freaks, decapitating them as I passed. With a quick somersault, I landed in the aisle, facing their rotting corpses. I don't know where the gymnastics stuff came from, I swear. Kyle and Murray were just standing there with their mouths hanging open.

"Guys! Get with it!" I called to them as I stabbed another ghoul.

Mr. Deason charged Murray, knocking her to the ground. She wrestled with her sack and managed to hit him in the head with a bottle of the garlic/holy water solution, nearly burning away the entire left half of his face. The flesh melted away, leaving his open tongue wiggling among his fanged teeth like a worm.

Yeah—*gross!*

Deason fell to his knees with his one black eye whirling around, staring at nothing but seeing everything. Murray kicked his hand away as he melted into sludge.

Kyle iced over with a solid sheet of fear. He stood there watching the commotion, trying to figure out where he fit in. Feeling a tap on his shoulder, he turned to see the petite Mrs. Linden glaring at him. Her jaws appeared to come unhinged as she roared at him like a bear, jumping onto him. They fell to the floor as she clawed and snapped at him with her mouth that, in my opinion, had always been on the large side.

"Oh, crap! Oh, *crap!*" I heard Kyle say as he blocked her advances.

As he wrestled with her, he reached into his sack and grabbed one of the sharp wooden spikes. He jabbed the first one through her right eye, causing her to go wild. He pushed her from him and stood up as she pulled the smoldering stick from her socket and growled at him like a dog. Then, she began to run—not like you or me—but in a strange spider-like manner. As she leapt for him, Kyle stabbed her chest with the spike and threw her over his head. Her melting body exploded with a *bang* before she hit the ground.

"There, *bitch!*" he shouted triumphantly.

I was making quick work of most of the Grunts, if I do say so myself. One organized a little ambush for me. He had two of the others hiding under seats while he dared me to come to him. So, I decided it was time to try the Morningstar. Oh yeah—one of us was going to lose a finger! I took the metal orb out of my pack and pushed the button to arm it. The blades shot out of it, cutting my sleeve before I dropped it forward, allowing it to dangle by its chain.

The creep had the audacity to put a hand up and motion for me to come, but his overconfidence cautioned me, letting me know something was up. I ran at him as the others slithered under the seats like snakes. I could see their shadows moving along the floor as I targeted them. I jumped into the air and swung the Morningstar by the chain, using my neck and shoulders to guide it. I could feel the blades of the ball cutting through their flesh like a Thanksgiving turkey; I could hear the slices and the blood splatter to the ground. By the time I hit the floor, the three of them were nothing more than goo.

I turned to see a group of vampires pouring in on Kyle and Murray. They tried as hard as they could to handle the creatures, but there were too many of them. I was never going to be able to get to them all in time. Then, Kyle got an idea. He fumbled in his pack, grabbed one of the Squealers, and pulled the pin just as the things were about to jump them.

I heard nothing, not a sound. Yet the vampires all stopped and began looking around themselves, peering at the ceilings and windows, wondering where the noise was coming from. Then, they began screaming as if they were on fire. Whatever they were hearing was far too much for them to take.

It was fabulous!

The remaining freaks began to scatter, but I was focused on the stage. Xavier's emotional balance appeared to go between excitement and despair through the whole battle. I hand-sprung onto the stage as he fell to his knees in surrender. My stake stopped just shy of his chest; I had no idea why I didn't follow through. Maybe it was because he was Rod's father; maybe it was because he seemed to want me to kill him. I didn't know. He kept his eyes down as tears streamed from them.

"Please…do it," he said. "I can't do this anymore, Victoria. He's not going to let me go, ever, not while I'm alive."

Suddenly, a smoke whipped around Kyle's hand, breaking the Squealer in two.

"Vickie!" yelled Murray.

It was too late. While I had been focused on Xavier's plight, the smoke had crept up on me, wrapping around my wrists and waist. I fought to get away from it, but it was no use. It was as if I had fallen into a vat of glue, a thick tar I couldn't get off me. The really creepy part was when it *spoke!*

"Hello, there," said the fog in a hissing tone. "And what is your name, little girl?"

I screamed, "Let me go!"

You know, because screaming *let me go* always works in the movies.

It patronized me. "That doesn't sound like a pretty name. Now, I know you have a pretty name. What is it?" Murray and Kyle began moving toward the stage. "*If you come any closer, I will rip her heart from her chest and eat it in front of you.*"

They froze.

I was at a loss. I mean, how do you fight *nothing?*

"Vickie—my name is Vickie Jenkins," I said, taking its attention from them.

It laughed. "Oh, now, I don't think you are being very honest with me. You seem to be astonishingly gifted. Are you certain that is your real name?" I didn't answer. I closed my eyes. "No matter. The scent of your blood will tell me. I am *thirsty.*"

It opened its cloudy mouth as it materialized, becoming part mist, part beast. It moved toward my neck. No matter how I struggled, I couldn't get away. Its strength was astounding. Kyle and Murray ran toward the stage as the mist completely morphed into Vladimir.

Slowly, he leaned his head back, preparing to bite into me, when, out of nowhere, a voice sang, "Say cheese!"

Vladimir looked up in time for the flash of a Flare to singe what was exposed of his flesh. He dropped me, and I scurried back to a safe distance. He screamed and thrashed about, transforming in and out of the fog-like state.

Yeah, he was going to be pissed.

I wasn't prepared for the Flare, of course, so it took my eyes a second to focus on the fact that it was Rod who had saved me.

"Am I late?" Rod said cleverly.

I smiled. "No, you're right on time."

Vladimir roared as his anger engulfed him. He began to heave and breathe at a rapid pace, taking it in, preparing.

"Well, I think we'd better get out of here now," Rod said, taking me by the hand.

I said, "I think you're right."

"Vickie, Rod, get out of there! Come on!" Murray called from one of the auditorium doors.

Vladimir's bones began to crack and bend, like a puzzle with broken pieces. He began to expand, to change. As he knelt down, he growled, "The children of the night—what sweet *music…they…make!*"

He began running at us like a canine on all fours, and as he jumped from the stage, his flesh exploded into mounds of black and gray fur. Vladimir was now a giant wolf-creature unlike anything we had ever seen!

We slammed the doors just in time to lock it inside the auditorium. We held both sets of doors while it thrashed against them, howling and yelping. The doors jarred so much I felt like I was on a roller coaster. Suddenly, the struggle stopped. There was no noise or tremble. We stayed pressed against the doors waiting and waiting, until …

*Crash!*

The thing busted through the glass of the front doors beside us. We ran as it galloped after us, but it was far too fast; I knew that. It was gaining on us quickly. I reached around my back into the weapons pack and grabbed what was on top: two fistfuls of holy powder. We were about to see just how potent this stuff was.

I kicked my foot like a figure skater and spun around to face the wolf just as it neared my back. It was so close to me I could smell its breath, and, no, it wasn't minty. It reached for me with its paws as I blew the handfuls of powder into its face and eyes. It yelped as it fell to the floor and slid across the tiles, knocking our legs from under us. Through a sizzling steam, the acidity of the powder ate away at its fur and flesh. With a loud howl, its flesh began to quiver and quake and, in an instant, it erupted into dozens of great big, ugly *rats!*

Yes, you heard me correctly. *Rats!*

They scattered around our feet, making their escape. It was *so* gross! We tried to remain still as the nasty things ran around us. After a final rat came from the corner and ran out of the broken doors of the school, we jumped to our feet, rubbing our arms, disgusted.

"*Woo, that was fun!*" Kyle yelled nearly causing Murray to jump out of her skin.

"Dammit, Kyle!" Murray yelled.

"You did a good job, Vickie," Rod said.

I looked at him and ran into his arms.

"Don't you ever run off again," I said with a bit too much drama. But give me a break—I had just fought vampires, for crying out loud.

We hugged one another, but our celebration was a bit premature. From the janitor's closet, we heard a noise, a scratching at the door that caused us to look suspiciously at one another. I armed myself, because I wasn't taking any chances!

We neared the closet.

I grabbed the door and slung it open. With a crash, brooms and mops fell to the ground. Nothing was there.

"Forget this! I am going home!" Kyle yelled, walking away.

We began to laugh, and I closed the door. That's when I saw Xavier peering into my eyes. He had been standing behind the door like a vacant zombie. How I could have missed the smell is beyond me. The putrid rot of death filled the hallway. Murray screamed. He didn't charge us or even acknowledge our presence, until he looked at Rod. And when he did, his pale face cracked into an expression of sorrow.

"Dad?" Rod said, overwhelmed. "Oh my God, Dad, what did he do to you?"

Then, Xavier began to weep. "Oh, please, please don't look at me." He fell to his knees. Rod stepped closer, and Xavier crawled away in fear. "No, no. Don't look at me. *Go away!* Please!"

"Dad?" Rod said.

"Your father is *dead*," Xavier said coldly.

In a way it was true; Xavier *was* dead—anyone could see that. But to Rod, Xavier died the night he used his only son as a vehicle to bring Dracula back into the world. At that moment, Rod had become an orphan—he just didn't know it. Rod stared back at him, torn between pain and disgust.

Without emotion, Rod said, "Come on, guys. Leave him to rot."

Xavier began to sob once again as we walked away. It was almost too much. It was horrible to listen to him cry. A part of me wanted to walk Rod back over to Xavier, to see if we could save him. But I knew we couldn't, not really. There was nothing left to save, so I took Rod by the hand.

We had survived the battle, but would we survive the war? I knew Drac was now suspicious about the Van Helsing bloodline and me. He had apparently been watching me during the fight. My past would not remain a secret forever, but the longer the better.

As we walked out of the front doors, Kyle hopped up on the concrete railing of the steps, balancing on it.

"Rod, dude, I'm sorry about your dad," Kyle said.

"Thanks, Kyle, but really, I'd rather not talk about it," Rod replied.

"That's cool. I get it. You can still stay with me if you'd like, man. My mom and dad don't care that you're there. Mom really likes you," Kyle said.

Rod said, "Thanks, Kyle. I'd like that."

"I don't know about you guys, but I'm hungry," I said. And I was, believe it or not.

"Are you nuts? I couldn't eat after that crap and I live on horror movies!" Kyle replied.

"Food may do us good. Where do you guys want to go? I'm buying," Murray said.

"Hot! I say we go to—"

It came from the bushes, tackling Kyle as he walked along the steps. It was one of the board members lurking in the shadows.

"Help!" Kyle screamed.

I pulled out a stake from the pack and stabbed it in an instant, but it was too late. Kyle had been bitten in the leg. As the creature melted away, I knelt down, pressing on his wound.

"Oh, no. Oh, oh, Kyle," I rambled, sudden tears burning my eyes.

Rod and Murray gathered around us. The thing had bitten through his ankle.

"Guys…guys, I'm about to turn. I can feel…" Kyle's eyes faded into black but then returned to normal. His body was fighting it, but barely.

"Quick!" Murray said. "Give me something to tie it off with. Hurry!"

Kyle began fading in and out. His eyes rolled over and fangs sprouted from his gum line.

"Oh, God! It burns!" Kyle screamed.

"Hang on, man. Hang on!" Rod begged.

Rod ripped the bottom of his shirt and handed it to Murray, and she used it to tie off the wound to keep the virus from spreading as much as possible.

Murray said, "Okay, hand me the small black bag inside my sack. Hurry!" Kyle changed and lunged forward as if he was going to attack Murray. "Hold him!"

Rod bent down and held Kyle's hands. I found the black bag and handed it to Murray. Inside was a green solution, a hypodermic syringe, and a stick.

"What is that?" I asked.

"Anti-venom," Murray said.

"Will it work?" I said.

"I don't know! I don't know! I've never tried it," she replied.

"Hang on, Kyle," Rod said.

Kyle continued to vamp in and out, screaming in torture.

Murray said, "Kyle! Kyle, I need you to listen to me, okay? Listen. The virus hasn't had time to spread. It's a leg wound, so we may be able to save you, okay?"

"Kill me!" he screamed.

"Kyle! Listen! This is going to hurt," she warned.

She stabbed the syringe into the wound, injecting the solution directly into it. He howled as tears ran from his eyes.

"Vickie, get a stake," Murray said.

"What!" I said. I couldn't believe what I was hearing!

Murray yelled, "Get it!" I pulled out a stake. "Rod, hold him as tight as you can, and don't let him bite you, whatever you do. Listen, guys. I'm going to pull off the tourniquet, and one of two things is going to happen. Either the solution will work, or he will completely change and attack us. We *have* to be prepared."

"I'm not going to kill him!" I yelled.

"Fine!" Murray yanked the stake from my hand.

She looked at us both as Kyle continued to scream into the night. I couldn't believe I was about to watch my best friend be killed in front of my eyes. Murray took a deep breath and yanked the strip from his leg. He lunged forward, eyes black, fangs bared, completely altered. Murray closed her eyes and swung the stake at his chest.

*Silence.*

# A Fool In Love

Murray gripped the sharp stake tightly in her hand, so tightly her knuckles were turning white. Kyle's eyes regressed into his own, his teeth now the normal, white, perfect set of which I'd always been jealous. I held Murray's arm firmly, keeping her from slamming the wood through his heart. I knew that Kyle wasn't going to change. I didn't know how I knew it, but I did. Murray's eyes grew wide at the realization that the serum had worked. Yeah, she had nearly killed Kyle.

"Vickie," Murray said with a shiver in her voice.

"Stop, it's all right, Miranda. Let go of it," I said.

Murray dropped the stake and put her hands over her mouth in shock. Kyle had turned human the instant she had swung toward his scrawny chest. She would have pinned him like a butterfly to a mat. I laid my hands on Murray's shoulders. I could see the damage in her face, the horror of what might have been.

Kyle began to stir.

I said, "Miranda, come on. Let's get him into the truck. It's time to go home now."

Still trembling, Murray got to her feet. Rod used his stocky frame to lift Kyle like a feather and carry him to the truck.

"Is he going to be all right?" Murray asked, quivering.

Holding on to Rod like a knight in shining armor, Kyle sighed, "Oh, Rod, you're so sexy."

"Oh, he'll be fine," I said with a smile.

Murray remained quiet on the drive. I sat in the small back seat of the cab, comforting Kyle while Rod kept his hand on my leg from the front seat. None of us said a word. Kyle peered out of the window with a blanket wrapped around him, watching the street lights go by. In many ways, I'm sure he thought it was awesome: he had been bitten by a vampire and lived. *Who can say that?* He was far too weak to express real enthusiasm, though. However, I can assure you, he hasn't shut up since.

I could tell Rod was lost in thoughts of Xavier. Inside I was beginning to wish that Xavier had used my blood instead, knowing it would have at least saved Rod the grief of feeling betrayed. Who was this thing, this creature that once was Xavier Rainfeld? I worried for Rod. What was he going to do? He couldn't remain with Kyle's family for an eternity. Eventually, they might want him to leave. None of it mattered. What mattered was staying alive, staying strong.

Me? Well, I was pissed, to say the least. My mind was calculating our next steps, which were obvious to me. Dracula had to die at all costs, even if it meant my own life. I knew only one thing: I could no longer put my friends in danger. Seeing Kyle writhe in agony was simply too much for me. Of course, I was sure they didn't want to see me be killed. Either way, it meant I had to go alone. How I was going to accomplish that was a separate matter altogether.

"Vickie," Rod said. "Where do you think Dracula is hiding?"

"I have no idea," I replied.

However, I did have an idea, a very good idea. I knew without a doubt that Dracula and his remaining suckers were hidden deep within the rotting walls of Simmons Mortuary. They had to be. So, the next step was to get away, alone and unnoticed. That was going to be a concern, especially with school. I had no idea how I would slip away unobserved, especially by Murray, who guarded me like a hawk.

We pulled into Murray's driveway. Kyle was beginning to feel much better by the time we arrived. Murray made some *super sweet tea* that provided the caffeine/sugar boost both Kyle and his mouth needed.

"So, what's next?" Kyle asked, sipping on his tea and eating his cheese sandwich.

"I'm not sure, Kyle," Murray said.

"We wait. We have to," I said. "We don't know where Vladimir is, but we pissed him off, so he'll be back soon. We go on just like we were going to do. We go to school. We act normal. Just like we talked about before, everyone who knows about this is at risk, whether they believe us or not."

Rod got up and walked behind me, placing his hands on my arms, rubbing them gently.

"Well, I don't know about you guys," Kyle said. "But I am ready to hit the sack. If we've still got to go to school in the middle of this, I need my beauty sleep."

I stepped onto Murray's porch, searching for silence and some fresh air. The October breeze was clean and crisp; the leaves scattered across the ground. It wasn't too long before Rod joined me.

"Are you okay?" he asked.

"That's funny. We see the condition your dad is in and you're asking *me* if I'm okay. Forget me…how are you?" I said.

"God, I don't know how to even answer that," he said, rubbing his face. He sat down in the front porch swing and began gently rocking back and forth.

"I know how you are," I said, sitting next to him. "You're messed up. Anyone would be. You've been through a lot in the past few days."

He said. "Me? Look at you. You have, too."

I looked down. "Yeah, I think we all have."

"You know, I wasn't going to walk back up to your door the other day," he said.

"When? Oh, with Jessica *Whores?*" I replied.

Rod laughed. "Jessica who?"

"That's what I call her." I smiled.

"You are so wrong for that!" he laughed. "Now, come on, she's not that bad." I gave him one of *those* looks. "Well, okay, yeah, she kind of is," he confirmed.

I laughed. We sat there for a second, trying to think of the next subject to address, anything besides the obvious.

"I've been meaning to ask you—how did you, of all people, end up…well…you know. Someone like you end up a…"

"A virgin?" he said.

"Yeah," I replied.

"I don't know, actually. Not that I haven't had offers before. My mom just had this idea that it should mean something, you know? I guess after she passed, I've kept that in my head," he said.

"I'm sure," I said in a half sincere/half sarcastic tone.

He said, "Really! Well, what about you? Are you a…well…you know …"

"Of course, and that guys haven't wanted to get a piece of this shouldn't surprise you," I said.

"It does, though. It does surprise me," he said. "You know, I've watched you for a while, Vickie. You've never been like the other girls at school. You're not, like, into all the clothes and make-up and stuff."

"That's because I'm a dork," I said.

"No, it's because…it's because you're real. I mean, there's no fake stuff with you—at all. What you see is what you get. And I like that about you. I like *you*," he said.

You know, I wanted to believe that so much. I needed to believe it. The quarterback of the football team, the hot and lovely Rod Rainfeld, thought I was pretty and far from the *plain-as-toast-blah* I felt I was. It was nice.

"I wish I could believe that," I said.

He smiled and looked away with shyness. "I do, too, because it's true."

"Is it?"

"Yes," he said. His eyes shined so brightly in the dark, like a lighthouse that my heart was sailing toward. He added, "You know, Vickie, I don't claim to understand any of this—all of the vampires and monster stuff. I don't get it. I can't process the things I've seen over the past few days. But I can process the fact that I've come to know a lot about you during this, and I like those things. Also, the fact that you could whoop my ass helps."

We laughed.

"So, what's your favorite song?" I asked.

"*Open Arms* by Mariah Carey," he replied.

"Journey did it first."

"Who?"

"Oh," I said patting his hand. "Bless your heart. It's a good thing you're pretty."

He smiled and scooted back into the swing facing me. He put one of his legs on the porch and opened his arms, motioning for me to lay into him.

Did I?

Well, *yes I did!*

I snuggled into him like a bed of cotton. His solid frame comforted me. He wrapped his arms around me, his thick forearms crossed in front of my stomach. I could see the blonde hair on them glistening in the glow of the streetlamps. He began to rock me, steadily and gently. I could smell the wonderful combined scent of his cologne and fabric softener. I know that sounds stupid, but I could, and I can still smell it today when I close my eyes.

The following day I would sneak out of school before Murray would notice I was gone. I would get to my house and tell my parents I loved them. Then I would leave hoping that I would see them once again. Then, I would make my way to Simmons Mortuary in the safety of daylight, where I would locate Vladimir. I couldn't guarantee many things, but I knew that after the following day, either Dracula or I would go into the ground—for *good*.

I *really, really, really* hoped it wasn't going to be me, though …

I felt Rod breathe—in, and out…in and out. The air from his nose blew gently against my bangs. His goatee would catch random strands of my hair. He rubbed my hand with his thumb. I noticed both of my hands could probably fit into one of his. For that moment, that single moment in time, I was not a Van Helsing; I was not a dweeb; I was not a know-it-all; I was not a savior. I was a just girl falling in love.

*Ain't that the sweetest thing?*

# ONE PHONE CALL

The morning P.E. class was going to be used as football practice for the team. Rod hated morning scrimmages. That night was the big game: Rutgers Rottweilers against the Rule High Golden Bears. The battles were legendary, and we were tied in wins. We had only been ahead once. If we could win that night, it would be the first time we were in the lead in over a decade.

Rod couldn't think about football, crowds, or beating Rule. He sat on the bench in the locker room, drifting. All of us who were aware of what was happening knew it had to end soon; we were having a hard time pretending a monster wasn't loose in the city.

Rod could hear some of the team members in the locker room barking the traditional Rutgers High bark. Typically, it excited him, but that day it only annoyed him. Personally, it *always* annoyed the crap out of me. I never understood the point of barking like an idiot.

Pete Thorning was closing his locker door. "Man, have you heard from Russ?"

"Uh, uh…no, Pete. I haven't seen him," Rod answered.

Rod couldn't say the last time he had seen Russ that Russ had tried to eat him. As Pete bent down to his duffle bag, Rod noticed the crucifix that hung around Pete's neck, a present from the boy's father. I saw Pete kiss it all the time. Crucifixes had taken on a new meaning for us by then. We could see them everywhere, in all sorts of things.

Pete said, "Boy, his mom was in the office yesterday and she is pretty p-o'ed. She's thinking his dad convinced him to come live in Indiana. I mean, if he did, there's really not much she can do. Next month he turns eighteen, anyway."

"Yeah, that's true," Rod said vaguely.

Pete looked at him and then sat down. "So, how are things with Vickie?"

Rod said, "They're pretty good. She's interesting. I like her."

"Yeah, me too. Vickie's cool," Pete said.

"Yeah."

Pete went quiet for a moment. "So, I guess you've heard, huh?"

"What?" Rod asked.

"Well, you've been really stand-offish with me the past couple of days and I think I know why," Pete said.

"You do?" Rod said.

Pete looked down. "I haven't said yes, yet."

"To what?" Rod asked.

"To Jessica. She asked me to the dance."

Now, you shouldn't be shocked by that at all. I know I wasn't. It was just like Jessica to try to catch a date with Pete to try to make Rod jealous. Jessica had always flirted with Pete—*always*. It gave her some type of ego boost to think she was tempting Pete into sin.

Rod said, "Pete, listen, she's just doing it …"

"To make you jealous. That's why I didn't say yes. I wanted to ask you," Pete said.

"So, do you want to go out with her? Even though you know she just wants to piss me off?" Rod asked.

Pete looked at him. "Listen, man, I don't like Jessica. I think she's a…well, let's just say I don't think she's a very nice person. But, when chicks know you're going to be a minister, they don't tend to get too excited about dating you, even though a minister *can* date. I've told everybody that, like, two billion times! If my going with Jess will bother you, I won't go with her. I promise you—even though it will make me a dateless loser. I'd rather go with someone else, yeah. But Jess is kind of popular. Maybe if some other girl sees me with her, she'll get interested in me, you know?"

"A bad date's better than no date at all," Rod said with a smile.

"Exactly! But, you're my bro, Rod. I've known you since, like, third grade, and that's the important thing to me. So, your call," Pete said.

Rod said, "Okay, you can go out with her. *But*—you have to act like I am pissed off, I mean furious. Tell her that I cussed you out, that we fought—"

"And that I kicked your butt!" Pete laughed.

"Well, now let's not go that far. Let's just say we argued," Rod replied with a smile.

Pete gave him a big old bear hug. "You got it, man. Thanks! Now, let's get out there tonight and whip some bear tail!"

Bears were the least of our worries.

Rod wasn't the only one preoccupied. I had been out of tune the whole day, and for good reason. How was I going to get out of that school and on my way to ridding us of our little pest problem?

Kyle was fumbling with his iPod as he trailed behind me. "What's wrong with you today?"

As if he had to ask.

My mind was spinning as we walked from class. Completing my task in the daylight was essential, of course, so I had to find some way out of school. In darkness, it would be somewhat pointless, don't you think?

The news that morning was riddled with strange sightings and accounts of missing people, including Rachel Stevens. Rachel was in my Geometry class, but not that day. I was certain there would be other missing persons to come. Old Drac had been quite busy. No doubt through the night he had built the beginnings of a *monster militia*.

We walked by the front doors that were boarded up from where the Vladimir-wolf had busted through the glass. The school was buzzing about the "vandalism" and the few students who were inexplicably missing from classes.

"Are you even listening to me?" Kyle asked.

"Yeah, yeah. Sorry," I said.

I wasn't listening, though. To be honest, where Kyle was involved, I hardly did.

"What is wrong with you? I mean, I was the one who was bitten. I should be the one all freaked out today," he said, playing victim.

"Kyle, I'm just out of sorts today, okay? I've got a lot on my mind," I replied impatiently.

Kyle said, "Well, excuse me!"

I didn't have time to be concerned about my attitude. I only wanted to act before it was too late, before someone I loved was killed. Dracula was taking over the city, and at the rate he was going, the entire town would be blood-sucking sots within days.

"Hey, Vickie," said a familiar voice. *Oh, God, not Jessica.* At first, I said nothing. "So, listen," she sweetly went on, "I just wanted to come by and say good luck for tomorrow night."

"Tomorrow night?" I asked. Of course, I didn't buy this considerate Jessica imposter for one minute. It was as fake as the nose on her face. But, would I play? Sure. Why not?

"Uh, yeah…the queen of Halloween?" Jessica said.

Of course, how could I have forgotten? After all, I only had monsters chasing me.

"Oh, yeah, yeah. Well, thanks, Jess. I appreciate that," I said sounding as sticky sweet as possible. "Good luck to you, too, but I don't think you're going to need it. That title was created for you!"

Really, I knew if anyone should be queen of the scariest night of the year, it was Jessica.

"Well, thanks, Vickie!" she said. "So, I've got to run! Got a lot to do before tomorrow night!"

I waved at her and turned to Kyle, whose mouth was hanging wide open.

"What?" I said.

"What was that all about? *'That title was created for you'*?" Kyle said.

"Oh, please. I don't feel like wasting time with her today. I can be fake, too." We passed the girl's restroom. "I'll meet you later."

Kyle left me as I entered the bathroom. After hovering over a toilet of questionable cleanliness, I walked over and washed my hands. I took the cold water into my palms and lightly ran it over my face, staring at my reflection. I took a deep breath and said to myself, "Vickie, you're going to drive yourself crazy."

"You're already crazy. You got a light? I used my last match," said Missy Lynn, stepping out of nowhere.

"Uh, nope," I replied.

I hadn't seen Missy and her two flying monkeys in the bathroom when I had entered. They were probably hiding in one of the stalls, huffing model airplane glue or something.

"Are you sure?" Missy said.

I dried my face and looked at Missy through the mirror. "I said I didn't have one. I don't smoke."

"Okay, so smoking is bad?" Missy said.

Now, what kind of idiotic question was that? See, there was the *stupid* thing I just can't take.

I said, "Well, yeah, if you listen to the Surgeon General and the other ninety-five percent of the world."

"Yeah, she's better than us!" said one of the flying monkeys.

I tried to let it go. I said, "Listen, Missy …"

*Wham!*

Missy slammed her chunky hand against the paper towel holder, blocking my way. She mumbled, "You know, I've been waiting to find you by yourself, Vickie. I wanted to tell you that I got hired the other day."

I said, "Yeah, well, good for you, sister. That's great. I'm glad you passed the background check. Listen, Missy, I don't know what your deal is, but I think it would be best if you left me alone because—"

"And my boss is going to pay me a good chunk of cash to beat the crap out of *you*," she said.

Who would pay Missy to get me? Jessica Whores, that's who. No wonder she was being so sweet. Her attempt to avoid suspicion by being nice to me only made her involvement more obvious. Then, it came: the anger. It flowed through me, forming a protective shield. I turned to Missy and looked at her defiantly.

"Well then, it's a shame you're about to be laid off," I said angrily.

Missy swung her fist toward my face. It was as if time slowed to a crawl, like a Matrix-type deal, yet the events were occurring so quickly I didn't have time to think about choreography. I ducked, allowing Missy's fist to belt against the paper towel dispenser. Her knuckles cracked against it, and she wailed like a hound dog. I know it had to hurt like a bitch. Missy began swinging repeatedly, and I dodged her advances like the wind. She was *no* vampire, let me tell you. Then, like lightning, I popped her in the ribs three times and came up with an uppercut to the jaw. The flying monkeys stepped back in panic. I twirled with the grace of a ballerina with a flying back kick to Missy's nose, dropping her to the floor. The smallest monkey ran from the bathroom.

Missy yanked my legs from under me, and I toppled. Then, she used her *substantial* weight advantage to straddle me…well, because she's a fat ass. She hit me in the face once, and then she raised her fists to really let me have it, but as she came down, I dodged her blow and used the shift in balance to throw her to the side, kicking her in the ribs. Then, I went nuts. I had hit her face so many times and with such fury that I couldn't stop myself. I rose to my feet and was just about to stomp my foot into Missy's gut when Mrs. Black, Mrs. May, and Mr. Hillard grabbed me.

"Vickie! Vickie, stop right now! Leave her alone," Hillard shouted.

I fought against them. It was as if I couldn't stop the attack. They dragged me into the hallway as Missy lay on the bathroom floor, moaning, holding her face and her side with Mrs. Black tending to her.

So, you can guess what was next, right? Hello, office!

As we sat in the office, Missy's mother demanded that the police be notified. Missy, not wanting to admit that little me, and me alone, had done the damage to her, said that there were others involved. Missy's redneck mother demanded justice. Justice for Missy seemed ridiculous to me, especially knowing hardly anything she did was justified.

"Mrs. Lynn, when I entered the bathroom, there was no one else in there but your daughter, Susanne, and Vickie. I assure you that if Missy had been attacked by a gang of girls, we would have seen it," Hillard said.

He was obviously perturbed at her accusations. I was certain no one could count how many times Missy had been the leader of fights and uproars at Rutgers.

"Well, I know my daughter. She can defend herself. And if you expect me to believe that that skinny little bit of nothing cracked three ribs, a nose, and dislocated a shoulder—well, I'll just give you five hundred dollars right here!" her mom said.

There wasn't much sunlight in the autumn days. I had to find a way to get out, and opportunity appeared to be knocking. Of course, if I ended up in juvenile hall, that wouldn't help. I couldn't sit there and waste time.

Then, the police walked through the door, and Missy's mother began spilling her BS. I just kept my head down as I focused on the tiles of the floor, recounting their shape and similarity to one another, each one different but the same. It was almost hypnotizing.

*Buzz, buzz!*

My cell phone vibrated in my pocket. The call passed, going to voicemail, but then it began to vibrate again. *Who is it? God, I don't have time for this!* I thought. Seeing that Hillard and the group were distracted with the police, I reached into my pocket and pulled out my phone to glance at the caller ID. I had no idea who it was; I hadn't seen the number before. The call again went to voicemail. Another round of buzzing began. Whomever it was wanted to speak to me pretty bad. Then, I began to grow worried about Mom and Dad. My mind began creating details, trying to think of paths that would have led Dracula or Xavier to them.

*Buzz! Buzz!*

I looked to my bud, Mrs. May, who was trying to tune everyone out, and said, "Mrs. May, is it all right if I step to the restroom."

"Lord, yes," she whispered through the debate. "Take me with you!"

I smiled and stepped into the hallway. Once I was where I couldn't be seen, I flipped my phone open in mid-buzz.

"Hello?" I uttered in a whispered tone.

"Hello, Vickie," said Xavier.

I could have passed out. My stomach immediately grew cold. *They have them. They have my parents*, I thought.

"How did you get this number?" I said.

"That's not important," he said. "What is important is the information that I need to give you. I'm allowed one visitor, and since my son no longer wants to speak to me, I thought you would be the next best thing. If I know Vladimir, I won't be alive when the sun goes down. So, you have to hurry. There is much to discuss."

"What are you talking about? Where are you?" I said. It was difficult to hear with the noise of conversations going on behind him.

"I'm being held at the detention center downtown. Be here within the hour. Tell them you are my niece. We've got to get everything ready before nightfall," he said.

Though I was confused, I knew I had to go. "Okay…okay. I'll be there."

"Oh, and Vickie?" he said.

"Yeah," I said.

"Please don't bring Rod with you. He has seen enough," Xavier said.

I folded up my phone and placed it back into my pocket. I looked back to the office door and heard Hillard ask where I was. I bolted toward the exit doors. I had just enough money on me for a cab…and a Milky Way.

# EATING OODLES OF POODLES

I had never been to a police station but had seen them on television. It was apparently a busy day for the force. Rows of names were listed on a large whiteboard in the middle of the room, the names of those who were missing. Officers hustled around it, adding names and talking about who had been reported. I was certain that they would never account for everyone. I stood there for what seemed like forever while the clerk lady chomped her gum. I tapped on the glass to draw her attention while she was stapling papers together.

"May I help you?" she said.

I said, "Yes, I'm here to see Xavier Rainfeld."

I imagined I could have said I was there to see the Dalai Lama and not received a stranger look.

She said, "And are you family?"

"Yes, um, he's my uncle," I lied.

The clerk gave me a suspicious glance. Nevertheless, she got an officer for me, an Officer Malone, who met me in the lobby.

"Hello there! Hey, I think I know you. You're from the high school, right?" he said.

Officer Malone usually comes to Rutgers every year to give us lectures on being law-abiding citizens, and I used to crush on him a little. I always sat in the front of the auditorium and asked the best questions, questions I would rehearse days before.

"Yes, my name is Vickie Jenkins," I said.

"Vickie, yeah. The question girl. What can I do for ya, Vickie?" Malone asked.

"My uncle called me and said he was being held here. His name is Xavier Rainfeld?" I said.

He looked at me without saying anything. I could immediately tell he didn't believe me.

"He's your uncle?"

"Yeah."

"You sure?" he said.

"Yeah. My cousin is Rod, his son," I added for effect. "What is he being held for?"

Malone leaned into me as if he didn't want to be overheard. "Well, Vickie, at the moment he's being held for disturbing the peace, trespassing, and animal cruelty."

"Animal cruelty?" I said.

He thought for a moment and then said, "Okay, come with me. Let's just say we've had a very interesting time with your uncle."

"Is he all right?" I said, trying to sound concerned.

He said, "Well, we're not sure. Listen, um, can your mom or somebody come down here with you? All this is a little strange and your—"

"No," I said. "My parents are out of town." I could tell he didn't want to let me in. "Listen, Officer Malone, I really have to know what's going on. I have to see my uncle. If I don't talk to him now, it could be too late."

He sighed. "All right. But, let me warn you, this stuff is pretty disturbing, okay?"

I said, "I got it, trust me."

He motioned for the woman to open the gate, and we began walking back to his office.

"Can I see him now?" I said.

"The doctors are looking at him right now. We can go to my office for the moment. There's something I think you need to see. Then, if you still wanna see your uncle, I'll take you to him." I sat down across from his desk as he pulled out a video tape. He popped it into the VCR. "I picked him up last night when we got reports that he was…wandering the streets." He sat down on the desktop, facing me. "Do you know of any medical conditions that your uncle may have?"

I said, "No, nothing that I am aware of. Why?" As if I had to ask.

"There is something…*wrong*…with your uncle, Vickie, medically. He's having some delusions and his health seems to be going downhill," he said.

"Is he dying?" I asked, even though I already knew the answer.

"Well, that's the odd thing. To look at him, you'd think he was already dead. But, he acts like nothing is wrong. He's not even running a fever; actually, his temperature seems to be slowly decreasing. Last I heard, it was sitting at about eighty-nine degrees. He's eating, but he doesn't seem to have an appetite for…*regular* food," he said, holding the remote to the VCR.

"What do you mean?" I asked.

"Well, last night I had just parked to eat and got a call about a suspicious person near my patrol. By the time I turned into West Haven, I saw nobody out of the ordinary around. I circled for about ten minutes and still didn't see a thing. Then, I thought I heard someone yelling in the distance. I reached over and cracked my window and could tell someone was definitely hysterical.

"I drove forward and turned on my emergency lights, but not my siren. You don't want to scare off a perp, ya know. Then, I saw something, a man, in the dark along the road. He sat in the grass on his knees, stooped over…*something*. A woman was running around in the yard, screaming with a phone in her hand like she was on fire saying, 'Help, he ate my baby! He ate my baby!' Well, I was sick thinking something had happened to a kid, or worse.

"I pulled my gun and yelled for him to put his hands on his head and back away. Then, I could see tufts of white, curly fur floating all around him, like snow. He was going at this woman's poodle, *eating* it! Personally, I breathed a little sigh of relief, you know, cause I kinda hate poodles. All of a sudden he stopped, put his head into his hands, and started to cry—like *really* cry. When I saw that, I felt sorry for him. I cuffed him and asked his name. You could imagine my surprise when he told me who he was."

I couldn't believe it. Whatever Vladimir had done to Xavier had made him mad, just like R.M. Renfield. And like Renfield, he obviously developed an appetite for some pretty gross crap! Malone pushed play on the VCR, and I watched poor Xavier tell his story.

I could see him seated at the table alone, thinking, wondering. Soon, Officer Malone and this ass named Detective Hernandez joined him.

"Hello, Mr. Rainfeld. I am Detective Hernandez. Officer Malone here tells me that you've had quite an interesting night," said the pompous Hernandez.

"To say the least," Xavier said.

Hernandez seemed to be taking some pleasure out of the fact that Xavier, once a prominent member of the community's elite, was now a withered wreck shivering before them.

Hernandez said, "So, you like eating dogs?"

Malone shook his head and rolled his eyes in disapproval. I don't think he was too pumped that Hernandez was assigned to Xavier in the first place; now he had to listen to him take jabs at someone who was clearly so weak he didn't have the strength to retaliate.

Xavier replied, "That seemed to be what was on the menu tonight."

Officer Malone liked that line.

"Do you eat cats, too?" Hernandez mocked.

"Cats don't sound too bad. I have allergies, though," Xavier said.

Hernandez smiled. "Listen, Mr. Rainfeld. I know that out there, you're this bigwig rich guy who's bought half of this city, but in here, you're nothing but another freak. Now, tell me what happened."

"No," Xavier said.

Hernandez leaned closer to Xavier. "You'll tell me, or you'll never get out of here."

"That's what I'm hoping for."

Hernandez began to get angry at Xavier's uncooperative attitude. "You know what I think? I think you've been doing all kinds of bad things. Tonight alone, we've received a whole boatload of calls about missing people. Now, who do you suppose is responsible?" Xavier said nothing. "Would you happen to know?"

"Yes," Xavier said.

Hernandez chuckled. "Well, I would love to hear it. Tell me."

Xavier shook his head. "No."

Hernandez threw his hands into the air in frustration. "What do you mean, no?"

Xavier ferociously looked into Hernandez's eyes, causing him to freeze. "I'll tell him," Xavier said coldly, pointing to Malone.

"Malone? Well, you can tell me anything you would tell him," Hernandez said.

"No."

"Fine! I'll let you two get acquainted," Hernandez said, getting up from the table and stomping out of the room.

Malone took a deep breath. Xavier looked at him, waiting for him to say something.

"Eh, you like some water?" Malone said.

"I'd love some water, Officer Malone. Thank you."

Malone got up, poured a small cup of water, and sat back down. Xavier drank it in one large gulp. Malone sat the pitcher on the table so Xavier could help himself. Obviously, he was near dehydration.

Malone said, "So, you want to tell me what happened?"

Xavier looked at him for a moment and said, "Yes. Now, what I'm about to tell you won't make sense, and you won't believe me, but I assure you it is the truth."

"Okay," Malone said.

Xavier took another sip of water. "It's no secret to anyone in this town that I collect rare artifacts and antiquities. However, I recently added something to my collection that turned out to be a huge mistake. Now, that piece of my collection is out there roaming the streets of the town and…and …"

"Killing people?" Malone said.

"*Changing* people," Xavier corrected.

"Okay…and what is this artifact?" Malone said.

Xavier looked at him. "Dracula."

"Uh, do what?" Malone said.

"Dracula," he repeated.

Malone leaned back into his chair and looked to the two-way mirror where he knew other officers were watching them.

"Mr. Rainfeld," he said cynically.

Xavier slammed his hand down on the table. "Don't patronize me, Officer Malone! You have to believe me! Look at me! Look into my eyes. Can't you see it?"

If someone couldn't plainly see something wasn't right with Xavier, they were either blind or stupid.

"All right," Malone consoled. "So, let's say I believe you. How did *Dracula* come back?"

Xavier took another sip of water. "Tell me, have you ever read Bram Stoker?"

"Uh, Dracula—the book? Well, no. I saw the movie when it—"

"Good enough. So you will understand that what we are dealing with here is a chess game that has been going on for hundreds of years."

Malone said, "No, I don't think I do."

Xavier leaned in. "Officer Malone, I had a brother once. Alexander was his name. It all began with him. One day, he started complaining about dreams, wild dreams. It went on for months. He complained of nightmares filled with images of bugs and insane asylums. Of course, I thought he needed to be in one. His dreams led him to an old bookstore in Manhattan. There, he happened upon a small book, an old diary written by a mad man that someone had just tossed into a pile of used books to give away. He took the book and began to study it, and that's when the obsession really began. Somehow, the dreams and the diary led him to uncover that our family carries the bloodline of R.M. Renfield, the diary's author. Do you know who R.M. Renfield is, officer?"

"Wait, Renfield…Dracula's henchman guy?" Malone said.

"Yes," Xavier replied. "Alexander became obsessed with him and the history of Dracula. He'd always come to me asking for money for his latest mania—be it plane tickets, hotel rooms, you name it. I'd usually give him what he wanted just to be rid of him. He used every bit of money he could get to travel the world searching for clues."

"Clues to what?" Malone asked.

"The location of Dracula's remains, of course. Alex was convinced that vampires were real, that Dracula was real, and he wanted to bring him back from the dead."

"Why?"

"To live forever," Xavier said. "God, I thought he was crazy, especially when he showed up with the ring."

"What ring?" Malone asked.

"He said it was Dracula's ring. He bought it in a little obscure market in India. He showed up at my house at four in the morning, showing me this ring with a bat on it set with a large ruby. He went on and on about the thing. I didn't have time to listen to it. My wife had cancer and I was taking care of her full-time. My patience was thin. We began to fight when he told me he needed more money to find the Van Helsing bloodline," Xavier said.

"The vampire hunter?" Malone asked.

Xavier smiled. "That's the one. He said that he was close to finding Dracula's remains and that one of his dreams told him that ancestors of Abraham Van Helsing were the only thing that could ruin his plans. Then, he told me he needed one hundred thousand dollars so that he could hire someone to hunt them down. He knew they were living in Tennessee somewhere. Well, I completely lost my mind. I threw him out and told him not to come back. I didn't care what his plans were."

"And what were his plans?" Malone asked, trying to take it all in.

Xavier drank the last of the water. Then, he reached into his mouth and pulled what appeared to be a bit of poodle fur from his teeth. Both of them tried to act as if he hadn't.

"I didn't hear from Alexander for quite some time. About five months later, he called me one night needing money again. He had been living in Tennessee working as a janitor at a college there. He had found a young newlywed couple in the school who had just had a baby. Yes, their name was Van Helsing. Alexander told me he had been following them for months, stalking them. Well, I absolutely lost my mind. I promised him I would send money and called the authorities to report him, but nothing came of it. I finally called the Tennessee Bureau of Investigation and reported it to them. They said they would investigate, but it was too late. The night before they were going to question Alexander, he followed the couple. On a rainy night while they were driving home, Alex tried to run them off the road. They all lost control, including Alex."

"Did anyone survive?" Malone asked.

"I don't know…I don't know. I think so. For our sake, I hope so. It was rumored that their baby lived, but I've never been able to prove it. However, I think I saw her tonight," Xavier said.

"Do you want to find the kid?" Malone asked suspiciously.

Xavier rolled his eyes. "Malone, I realize under the circumstance it's hard for you to believe that I would never want to harm a soul intentionally, especially a child. Have you ever watched someone you love die?"

Malone sighed. "No…no, I haven't, Mr. Rainfeld. I'm sorry for your loss."

Xavier said, "Yes, I was, too. Before Angela passed, I became afraid. I was terrified for myself and especially my boy. Then, I heard of Alex's death. My brother had left me four things: the ring, the journal, his research files, and a twenty thousand dollar debt. In Angela's last days, I began reading the diary. The more she withered away, the more I became obsessed with immortality. I never wanted to watch someone I loved go through that again."

"I can't imagine what it was like," Malone said.

Xavier said, "It wasn't enjoyable. Fear led me to study my brother's research. You see, I had one thing Alex didn't have: *money*. I could go anywhere. I could do anything. I had unlimited resources. I started making journals of my own, keeping notes of every detail. Then, I started having the dreams, the dreams that wouldn't go away. They led me to commission an excavation in a little village near Transylvania where I believed the body of Dracula to be buried. I found that it was all true, every bit of it. They found the coffin sealed tight, and I had them remove it and ship it here."

"Okay, let's say I believe you. How'd you bring Dracula back to life?" Malone asked.

Xavier grew silent. "Let's just say I found a way without anyone having to die."

"And you brought him back," Malone confirmed.

"Yes, obviously, because he's out there right now, in your city."

Malone sat there, astonished, trying to digest it. "Mr. Rainfeld, you gotta understand how unbelievable all of this is."

Xavier said, "I do."

Malone asked, "Is there any proof of this stuff?"

"Reach into my jacket pocket," Xavier replied.

Malone got up and cautiously approached him. Xavier raised his hands as Malone reached into his pocket and pulled out R.M. Renfield's diary.

"The diary?" Malone asked.

Xavier nodded.

Malone began flipping through its worn pages. "Well, this is really interesting, but I need ..."

Xavier stopped him. "If you go to Simmons Mortuary, you'll find him there."

"Is that right? So, if I go there right now, he'll be there? Dracula, alive and well?"

"Yes. However, for you and your friends behind the glass there, I wouldn't recommend going in the dark. There are bad things in the dark, and I'm afraid if you go, you'll end up anything *but* alive and well. I mean, look at me, officer. Take a good look. What do you think this is? It certainly isn't the flu," Xavier said.

Malone looked to the two-way mirror. He took a deep breath, stood up, and began to walk out of the room.

"Thank you, Mr. Rainfeld. We'll check it out."

"Also, don't take your guns. They're useless," Xavier said.

"Then, what do you suggest?" Malone asked.

Xavier said, "Read Stoker's book, watch *The Lost Boys, Fright Night,* most any vampire movie. You'll know what to do."

Malone looked at him and nodded his head. Before he closed the door, he added, "I'm really sorry for all of this. I'll…I'll pray for you, Mr. Rainfeld."

Xavier smiled. "Don't bother, Officer Malone. I think I'm already spoken for." As Malone went to close the door, Xavier said, "Malone, I do get one phone call, correct?"

Malone nodded and then left Xavier alone.

# UNCLE XAVIER

The interview ended, and Malone turned off the VCR. Yes, Xavier's brother had killed my birth parents. You'd think I'd have gotten upset, but I didn't. My birth parents were only an idea to me, a concept. The truth was I loved my life and my mom and dad. I couldn't imagine my life without them. It was meant to be.

"You okay?" Malone asked.

"Sure, yeah. I'm fine," I replied, trying to act as if I was at least a little shaken up. Truth was, that interview didn't compare to the other stuff I had seen. No way. "So, did you go?"

"Where?" Malone said.

"To the mortuary, like he said. Did you check it out?" I asked.

"We started not to, but yes, we did go this morning. We thought it best to go in the daylight," he said.

I knew then that even if they didn't believe Xavier, they at least thought enough of his story to not venture to the mortuary in the dark.

"Did you find anything weird?" I was interested to know, to confirm I was right about the mortuary.

"Nothing, not a thing out of place," he said. "We searched everywhere."

So, this meant that either the police missed something, or I did.

I said, "Can I see him now?"

I could tell he still didn't want to take me back. Nevertheless, Malone picked up his phone to confirm Xavier's examination was over and then said, "Okay, we can go back. But Vickie, I gotta warn you, his appearance is freaky to say the least."

We started through the double doors to a secured holding area. I smelled the cleanliness, like a hospital wing.

As we neared the conference area, Malone said, "Last night he refused to go the hospital. Today he's been getting worse, so in about an hour we gotta get him to Community General and have him tested and treated. At around 6:00 a.m. we moved him here to keep him away from the other detainees."

I sat down in a chair in front of a thick glass window, the type you see on television with the phone to speak to the prisoner, the whole nine yards. The phones on the other side of the glass had protective covers to prevent the spread of germs. The officers looked like nurse/cop hybrids.

Then, they led Xavier in. I cringed. He looked much worse than he had the night before, like a corpse, yet his mannerisms showed nothing out of the ordinary. He didn't appear to be ill by action or attitude. The officers that led him to the glass maintained a safe distance from him to avoid possible contamination, but I knew what he had couldn't be spread, at least not by touching him. They sat him down, and I looked up at Malone.

He asked, "You okay?"

"Yeah, yeah. I'll be okay," I replied.

"All right, I'm gonna be right outside this door, so you press that buzzer there if you need me," he said as he began to leave.

The door clicked shut with a buzzing sound. Xavier looked at me with his white eyes. Some dry flesh on his face flaked and fell away, floating to the table. He reached over and picked up his phone. I did the same.

"How's Rod?" he immediately asked.

"He's okay. How…how are you?" I thought that it was a dumb question based on his appearance.

He laughed. "You know, believe it or not, I feel fine. I mean, I look like hell, but on the whole …"

I stared into his foggy eyes. "Mr. Rainfeld …"

"Xavier. Call me Xavier," he said.

I said, "Okay…Xavier. So, I saw your interview with Officer Malone."

Xavier smiled; rotten teeth lined his receding gum line. "Not my best television appearance, I'm sure."

We talked about the shipment and the night Dracula arrived. He kept me engaged in conversation, filling me with details, as if his loneliness needed my company.

"Xavier, what did he do to you?" I said.

"I wish I knew," he replied. "He sent me out the other night, to get him *a snack*. I found this woman and brought her back for him, but I couldn't let him do it. I barely got her out of the house in time. Vladimir wasn't too pleased that I'd let her go. He needed more control over me—needed me to think less. He bit me that night, but he didn't turn me into a vampire. He turned me into something…worse. Every time the insanity would begin to subside, he would sink his teeth into me again. In all the commotion last night, I managed to get away. Since then, my mind has improved, but, well, look at me."

I felt so sorry for him at that moment. I wanted to help, though I didn't know how.

"What information do you have for me?" I said.

"Tell me more about Rod. How has he been?" he said.

"Xavier …"

"Please …"

I looked at him. "He's been doing well, all things considered."

"He must hate me," he said.

"No, I don't think he hates you," I said.

Xavier laughed, "Oh, please. He thinks I tried to kill him!"

"Well, didn't you?" I asked.

"No, no, I never wanted to do that. I wanted him to live forever." Xavier put his head in his hands. "I never wanted him to get sick or die or know the pain of growing old. I wanted him to have it all, more chances than I had, more chances than…his mother had. Vladimir had that power."

"I have to stop him," I said

"I know. This is why you are here, Miss Van Helsing."

To hear someone say it tripped me out. I acted as if I didn't know what he meant. "What are you talking about?"

He smiled. "I saw you, the way you moved through all of them, the ability you had. Don't worry; I haven't told Vladimir. Though I'm sure he suspects, anyway."

"What do I need to do?" I said.

Xavier leaned in. "I tried to tell them, you know. They looked at me as if I were insane. I told them that he was there at the mortuary with all of the ones he had infected, like an ant colony. They said they went this morning and checked it out and nothing was there, but he's there. I know it."

"Simmons," I said.

"Yes, and if you don't get to him before tomorrow night, I am afraid he's going to make your little Halloween Ball a buffet," he said.

My eyes flew open wide. "What? What are you talking about?"

"Last night, at the school. He saw all of those flyers on the walls advertising the ball; he knows it's going to be full of kids, the youth he needs for a prime army. I've heard it all over the news. This place has been buzzing with all of the missing persons. They thought it was me at first, but then people kept disappearing even after they had locked me up. Vickie, he's been hunting all night long trying to get enough soldiers together to attack the school—you know it and I know it. You and your friends have to stop him," he said.

I knew Xavier was right. It was perfect. A large gathering of students, barely even eighteen, with the youth and strength Dracula would need. Yes, that was the plan all right. There was no turning back now.

I couldn't allow vampires to ruin my big night—I had a date!

I said, "I have to go alone. I can't involve my friends anymore. I can't risk one of them getting hurt."

Xavier looked at me. "Then alone it must be. Hurry, while there is still time. You have to get there while there is still daylight. You can't miss his coffin. It should be sitting in the center of the room with at least seven feet between his and the others. It is red with gold lettering. But it's protected and locked from the inside."

"Well, then how am I supposed to open it?" I asked.

"On each side of the coffin, there are small golden buttons. There is a specific order to them, the sign of the cross." Xavier did the sign to show me. "Top, bottom, left and right. Push them in that order and it will unlock his coffin. And be careful. Not all vampires sleep in coffins; some aren't allowed to—the lesser ones, the dogs."

"I don't have much time," I said.

Xavier said, "Yes, you have to hurry."

I grabbed my things and started toward the door. I looked to the weary Xavier and felt a twinge of sadness in my heart. I knew I wasn't going to see him again, and maybe he felt that was best.

"Is there anything I can do for you, Xavier? Is there anything that will reverse whatever is happening to you?" I asked.

"Unfortunately, I don't think so, Vickie. I think I died days ago." He smelled himself. "Whew! Yeah, I think I'm gone. Now, go. Go on and put him to rest for good."

I pressed the buzzer on the door, and Officer Malone opened it for me.

"Oh, and Vickie?" he said. "Tell Rod that no matter what he thinks, I always loved him."

I smiled at him and nodded. I walked away with Officer Malone, and as we made our way toward the doors, I pulled out my cell phone. If I was to tell Rod anything, I thought it best to do it while I was still alive.

# BREAKING AND ENTERING

Officer Malone was nice enough to give me a ride home. Mom and Dad were elated to see I was alive. Mom nearly crushed my rib cage with her embrace. I would have loved to sit down for a visit, but time was of the essence. We took a seat at the kitchen table.

"Guys, I just wanted to come by before tonight. Something…something bad may happen and—"

"What do you mean something bad?" Dad asked.

"I mean, this all has to stop one way or another, and I have to finish it," I said. "But…but, I had to see you guys first and tell you that I don't want you to feel guilty for not telling me about my birth parents. I'm glad they, like, gave me *life* and all, but you have always been my parents. I couldn't have ever asked for better than you."

I noticed Mom's eyes began to glisten with tears. They both leaned over and took my hand.

Dad looked at me and said, "Okay, how can we help?"

I smiled. "Well, I'd like to borrow the car?"

"Well, the starter really needs to be replaced on—" Dad began.

"No," I added. "I mean the Mercedes."

I very well couldn't take a cab to *Creep Corner*, and Mom's heap would only lead to one of those idiotic horror movie car-won't-start-in-time moments. I needed a dependable vehicle, some way to get there and get out and quick! A V6 Mercedes would do just that. Dad sat there, looking at us and mumbling. He didn't want to say no, but he sure didn't want to say yes.

Mom and I found it best to let Dad cook on it while we visited the attic to search my parents' chest for any useful items. There were a few bundles of stakes, some small vials of holy water, and a sack of assorted crucifixes. This stuff was far from the high-tech artillery Murray had collected. Unfortunately, it would have to do. I began packing the items into my backpack, wishing I had the cool stuff. I turned around to take the main weapon I had come for, Abraham's bow. I grabbed the bow and quiver full of arrows from the mirror.

"Darling, now you've never shot a bow," Mom said. "What are you going to do with that besides put your eye out?"

"Yeah, I have, Mom. Remember? Back in camp when I was ten? Mr. Morrison gave me lessons," I said.

I slipped the arrows around my neck and took the bow in my hands to show her I knew how to hold it. It was then that I noticed a spider creeping its way along the far wall—one of the big, hairy, *hide-under-your-bed* things that I despise. Immediately, I reached over my shoulder, armed the bow, and sent the arrow soaring through the air. It smacked firmly into the wall. If not for the eight hairy legs sticking out around the arrow's shaft, you wouldn't have known a spider was once there at all. After a few seconds, its legs slowly wiggled to a halt.

Oh yeah, I was the *shizz!*

Mom's mouth fell open. "Eh, well, Mr. Morrison was a really good teacher, wasn't he?"

I gathered as many of the weapons as I could and left the attic. Dad stood in the hallway waiting on us with the keys to his prized possession in his hand. Yeah, you heard me right. I just looked at him, not knowing what to say. Slowly, I reached for them. He snapped his hand closed and shut his eyes, as if he was holding them for the last time. Then, he reluctantly dropped the keys into my waiting palm.

I said, "Dad, I don't have to really. I can take Mom's car."

"No, no, you take her," he said. "You need something fast."

I smiled and began to walk away.

"Do you want to look at her again before I go?" I asked.

"No, no. I'd better not," he said.

"Oh, for Pete's sake, John. It's just a car! For crying out loud. Vickie, be as careful as you can with it, but more than that, be careful with *you!*" Mom walked around us and patted Dad's shoulder.

Dad reached out and hugged me.

"Listen," he said into my ear. "I don't know if I believe all of this, but I do believe that you are the best daughter I could have ever had. I love you."

"I love you, too, Dad," I said.

I started up the car, and she purred like a kitten. They waved to me as I cautiously made my way out of the driveway. I did all the good driver stuff to try to keep Dad calm. I made certain to look both ways and even turned on the signal when I pulled away. I came to a complete stop at the stop sign.

I had just about an hour of daylight left. Once safely away from their line of vision, it was time to see what Dad's baby could do. I peeled away from the intersection and raced into the distance.

By the time I arrived at the mortuary, daylight was dwindling. The sparse glow of sunset shined on what remained of the day. Would it be enough? I didn't know. Pulling into the worn lot, I cut the engine and looked at the old building, noticing how much creepier it appeared to be now that it was abandoned.

I took a deep breath and pulled the keys from the ignition. I began to put them in my pocket but thought it best to leave them under the seat. I got out of the car, leaving the doors unlocked. If Kyle had taught me *anything* it was that in a horror movie, you didn't race to a locked car and wrestle to find keys that you unintentionally lost while fighting for your life.

Oh, no, no.

Leaving the car open and ready was my best bet for a quick escape. And, yes, I know what you're thinking—I would check the back seat before getting in, too. Creeps loved to hide in the back seat.

I gathered my things and softly shut the car door. I unconsciously checked the body of the car, making certain there wasn't a scratch on it. I couldn't help it. If I lived through all of it, my life would still be in jeopardy if Dad found something wrong with the car.

I slithered toward the front door, listening, moving carefully. The old porch creaked under my feet. A large chain lay to my right. It must have been removed from the door when the police had visited that morning. Leaning my head against the door, I heard only silence. The door was locked tight, of course.

Things can never be easy. I closed my eyes and gave the door one hard shake, but it didn't budge. With a sigh, I walked away to explore other options.

Crickets were beginning to chirp in the distance. I adjusted the bow around my shoulder so that it wouldn't slip, and placed one of the bulkier crucifixes into my pocket. With my bag weighted with artillery, it was difficult to be agile, but the load that I carried was my only protection. I would've pulled a refrigerator behind me if I thought it would help. The large doors at the back of the building where bodies had once been delivered to the mortuary were completely boarded shut. No luck there. There had to be a way inside and I had to find it fast.

Then, I happened upon a cellar window.

Yeah, it had to be a creepy *cellar* window. How *Salem's Lot* is that?

I knelt down to it and looked inside, but couldn't make out anything of the interior. I tried to push it open, but it was also locked. Taking the bow and quiver from my shoulders, I removed my over shirt, leaving my upper body covered with a thin tank top. I bundled the shirt around my fist and slowly pressed on the windowpane until it cracked. I then removed a broken section of the glass to reach in and unlock the window. I didn't want to go all Bruce Willis and start busting out glass and waking up the dead!

I lowered my bags and bow into the cellar first, then opened the window wide to allow my junky butt to slide through easily and to keep as much daylight as possible flowing in. As I attempted to drop quietly to the floor, my left foot came down on my bag, causing me to lose my balance. I clumsily fell forward, arms flailing in front of me, hoping to stop my plunge. They found something to hold on to, all right: a large ruby red coffin covered in strange symbols.

Frantically, I stumbled back from it.

*Oh, no, crap! I hope I didn't wake him up!* I thought.

I looked around and saw dozens of closed coffins surrounding Vladimir's, about seven feet away from where it sat, just like Xavier had said they'd be. Off in the distance, I could see what appeared to be creeps who were not in coffins. They slept on the dirt floor like dogs. These were the lesser ones, the Grunts. My heart beat wildly inside my chest as I looked down to the floor and quickly gathered my stuff. There was no sound, no movement. Amazingly, I had entered unnoticed. The remaining sunlight shined perfectly on Dracula's coffin. All I had to do was open it, expose him, and let the sun do the rest—*if* I could hurry.

Stepping to the head of the casket, I saw a small gold button with three others positioned around the perimeter. *The sign of the cross, remember.* I could see the sunlight pulling away from the room, dripping into darkness like an hourglass. There was no time to think it through.

I began.

I did just as Xavier had said—top, bottom, left, right. As I pushed in the last button, a clamor of clockwork began. It turned and clicked so much that I expected the thing to chime with a cuckoo popping out of the lid! One by one, the locks began to crack open. Staying in full sunlight, I stepped away from the coffin, never taking my eyes from it or the other vamps that were beginning to stir. I took the bow and armed it, pulling the cord tightly and aiming for where I thought his heart would be. I would be certain not to miss—it was my only opportunity.

Then, the door of the coffin popped open. I stood there waiting on Vladimir to lift the lid himself and slither out, but again only silence. My breathing was erratic and my hearing focused on the rustle of the waking vampires. Waiting for Dracula to show himself, I kept the bow pulled at full tension and looked around. Nothing.

"Screw this!" I said.

Impatiently, I threw the bow over my shoulder, took the arrow in my hand, marched to the coffin, and threw open the lid. I raised the arrow high into the air and plunged it downward into the dirty satin of the empty casket.

Uh…*check, please!*

# A Fond Farewell

I wasn't certain if Rod would go to see Xavier or not, but I had hoped he would. You only get one chance to say farewell in this life, and I could tell by Xavier's appearance that his end was near.

Rod stood outside of the room with Kyle, waiting, wondering if he should enter or leave.

"Man, this guy smells like hell!" he heard one of the nurses say as she passed.

They obviously didn't know he was Xavier's son. Rod gathered that his father had met no warmth or kindness on his short journey to Community General. Maybe they were afraid Xavier was contagious; maybe they thought he was a freak.

A nurse walked past Rod and went in to take Xavier's vital signs. Rod could see the IV wasn't comfortable for his father, but he was trying to tolerate it as best he could. The nurse handled Xavier with care and looked at him benevolently as she laid a gloved hand against his forehead.

"Mr. Rainfeld, I know this is a ridiculous question, but how are you feeling?" she said.

Xavier smiled. "Well, I've felt better, but I think this is the best I've looked in years."

Though Rod couldn't see it, he could tell she was smiling under her thick mask. She checked his IV and then walked out of the room, leaving him to his thoughts.

"Dude, we can leave if you want," Kyle said.

Rod didn't reply. He stood there for another moment and then walked to the nurse's station. After they had suited him up, he walked back to where Kyle was standing and took a deep breath. Then, he opened the door.

"Dad?" he said softly as he entered.

Xavier nearly leapt from the bed with fright. He turned to see Rod looking in at him, dressed in full sanitary garb.

He turned his face away in shame and said, "Son, you shouldn't be here. I didn't want you to see me like this. How did you know...?"

"Vickie called me," Rod said, walking in farther. He stood at the edge of Xavier's bedside, wondering what to do next, thinking of what to say. "She told me that I needed to come see you."

"Well, I didn't tell her to do that," Xavier replied with an impatient tone.

Rod looked down. "Well, okay then. I'll go."

"No! Wait," Xavier said, causing Rod to stop. Xavier reached up and turned off the light above his bed so that his face would not be so obvious.

"I'm sorry about all of this junk," Rod said, pulling at the smocks. "They wouldn't let me come in without it. But I know that whatever he's done to you isn't contagious or anything."

"It's fine, son," Xavier said.

Rod had not heard that voice in years, that fatherly tone, soft and quiet—not since the death of his mother, before Xavier's heart had turned cold.

Rod said, "Does it hurt?"

"I don't feel much," Xavier said. There was a moment of silence, a comforting quietness between them. "So, Rule...the big game."

"I don't really feel like playing, Dad," Rod said.

"Listen, Rod, I wanted to tell you—" Xavier started.

"You don't have to say anything, Dad," Rod said, stopping him.

"No, I do," Xavier replied. "I really do. Listen to me. I didn't mean for any of this to happen, Rodney. I didn't. When your mother died, a part of me died along with her. It destroyed me to watch her fade away. I vowed right then and there that I would never let that happen to either of us."

"And that's why you called Dracula back," Rod said.

"Yes. That's why I did it. I…I shouldn't have, Rodney. I just thought…I thought that if he came back, he would be grateful to me for doing it and he would give us the ability." Xavier stopped trying to explain. Trying to articulate it seemed to cause him physical pain.

Rod took the glove off his hand and laid it on Xavier's cool flesh. "Dad, it's all right."

Though he could not see it clearly, Rod could have sworn a tear ran down his father's cheek.

Xavier smiled at him in the dimness. "So, how are things going with Vickie? She's really cute."

Rod smiled. "Dad, we don't need to talk about that."

"No, I want to talk about it," Xavier said. "I need to…to think of something else."

Rod looked down. "You know, I don't know yet. I mean, with all of this stuff going on. But she's cool. I like her a whole lot better than Jess."

"Good," Xavier said with a crooked smile.

Rod smiled. "Who knows? We'll see what happens." Rod looked down, not wanting to let Xavier see him cry. "I'm going to get him, Dad."

Xavier said, "Now, Rod, I can't have you putting yourself into danger. Vickie has the power to do this. You have to let her lead. It was meant to be that way."

"Isn't there anything we can do for you?" Rod asked.

Xavier looked up at him and squeezed his hand. "Son, you already have. You've done the best thing of all. I know you don't want to hear it, but your Aunt Phyllis has all my policy information, okay? She can be on a plane from Florida in no time. You won't have to worry for anything, at least not for a while, okay?"

Rod squeezed his hand in return. "Dad, I don't care about any of that."

Xavier smiled and said, "Well, I do. You need to be taken care of." He turned to the window and noticed the dwindling sunlight. "Now, it's getting dark, son. You get along and stay safe. Get with your friends and stay together. You can't lose if you stay together."

Rod didn't want to leave. There was much more he wanted to say, though the words escaped him. It was one of those times where he just wanted to keep talking, about the weather, about sports, about anything, just so long as the conversation kept going.

"Dad, I'm not going to see you again, am I?"

"Rodney, it's time to go now," Xavier replied. Rod shook his head in agreement and slowly began to walk away.

"Son? I love you, son," Xavier said.

"I love you too, Dad."

Kyle waited on Rod in the hallway and walked with him toward the exit doors. I'd like to think I did a good thing, having Rod go there and all. I didn't make him go, of course. I left it up to him. In the end, at least they both had absolution…forgiveness from one another.

Xavier's room sat to the east, and once the last beams of the remaining daylight left, his final visitor entered.

Good-bye, Mr. Rainfeld.

# Round Two

*Oh, God! Where is he?*

I stumbled backward toward the window as the last rays of sunlight seeped out of the room. I could hear them, the ones who were beginning to awaken. They rustled inside of their tombs, preparing to come out for breakfast, and there I was without bacon and eggs! I could hear the creaking and popping of hinges. Looking to my left, I saw a hand sliding from under one of the coffin lids. It slowly took hold of it and began to push it open.

It was definitely a *get-the-hell-out* moment.

Grabbing my stuff as quickly as I could, I raced toward the broken window. I could see the lid to the coffin opening wide. The thing hissed at me, but I didn't turn around because it would only waste time. I needed to get out before I was completely up to my elbows in the undead. I had no idea where Dracula was, but he wasn't in the mortuary.

I tossed the bow, bag, and quiver onto the ground outside the window and began to hoist myself up, being careful of the glass. As I slithered out, I didn't see one of them making its way to my ankle. It grabbed me. I screamed and began to kick at the creature. It was then I noticed that the thing was what I had once known as Mr. Parsons, the grocer from downtown where Dad bought all of our meats in bulk. My mind recalled how wonderful and kind his smile had once been, how he used to give me candy when we would visit the market—you know, all that crazy stuff that runs through your mind when you're freaking out? Well, he wasn't good old Mr. Parsons anymore, that was for sure. He was just another bloodsucker.

I kicked at him, but I couldn't break free. Jaws full of razor sharp fangs snapped at me like a rabid animal. I screamed again, kicking him in the mouth. I kicked repeatedly. Finally, he got the hint and bit down on the sole of my shoe—yes, my *brand-new* shoe. I could feel the pressure of his bite pressing down on my foot.

While I struggled, I knocked my bag over and out of it rolled nothing short of a miracle—one of Murray's Flares! It must have been left there from the Battle of the Board. I just had to remember how the friggin' thing worked. Pulling myself backward struggling against his strength, I could see others were beginning to awaken. A couple of them gathered behind him, snarling, growling, cheering him on. I finally grabbed hold of the Flare and began fumbling with it. His fangs started to work their way through the sole of my shoe. Finally, I had it. I closed my eyes and …

*Crack!*

It was just like at Murray's: a flash from a camera, just brighter and louder. My eyes opened in time to see Parsons and the two others burning and screeching. I squirmed back from the window into the remaining sunlight as they howled in pain.

Yeah, that was going to leave a mark.

"That's right! These are ninety dollar shoes, *asshole!*" I yelled as I got up.

Smoke from their burnt flesh filled the air and stung my nose. Steadying myself, I began running as hard as I could, my muscles burning with adrenaline. As I neared the car, my mind began spinning.

*What am I doing? I can't leave. I have to do this. But how do I find Dracula?*

The daylight completely sank into dusk. After I dropped the bag to the ground and opened it, I picked up the quiver and held the bow, tightening my grip on it. It was time to fight. I stood there waiting for them, listening like a fox, but they didn't come. Sweat dripped into my eyes, burning them. Still, they didn't come at me. Either they were scared of me, or they were waiting.

Okay. Was I, like, supposed to go and come back? Was I to leave a Post-It on the door? Then, I could hear Murray's warning in my mind.

*So, Vickie, you have to be very, very careful about accidents. If you hurt yourself and bleed, he will be able to smell it for miles.*

I reached back and grabbed an arrow from the quiver, and with a quick slice, I slit open the flesh of my palm. I squeezed my hand together, letting the fresh blood drip to the gravel below. That was when I heard them roar.

"Come on!" I screamed into the air. Then, the doors of the mortuary began to open. I saw them peering at me from inside. "You know," I said to myself. "Maybe I need to learn to *shut up*."

Two of them charged out of the doors, running on all fours. I braced myself, reaching back and grabbing two arrows from the quiver. I armed the bow just in time to send the wood through their hearts, turning them into dust. Others came. They ran at me from every direction as I countered with faultless precision. Again, my subconscious had taken over, and I was happy to let it. At that moment, I was no longer plain old Vickie Jenkins.

I was *Vickie Van Helsing*.

I back-flipped onto the hood of the Mercedes. With both hands, I threw stakes into the heart of one vampire and the neck of another. The wounded one charged me through the decomposing dust of its buddy.

*I won't miss this time*, I thought.

The vial of holy water shattered against its throat, severing its neck, allowing its head to roll from its shoulders. I looked for others as the thing fell to the ground, grabbing for its absent head. That was just…*so gross*.

As the flesh peeled from the headless thing like a rotten onion, I noticed that the others were now pretty freaked by me. They were no longer willing to charge me blindly. Of course, I felt like *Betty Badass*.

"Yeah! That's right! You're not so tough now, huh?" I screamed at them.

"My apologies for being late. I had to visit a sick friend," Vladimir said.

I turned around to see Vladimir standing on the roof of the car. Before I knew how to react, he sent my body sailing across the grounds with a punch to the chest. He puffed into smoke and reappeared at my side, placing his foot onto my chest as I struggled for air.

He was good at that puff-in-and-out thing.

He laughed. "You know, I knew that scent was you. You had to be a Van Helsing. You did remind me so much of Abraham." I grabbed his foot, causing him to press down harder. I grunted under the weight. For a moment, I thought he might stomp through my rib cage. "Now, now, just calm down. You're such a fighter. I like that. But alas…not too bright. All these others, these dogs, they've been no challenge, no fun at all. But you, oh, I knew you'd be a treat. You're like Abraham with all of the fun, but none of the threat. You have a certain charm about you, yes, but you lack experience. I could teach you. I could turn you into a warrior unlike any other. You'd be my right hand. If you were *really* good, I could make you my equal, a Host."

"Go to hell!" I screamed.

He laughed. "Oh, my dear, but we're already in hell, you and I. This place, this is hell."

"No, you haven't seen hell yet," I said.

I reached into my pocket and grabbed the crucifix I had shoved into it earlier, showing it to him like a shield. His eyes ran red with fear. He stumbled backward allowing me to get to my feet. He looked to me as he shifted into a more formidable, monstrous state. He roared at me with gaping jaws and charged, and I smacked the side of his head with a spinning back kick.

We started the hand-to-hand stuff. Swiftly, I blocked his attacks, but the faster I moved, the more he matched me. He was naturally far more powerful than the others I had fought. I threw my left fist forward, and he blocked it like a brick wall, spinning me around. I used the force of the spin to come back with a right hook that connected with his mouth, knocking him backward. He stumbled and grabbed his jaw. Taking a stance with both fists displayed, I showed him I was ready to continue. He spit a loose fang to the ground; he was pretty pissed.

"Now, that wasn't very nice," he said.

"Oh! Oh, my God! Are you okay?" I replied sarcastically.

He ran at me again. I dodged each swing, with the exception of one, which landed across my face. His claws scratched my flesh. He punched me in the stomach, knocking the wind from me again. I took a deep breath and came back with an uppercut to his jaw. He stumbled backward. I kept swinging, making contact with his face each time; I never missed. Suddenly, he was gone. Yeah, that *poof* thing again.

I was getting really tired of that.

In a second, he had me by the throat. I beat against his forearm, trying to loosen his grip as he choked me. I fell to the ground to throw off his balance. As he slid forward, I put my foot against his chest and flipped him over me, but I didn't hear the *thud* of his body hitting the ground behind me. With the force of my thrust, he had just sailed over me and landed upright like a cat, the cheating bastard.

Before he had the opportunity to turn to me, I rocked backward, and with the strength of my legs, sprang to my feet. With a turn, I shoved a stake completely through his back. I felt bones crack under the pressure of the wood.

Vladimir yelped in agony and fell to his knees. The other vampires began to advance. I grabbed my bow and took out four of them before they even charged. Then, I turned to Vladimir, who rested on his knees, looking up at me. His breaths were heavy and labored. I armed my bow and held the point of the arrow against Vladimir's brow. The other vampires stopped as he raised a hand in surrender.

"Stop! No…no more," he said.

"Tell them to get inside!" I shouted.

Reluctantly, they began to wander back into the mortuary, growling and hissing at me.

"You're not going to kill me, Van Helsing. What would you do without me?" he said slyly, the dark blood glistening on his lower lip. "I've given your bloodline a focus for centuries. Without me there would be no vampire slayer."

"*Slayer?* Dude, who do you think I am? Buffy?"

Vladimir laughed, though he didn't know what I was talking about. Guess he never had cable.

"There's that word again. *Dude.* What does it mean?"

"Uh," I said, not knowing quite how to reply. I kept the bow pulled tightly. "Well, it means 'man' or 'guy,' I guess. I've never thought about it."

"Ah! I see. Thank you," he said. He chuckled again. "Vickie, Vickie, Vickie, oh, Vickie. You can't get rid of me. I've survived more than *you*. I am forever. I am eternal. And I will continue to hunt you and your family. Your boyfriend would make a good addition to the team."

I looked at him and lowered the bow.

"Oh, yeah? Well, bring it."

With that, I spun around and kicked the stake completely through his ribcage. Vladimir shrieked in pain. He leaned backward, quivering and trembling as he began to melt away into a thick haze like lava. Then, he chuckled.

I didn't see what was so funny.

"You may have beaten *me*, but what about *them?*" he coughed at me. And just before the blob that was once Count Dracula faded into oblivion, it smiled one last time and whispered, "*You…have…company.*"

The others were casing me, though they didn't immediately charge. They had seen too much of me for that. I was hurting bad, but I couldn't appear weak, not when they were wary of me. If they sensed my disadvantage, they would lunge together and it would be dinnertime for them. I didn't have enough arrows to kill them all, but they didn't know that.

I took a crucifix from the bag and held it to them. The backed away, snarling and hissing at the relic in my hand. I couldn't defeat them all—I knew that. In a short time, they would know it, too. My best bet was to keep them contained somehow. I slowly backed them up one step at a time. I had to get them back inside the mortuary. One of the things broke from the rest of the group to test me. Without taking my eyes from the crowd, I chucked a stake into its chest, and with a shriek, it blew apart. The others continued to back away.

They began to retreat into the front doors of the mortuary. For added effect, I tossed a holy water vial at another, melting away its shoulder bone. It screamed as its right arm fell to the ground and disintegrated. Some of them began to scurry away in fear, and that is what I wanted. I continued to back them in, keeping my eye on the chain that lay on the ground.

Once they were all inside, I slammed the doors. I grabbed the chain and wrapped it around the door handles as the doors shook back and forth. Taking the large metal cross in my hand, I shoved it between the links of the chain to lock it into place. They howled and screamed as they began to beat the boards from the windows. One of them had already managed to get its head through the planks, and I put an arrow through its eye to stop it.

Of course, I had no idea what to do next; I had to hurry before they broke free. Then, I looked back to Dad's baby, his Mercedes. I ran from the porch and opened the car door, reaching inside and popping open the gas cap. *Dad, please forgive me!* I could hear them wailing. One had managed to make its way out of the mortuary and was coming at me. He soon found out that *arrow = dead vampire.*

I ripped my shirt and used one of arrows to push the fabric into the gas container of the car. *Oh, God—Dad, please be a lying, no good smoker!* I jumped into the car and popped the glove box. No matter how much Dad protested, I knew he still smoked in secret. Sure enough, hidden deep within the drawer was a plethora of lighters and three cigars wrapped in an envelope.

"Dad, you rock! If I live through this, I swear I won't tell Mom!" I said to myself.

I started the car, staked the gas pedal to the floor, lit the cloth fuse, and knocked the car into gear. A sickly feeling overtook my gut as I watched the Mercedes speed toward the mortuary. In an instant, the car rammed up the steps and through the front doors, exploding into brilliant flames. The gas lines of the building made the explosion grander than I had thought it would be, lighting up the night sky like fireworks. I watched as a few of the vampires ran from the burning house into the courtyard, flailing and squealing, and then smoldering away.

I turned and walked into the night. The bow was heavy around my shoulder, and I was weak and exhausted. I wiped the blood from my lip, knowing that the following morning would bring me nothing but aches and pains. My hand hurt like hell.

Still, it was over; it was all over. Yet, I wasn't as excited about it as I thought I would be. Maybe I'd enjoyed the adventure more than I wanted to. Maybe it felt nice for once not to blend into the plain white paint of life. Maybe I'd miss it. However, there were more pressing things ahead of me…like how I was going to explain the car!

# Alive

The boys told me they had been driving for what seemed like forever with no sign of me. All they knew was that I had disappeared and no one had been able to find me. Rod had ditched the Rule football game. Yeah, I still feel bad about that. He couldn't be bothered with it right then.

"I don't know where else to go," Kyle said, turning left.

"She's got to be around here somewhere," Rod said.

"What did Ms. Murray say? Did she see Vickie today?" Kyle asked.

Rod said, "Not after Vickie was taken to the office. She told me about my dad and hung up the phone before I could find out anything else. Murray was going to Vickie's parents' house to see if maybe she was there."

Rod sat in the passenger's seat, frantically gazing out the window, looking for any sign of where I could be. Then, they saw it: the smoke in the air. They could faintly hear sirens wailing in the distance.

"If I know Vickie, we should probably follow the path of destruction," Kyle advised.

"Go! Go!" Rod said.

They followed the sound of the sirens and the smell of smoke toward Simmons Mortuary. They grew anxious of what they'd find, not knowing if I was alive or burning up in the rubble. The sirens grew louder as the smell of smoke grew more pungent. Kyle pulled around to the street in front of the mortuary. Cops lined the grounds of the burning building. Two fire trucks sprayed gallons of water, attempting to douse the flames. Rod saw my dad's Mercedes imbedded into the frame of the building, burning out of control. He jumped out of the car.

"Wait! Wait! Rod, wait a minute!" Kyle yelled.

Rod didn't listen. He had spoken to his father for the last time that day and he couldn't let me slip away, too. He ran full force toward the building, yelling my name. The cops in the courtyard grabbed him to hold him back. Another explosion sent shards of burnt wood and rubble into the air.

"Somebody turn off the gas line!" one of the firefighters shouted.

Kyle sat there with his mouth open, not believing what he was seeing, wondering if I could really be dead. I could sympathize; I had the same feeling the night he was bitten. It was surreal. Another fire truck was pulling up in front of him. He put the truck into gear to move out of the way and, as he did, he saw someone unusually familiar down the street ahead of him. Whoever it was wore a dirty white tank top and was carrying a bag and a bow. They walked slowly, waving the oncoming police cars away from them.

"Rod! Rod! I think I see her!" Kyle yelled.

Rod broke free of the cops and ran to the truck; then they sped down the street towards the figure. Yeah, it was me—beaten, covered in soot and dirt. Granted, if I would've known Rod was going to be on the scene, I would've tried to look a little hotter.

"Hey!" Kyle yelled.

I didn't recognize the voice at first and thought it was another police officer asking me if I was okay or if I wanted to go to the hospital.

"I told you, I'm fine. I don't need to go to the hospital."

"Vickie!" Rod yelled.

That voice stopped me. As I turned to them, Rod jumped from the truck and ran to me, pulling me into his arms.

"Rod," was all I could say. I melted with exhaustion into his arms.

"Oh, God, are you all right?" he said.

"Yeah. Yeah, I'm fine," I replied.

Kyle got out of the truck and walked to us. "Dang, girl, you look like hell!"

I laughed. "Well, yeah. I seem to end up that way a lot these days."

Rod opened up the back of Kyle's truck and tossed my bow and backpack among the bulk of Murray's artillery; then he got in the back seat with me, allowing me to snuggle into him and make myself comfortable. He smelled a whole lot better than I did, of course.

As we pulled to a stop in front of my house, I realized I had nearly fallen asleep on the ride. Now that the ordeal was over, it was as if my nervous system was shutting down, preparing for hibernation. We could see Murray's car parked beside the spot where Dad's non-existent Mercedes used to sit. Mom ran from the door to greet us.

"Oh, my God—are you all right?" Mom said as she brushed my damp hair from my face.

I said, "Yes, Mom, I'm okay."

We walked into the house and was greeted by Dad. *Bear hug!*

"Oh, I am so glad you are okay," he whispered into my ear. "If something would have happened to you, I just couldn't go on. I can't imagine…Sweetie, tell me that's not my car on fire in that building."

"John, hush!" Mom said.

The television was overrun with news reports of the Simmons incident. It would be only a matter of time before the police would discover the car was registered to Dad and come for a visit. What would we say?

*Yes, sorry about that, officers. My daughter was killing off a gaggle of gruesome vampires and had to use the car to blow them to smithereens.*

"They'll be here soon," Murray said, referring to the police. She walked over to me and took me by the arms. "What did you do?"

"He's gone. I killed him."

"Why on earth would you do something so stupid by yourself? You could have been killed, or even worse," she said.

"I…I couldn't take you guys with me, not after what almost happened to Kyle. I had to do it alone." I said.

Murray looked into my eyes. I'm sure she could appreciate my sincerity; however, she couldn't stand my impetuousness. She gave me an understanding glance and said, "So, you're sure it's over?"

*Boom!*

Another explosion occurred on the live broadcast of the fire. We turned to the television.

"Oh, yeah. It's over," Kyle said. "What are you guys going to tell the cops?"

"Well …" Dad began.

"We'll tell them the car was stolen, that you had thought Vickie had borrowed it without telling, which is why you didn't report it," Murray said.

"Wow! You watch a lot of CSI?" Rod asked.

Murray rolled her eyes and grinned. It made sense, but it was a lie. Nevertheless, it was far easier to believe than the truth. We stood there for a moment, watching the coverage on television, lost in the fantastic possibilities of what could have been. Rod's cell phone began to ring and he stepped away.

"So, you go get cleaned up now," Mom said. "I'll get us something to eat."

The hot water ran over my worn body. The dirt, blood, and muck made a swirling pool of yuckiness in the bottom of the tub as I leaned against the wall with my hands and let the water run down my back.

Then, I began to cry.

I can't tell you why, really. As you can probably guess, I'm not really the boo-hooing type. It could have been the release of emotion that caused the response, the overwhelming feeling of *it's finally over.*

I sat down at the vanity in my robe and brushed my hair, looking at myself in the mirror. *Who am I? What am I supposed to do now?* I recalled Vladimir's words, how he had given my family purpose for hundreds of years. Now that he was gone, was I supposed to go back to my vanilla life?

*Yes. Yes, go back. Be with Rod. Graduate. Live,* I thought.

"Vickie, honey?" Mom said, stepping to my door. "I think you'd better come downstairs now and talk to Rod. They told him that his father passed away this evening."

The police had arrived by the time I got downstairs, and Dad was outside talking to them about the inexplicable theft of the car. I stepped onto the back deck where Rod sat staring into the darkness and reached out and touched his shoulder.

"Are you okay?"

He sniffed. "Yeah. Yeah. I'm fine."

I said nothing else, allowing him to remain silent in his thoughts for a moment.

"They said someone killed him, someone in his room. One of the nurses saw him, but she didn't get a good look. We both know who it was, don't we?"

"Yeah, we know," I said.

Rod took my hand. "Thanks for telling me where he was, Vickie."

"You're welcome. I just couldn't bear the thought of you two not talking before…well …"

"Yeah," he said. He told me about their talk and their reconciliation. I was thankful.

The last thing I thought Rod wanted to think about was the ball. Personally, by this time I didn't care where we were so long as we were together. I would've been just as thrilled to just sit with him, talking and getting to know one another.

I said, "Listen, Rod, this dance thing tomorrow. I don't think either one of us are in the mood to go. I mean, who cares who the Halloween queen turns out to be? Jessica can shove it up her booty implants."

Rod laughed through his tears. "Oh, no. We're going. I can't wait to see you win."

"But your dad?" I said.

He turned around and took my hand. "Listen, Vickie. I said good-bye to Dad a long time ago. If I just sit around it's all I'm going to think about. Right now I don't want to think about anything...but *you*."

The words ran over my heart like melted butter. He leaned over to me and I leaned in, preparing to kiss him. My heart pounded in my chest, a joyous anxiety, and the only thing I could think about was not burping in his face or doing something stupid that would ruin the moment. I could feel the heat of his breath on my upper lip as he neared my face. His breath smelled great, and that's a *big* plus.

"Dang! Your dad is slicker than snot!" said Kyle, killing the moment. "You missed it! He just poured that bull all over those cops!"

I could have mule-kicked him in the head.

"Thanks, Kyle!" I said.

"Oh, oh…were you two having a moment? Oh, my bad!"

Mom called us in and we ate finger foods, small sandwiches, and drank soda. We talked and laughed about many things: about the car, the insurance, the ball, hopes, humor, but we didn't talk about *fear*. We also didn't talk about my battle. Didn't anyone want to know? Sure, they did. Nevertheless, the focus was that we were all together and safe. We were happy.

We were *alive*.

# The Angel

I stood back from the mirror, not sure whose reflection was staring back at me. I had to admit, the dress wouldn't have been the first thing I'd have picked out to represent something heavenly, but it fit me well. When I had tried on the costume that afternoon, Mom had just fallen to pieces over it—an *angel*, of all things! I was many things, but an angel? No, I don't think so.

I did look a little blessed, though, so I was willing to let it roll. The wings rocked. They were super-real looking. The dress was tighter than I'd have liked, but for the first time I saw that I had curves, the curves of a woman, not at all like the little girl I used to be. And I don't care what Kyle says about my ass; it looked good. At least I had one. The only thing worse than having too much booty was not having enough!

I drew the line at false eyelashes. Mom would just have to get over it. My makeup was perfect. I managed to hide the majority of the scratches and surface wounds I had sustained during my fight with Vladimir. You could still see the wound to my face, but only barely. Mom swore that once I was inside the dark gymnasium, no one would notice.

The doorbell rang, and I heard *trick-or-treat* coming from children at the door. For a moment, I thought it was Rod. I hoped he would like the way I looked. There was no telling when anyone would see me that way again. I stood there still staring at myself in the mirror and smiling. The doorbell rang again.

*Trick-or-treat!*

I began thinking about the evening I was about to have. Was it possible for me to be the queen? *No, of course not. That's not going to happen.* But, *what if it does?* I smiled and fluttered my little wings.

"You're a beautiful angel. Have I died and gone to heaven?" Rod said from my bedroom door.

I spun around, my face flushing. "Rod! What are you doing up here?" He was dressed as a pirate. There was something very sexy about that, I had to admit. It was Johnny Depp-ish. He wore a bandana over his head and a patch, and smiled a grin with two teeth blacked out. I cracked up.

"That's a hot mess," I laughed, trying to lie.

"What? I thought I looked really good!" he said, standing beside me. "See, I don't look so bad. I couldn't do the long hair, though."

He couldn't help but notice my curves. Oh yeah, I saw him checking me out.

He smiled. "You know, you should have been my wench."

"Oh, yeah!" I said walking away. "That would happen. Come on. If I have to put up with you all night, we'd better get going."

He smiled. We walked down the stairs together with Mom and Dad waiting on us below. The flashes began as Mom, dressed as a witch, took more photos than the paparazzi.

"God, Mom, hold on!" I said.

Mom said, "Oh, shut up! You'll never let me dress you like this again!"

"Well, I hope she does!" Dad said with the smile.

"Me, too," Rod said.

I thought, *Yeah. Oh, yeah. I'll be dressing like this again. I may even wear it to school!*

"Where's Kyle? What's he wearing?" Mom asked.

"Well ..." Rod said rather uncomfortably. "I don't know what he's going to be. He was still trying to decide. He's going to meet us there."

"Marvelous," Mom said. The doorbell rang again. "Lord! Those kids are hungry this year! All right, you two, get out of here. Parking will be a nightmare."

Mom opened the door and overacted the witch thing as we shuffled past the ghouls and goblins on the porch.

"And be careful!" Dad said.

"We will!" I replied.

"And be home by midnight!" Mom said.

"We will!" we said.

"And have a good time!" Mom added.

We shut the car doors and I turned to Rod. "Now you see why people don't meet my parents."

"I like your parents a lot," Rod replied.

I said, "Well, that's because you're patient. That helps."

We drove to Rutgers, not saying too much on the way. Both of us were far too nervous for that. We kept looking at one another and smiling to the point where even our embarrassment embarrassed us. Rod held my hand the entire way. It felt right, like it was meant to be the way it was.

We pulled into the lot. Kyle stood there next to his truck in the parking lot, waiting on us. Worst of all, his costume—he was dressed as a *vampire*.

Now, how tacky is that, I ask you?

"Oh, what the hell!" I said.

"I didn't have the heart to tell you," Rod said.

Kyle was doing his best vampire impression. I rolled down the window.

"*I vant to suck your vlood,*" Kyle said in the classic Transylvanian accent.

"I want *you* to suck my butt!" I said. "You have some nerve showing up like that, Kyle." I got out of the car.

"Oh, come on, Vick! You've got to admit, I look pretty cool!" Kyle said.

I looked at him suspiciously. "Well, yeah, *but*—that doesn't matter."

The bad part was that he was right. One thing the boy could do was special effect makeup. If it wasn't for his fangs falling out every time his mouth flew open, you'd almost bet he was the real thing!

"Aw, come on. Get happy!" Kyle said, wrapping his arm around my shoulder. "You have Captain Jackass Sparrow as your chaperone tonight!"

I rolled my eyes.

"Gee, man, thanks a lot. It was your mom who said it looked cool," Rod said as he rounded the car.

Kyle said, "Well, yeah, and my mom also thought *Leave It to Beaver* was a porn movie!"

"Hey, it is! I own it!" Rod said.

"All right! Let's go in, guys," I said as I took both my men by the arms, leading them inside.

We walked in the front doors. The windows had been replaced from the night of round one, a night I didn't want to recall. I wouldn't even look at the new glass in fear the images would come to my mind. It was over. Period.

There, right inside the door, were none other than Jessica and Pete, dressed as a *nun* and a *priest!*

"Oh, our Father who art in heaven," I whispered to the guys.

"Hey, Vickie!" Jessica said in her bubbly manner. "You look great! See, it's like I was praying and an angel came to me!"

"Yeah, hire any other demons to jump people in the restroom lately?" I said with a smile.

"What? What are you talking about?" Jessica said, trying to deny it.

"Hey! Great costume, Rod!" Pete said, stepping between us.

"Thanks, man. I wouldn't have thought you'd wear something like that tonight, Pete," Rod said.

Kyle said, "Yeah, Pete, that'd be like my dad wearing his scrubs as a costume."

"Hey, this is a *priest* outfit. I am going to …"

"*Be a minister!*" we all said in unison with him.

"Right! I…I may even cuss tonight!" he said with a smile.

Jessica turned to him, placing a hand on his chest. "Oh, that would be like…*so* hot."

I rolled my eyes. Pete was with Jessica and he was Rod's friend, so just for the night, I'd play nice.

I said, "Okay, Sister Mary Hormone, let's go in."

We could hear the bass thumping through the walls of the gymnasium. My skin rushed with electricity. I felt excited, like I wanted to, well, break it down! I didn't even seem to mind Jessica, my sworn enemy. I had battled worse villains lately. Here I was with Jessica's ex, Jessica was with his best friend, and we all were acting normal!

*Talk about trick-or-treat!*

Murray met us at the entrance of the gymnasium. She was dressed as…wait for it…a *flight attendant.*

"I love it!" I said.

Murray said, "Thank you, thank you. I've always wanted to be a flight attendant. I don't know why. How are you, Rod?"

"Arrr," he replied.

"Kyle, now, that's just tawdry," Murray said.

"Mwah, ha, ha, ha, haaa," Kyle muttered, slipping into the gym with his cape covering his face like Béla Lugosi.

"All right, everyone. Buckle your seatbelts and put your trays in the upright position. Here we go!" Murray said, opening the gym doors.

We entered the ghoulish gym. Everything looked magnificent. The committee had done a great job with the decorations and the food. The cans had gone a long, long way. The fog machine was working perfectly, sending fog rolling from the stage that was lined with caskets and torches. Well, I could have done without the fog and the caskets, of course.

"Brewskie" Burns, another football player and famed DJ of Rutgers High, was spinning his music, dressed as a Mozart knock off. He had horrible taste in costumes, but good taste in music.

We had just gotten something to drink when Rod leaned into me.

"Want to dance?" he screamed at me.

"What?" I yelled over the *boom-boom-boom-boom*.

"Dance!" he said again, making a dancing gesture.

"Yeah!" I said, laughing.

We took the floor together in close proximity to Kyle, who was trying his best to pick up a girl with his vampish ways.

"I think he's going to lure Lucinda," Rod yelled near my ear.

Kyle was asking Lucinda Chandler to dance. She actually seemed charmed by Kyle's goofiness. I smiled. Lucinda nodded and followed the goober-like vampire onto the floor. Kyle gave me a sly grin as they walked passed. I laughed again. It was wonderful, magical, a feeling that I'd never felt and wanted to feel forever: that feeling of *belonging*.

We danced for what seemed like an eternity, but I didn't care. I loved it. The cheerleaders were showing off with their routines, of course. Brewskie slowed down the tempo, spinning a sexy tune. At first, I began to walk away, but Rod held me by the hand, not letting me go. He motioned for me to stay on the floor with him. He pulled me close. My face was just a bit higher than his chest, but not by much. I love a tall guy—I can't help it! I laid my head against his chest, and he wrapped his arms around me.

The moment was completely ruined when a large, ugly, gruesome witch overtook the stage. Mrs. Black sent a squeal of feedback through the microphone as she turned it on. Brewskie stopped the music.

"Hello! Hello!" Mrs. Black said as she adjusted the microphone and her witch's hat. "I hope everyone is having a great time tonight!"

"Look," Rod said. "Black's a witch, too. Like your mom."

"Yeah, but she *means* it," I said, downing my glass of punch.

"*Wiiiitch!*" someone yelled from the back.

I saw Murray laugh to herself.

"Okay! That's enough. All right, everyone. Now's the moment we've all been waiting for. It's time to announce the King and Queen of Halloween!" Mrs. Black said, holding up the crowns.

Everyone applauded.

Kyle walked by us. "She makes me want to take a dump. I'm going to the john. Text me when you win."

Black cleared her throat. "Now, could I have the envelope please?" Mr. Hillard walked up the steps to her. He was dressed as Sherlock Holmes. Fitting. He was always trying to figure her out, anyway.

Black ripped the envelope open with a dramatic movement. She unfolded the paper and said, "And the King of Halloween is...Matthew Stevens!"

There was an uproar of applause. Matt darted past Rod and me and playfully patted Rod on the shoulder.

"Better luck next time, man!" he said.

"Oh, whatever!" Rod said with a smile.

Matt jumped onto the stage, hugged Black, and yanked the black and orange crown from her hand.

"Yeah! Woo hoo!" Matt yelled into the microphone.

"Yes..." Black said cynically. "And, now, the winner of *Queen* of Halloween is..."

Hillard handed her the next envelope. I turned around and immediately met Jessica's gaze. We smiled at one another. I stood there wondering what was going to roll from Black's tongue. It was the first time I could recall actually wanting to hear the woman speak. I could suddenly imagine it clearly—she would call my name and I would smile. I wouldn't freak out at all. Calm and collected, I would walk up to the stage and tell everyone that I appreciated their vote. Then, I would walk off the stage and hug Rod. That was it.

Black ripped open the envelope. "The winner is..."

Then, the auditorium doors slammed shut.

# Harvey The Assman

Kyle stood at the urinals, singing to himself and staring at his image in the mirrors. I could tell he was already starting to crush on Lucinda, and I had a feeling she was just odd enough to crush back. He flushed and began to turn around when something in the mirror caught his eye. Something was behind him, something freaky.

He snapped his head around to see that no one was there except Harvey Martin from shop class.

"Hell, man! Why don't you make some noise or something?!" Kyle said.

Harvey stood there, hands clinched into fists, arms draping loosely at his sides, and his eyes aimlessly looking down at the floor as if he was in a trance. Kyle looked back to the reflection but saw a beast where Harvey was standing. It was shadow-like with large, leathery wings on its back and small horns lining its head. It was as if Harvey's reflection was revealing something else about him, his *true* self.

Kyle's eyes grew wide as he took a precautionary step back. Harvey slowly unfolded his hands, his fingertips lined with claws. He rolled his head slowly to the left and then upright, his eyes still closed.

"Assman?" Kyle muttered.

Harvey's coal black eyes popped open and he grinned with a fangy smirk. He threw a clawed hand at Kyle, who ducked the swing. Slipping through his legs, Kyle ran to the bathroom door. Harvey sprung from the floor to the ceiling and began scuttling along overhead like an insect. Kyle tried to yank the door open, but it slammed shut. He looked above his head to see that Harvey held the door closed from the ceiling.

"Oh, you've got to be kidding me!" Kyle said.

Harvey dropped from the ceiling behind Kyle and grabbed him around his waist, holding his arms in place. Kyle struggled but could not wrestle free. Harvey was about to bite into him, he knew it. He did the only thing that came to mind. Kyle threw his head backward, giving Harvey a jarring head butt, knocking him away. Kyle held his throbbing head and ran for the door.

Harvey was fast on his heels. All of the classroom doors were locked. Kyle had to find somewhere to go, a place to hide. Straight ahead was Mrs. Black's classroom. Kyle ran faster. He could still hear Harvey galloping behind him, swatting for his legs, trying to trip him up.

A wind blew around Kyle as he busted through the door of Black's classroom. He slammed it and locked it behind him. Then, he grabbed a long, sharp fire stick from one of the lab sets and spun around in defense, but nothing was there. The glow of Black's desk lamp was faint, barely enough for Kyle to see in front of him. He held the stick in his hand, not noticing that Harvey was already with him in the darkness. Without Kyle noticing, he had breezed into the classroom before the door had closed.

Harvey surprised him, tackling him out of the shadows, snapping and clawing like a panther. Kyle was using all his strength to keep him at bay, and Kyle didn't have a lot of strength—believe me. He couldn't allow himself to be bitten, not again.

Harvey almost had him. Drool dripped from his mouth, splattering onto Kyle's cheek.

"Oh, *gross!*" Kyle yelled.

 Kyle was barely holding Harvey's teeth away from his neck when he spied the cord to the UV lamps hanging beside him, the same UV lamps that gave light to the worthless plants we were growing. With a jerk, all of the lamps tumbled on top of them. The lights illuminated the whole room.

Harvey began to shriek and smolder as Kyle crawled backward, grabbing another lamp and turning the light directly on him like a flamethrower. Harvey jumped to his feet and wailed with fury through the scorching flames. He charged Kyle, full force, like a flaming steamroller. Kyle ducked behind the lamp using it as a shield and braced himself for the tackle.

*Bam!*

Harvey exploded into an ashy blaze of smoke before he reached him. Then, he was gone, leaving Kyle covered in his muck. I enjoyed that part because Kyle now knew what it felt like to be covered in vampire grime.

He slowly opened his eyes and looked around the room. He could smell the stench of cooked flesh all around him.

"Oh, God…Vickie!" he said to himself.

He scrambled down the hallway toward the gymnasium. He slid to a stop at the gym and grabbed the doors, tugging at the handles, but they were locked tight. He had to find a way in to save me, to rescue us all.

But how?

# READY TO RUMBLE

lack's eyes searched through the crowd and met mine. It was as if
she was purposely adding dramatic pause to the announcement
because she knew I was anticipating the results.

"Come on!" yelled a student from the back of the gym.

Black looked back to me and smiled. "Jessica Moores…"

The crowd applauded and, yes, I joined them.

Come on, you must have known it wasn't going to be me. It's no big deal;
don't be disappointed—I wasn't. I had only begun to step into the social life,
and I wasn't certain I even wanted to be there. Jessica thrived on things like
that; it was what she lived for.

She giggled, squealed, and jumped up and down as if she had won the
lottery. *Blah, blah, blah.* She made her way toward the stage waving to the crowd
as if we cared. I just smiled and shook my head.

Rod's grip tightened on my hand, causing me to turn to him. He smiled
sweetly, giving me a look as if to say, *It doesn't matter—you have me.* I smiled back
to him, because he was right. Jessica could have all of the crowns and attention
she wanted; just so long as I had Rod, all was right with the world. I leaned in
to him and kissed his cheek.

"I need a drink!" I yelled. "You want to come?"

Rod shook his head and began to follow me to the back of the gymnasium.

"Where is Kyle?" he said.

"Who knows? He's probably molesting poor Lucinda," I said.

Jessica walked up to the microphone. "I would like to thank all of you who voted for me. This is truly, truly an honor."

"Take it off!" yelled the voice from the back of the room.

"Shut up, Steven!" Jessica said. "Anyway, I am so glad to be named the first annual Queen of Halloween."

"I didn't know you were supposed to do an acceptance speech," I said.

"You're not. Look at Mrs. Black," Rod laughed.

Black kept trying to grab the microphone from her. I laughed. It was just like Jess to act as if she'd just won the Miss America title. However, something caught my eye. Behind where Jessica, Brewskie, and Mrs. Black stood, I could see the lid of one of the makeshift caskets begin to slowly open. Initially, I didn't think it was a big deal. I thought one of the teachers was going to jump out for added effect. Yet, through the darkness, I recognized the scarred face of the monstrous Mr. Parsons.

"Oh, God," I said, dropping my cup.

"What? What's the matter?" Rod said.

"We've got to get everyone out of here, now!" I broke into a full run toward the stage, trying to push my way through the crowd. Jessica remained at the mic, going on and on. "Jessica! Jessica! Watch out! Get off the stage!"

Murray noticed Parsons and ran to meet me. "We've got to get out of here!"

"I know. Help me get everyone out," I said.

Jessica squinted her eyes and looked into the crowd at me. "Vickie?" she said over the microphone.

"Run!" I said.

"Run? What are you talking about? See, Jenkins, I knew you'd act this way. You think you're so hot. You're not ruining this for me!" she shot.

Parsons shuffled through the darkness of the stage behind Jessica. As he worked his jaws, preparing to have dinner, I could see his face was damaged from the Flare I had released at the mortuary.

Jess continued going off on me in front of everyone, but I couldn't hear her. I tried to make it through the crowd as quickly as I could. Black turned around to see Parsons behind them and took two steps back, falling into the

DJ equipment and off the stage. Everyone laughed hysterically as music began to queue. Brewskie saw the thing and ran like a shot.

"Everybody, shut up!" Jessica protested.

I stopped at the front of the stage, completely out of breath. "Jessica!"

"What!" Jessica yelled.

"Get off the stage!" I screamed.

Parsons' long claws reached out to her.

"You know what, Jenkins? *Bite me!*"

Well...

Blood spurted from Jessica's neck, turning the white coif of her nun's costume crimson. The students broke into hysteria as vampires entered the gym from every angle. I stood there in a state of confusion—I didn't know what to do or where to go. I looked around and saw Rod running toward me. He grabbed my arms, pulling me down to the floor. Murray met us there.

"What the hell! I thought they were all gone?" Rod said.

I said, "I did, too! Are you okay? Where is Kyle?"

"I don't know. What are we going to do? We don't have anything to fight them with. Do you have anything?" Rod said to Murray.

"No! Who do you think I am? Batman? I don't wear a utility belt!" Murray replied.

The music from the abandoned DJ station pumped louder. As the bass began to build, I could hear an engine revving in the distance. Headlights shined through the cracks of the main gymnasium doors from the courtyard.

"Uh...I think we'd better move," I said.

I took them by the hands and yanked them out of the way just in time for Kyle's truck to shatter through the doors, throwing vampires in every direction. Kyle screeched to a stop in the middle of the gymnasium court and jumped out of the truck.

"Woman! Get with it! We got stuff to do!" Kyle said.

I smiled and grabbed Rod and Murray. "Come on!"

We popped the back of Kyle's truck to reach the artillery we had left inside. I grabbed my bow and loaded up new arrows.

It was time to play.

"What do we do?" Rod said.

"I'm not sure, but I think we'll want to avoid dying!" I yelled. "Here, pass these out to everyone. Get the football team together. Everyone has to fight if they want to stay alive."

The battle began. I began sailing arrows through the air, never missing my target. Other students had begun to fight as well. The music pulsed louder and louder. Three of the monsters galloped across the stage and leapt at Rod. He turned and let loose one of the Flares, flashing the vampires away. Matt ran to him.

"Dear God, man! What is going on? What do we do?" Matt said in a panic.

"Get the guys together. Hurry!" Rod replied.

Matt began to bark the Rutgers High bark, calling the other team members over. The panicked group came from all over the gym and huddled around Rod.

"Rod, man, what the hell?" David Rickets said.

"Come on, Rod. Tell us what to do," Pete said.

"Listen, guys. This is our chance to be the heroes. We can't let these things take over our school. This is *our* world—not theirs! Either we can fight, or we can die. And I don't want to hear any wimpy crap like, 'Rod, these are *vampires*, man!' No! None of that. We are Rottweilers, and we're here to whoop ass!"

"Damn right!" yelled Pete excitedly.

"Let's get it on!" David said.

"All right, guys. Take these. If you've seen a vampire movie, you know what to do. *Do not* let them bite you. Hit 'em hard, hit 'em fast. We've got the plays; we've got the talent. Are we ready?"

"Yeah," they said.

"*Dammit!* I said, are we ready?!" Rod yelled.

"Yeah!" I heard them yell.

"Then…*let's stick it to 'em!*" Rod screamed.

The team yelled their battle cry as they dispersed into the sea of goons. They tackled them, threw them into the air, and tossed them like rag dolls as they stabbed their chests. They began to run plays on them as if they were on the field with an opposing team.

I had to admit, it was the best I had ever seen them play.

Kyle had run out of weapons. He had to get back to the truck and restock as soon as possible before he was minced meat. He was just about to run back to the truck when nearly a dozen of the vampires cornered him. He didn't know what to do. He had nothing, no way to fight them. The funny thing was they didn't attack him. They just stood there, stupefied, confused at what they were seeing. To them, Kyle looked like another vampire.

After a second, the realization clicked with Kyle. Without missing a beat, he hunched over with a growl and began hissing and clawing. As he crept away, they followed as he led them all the way to the back of the truck. He dug for weapons as he snarled and hissed along with them, when suddenly his fangs flopped out of his mouth and down his chest to the floor. *Whoopsie!*

They looked down to the teeth and then back at him with a grumble. Kyle giggled nervously as they began to lurch toward him. He spun around and grabbed the Divine Light ball from the truck bed. He tossed it to the ground in front of them. They cautiously jumped back in fear. Kyle stomped the button on the top…but it did nothing, just like when we had tried it at Murray's house. The vampires smiled.

As they began to advance, Kyle stomped and stomped on the ball, but nothing happened. Then he spied a small lever on the side of the ball we hadn't noticed before. One leapt for him as he bent down and snapped the lever to the right. Then, the ball began to shudder and shine.

The vampires began to back away. The glowing ball rose and started to hover about four feet in the air. Suddenly, laser-like lights shot out from all around the orb, lights in the shape of small crucifixes. The ball began to rotate, burning the vampires as they ran off in fear. Some didn't escape in time and burst into flames, others melted, but all of them ran. After a moment more, the ball stopped and floated back to the floor, going dark. It was wicked. Seems Murray's son knew what he was doing after all.

"Dumbasses," Kyle laughed as he gathered more supplies to rejoin the fight.

Okay—cheerleaders. I don't like them. Hate them as I may, I saw that two of the vamps had backed Teresa and four other cheerleaders into the corner of the gym, preparing to pounce. I armed my bow and pulled the string tight, but I couldn't get a clear lock on them without endangering one of the girls. Then, I had a great idea. Maybe Brewskie's mix inspired me.

"Teresa!" I yelled. Teresa turned to me with tears in her eyes. "Teresa! Step back!" She looked to me, confused. *"Step back, Teresa!"*

As the music continued to beat on, Teresa realized what I was telling her. It was her chance to be the lead. On rhythm, she reluctantly broke into the routine as the other girls followed her. The vampires looked baffled. Of course, they didn't know what kind of fit the girls were having or what they were doing, but they seemed curious.

With a quick flip, Teresa landed on Tina's shoulders, giving me a clear shot at the heads of the creatures. In an instant, I sent an arrow sailing. The vampire's eyes grew huge with surprise as the arrow sailed between Teresa's legs, sinking through both of them. It pinned their heads together as they liquefied into an icky mess. Teresa looked back at me with a thankful gaze as we exchanged a thumb's up. Then, she fell with a thud off Tina's shoulders into the mucky mess below.

I reached into the mix of weapons from Kyle's truck, trying to find something fantastic, when I saw three Coldseekers. I threw the bow across my shoulder and held the large stakes. It was at that moment that I saw him standing there on the stage, patiently watching the battle. Vladimir smiled as he looked into my eyes.

Murray had spotted him, too. She pulled out two stakes and sprinted toward the stage. He never took his eyes off me for second, not even when he blocked Murray and grabbed her by the neck. He had no time to be bothered; he was there for me and only me.

"Oh, sweet, sweet, Miranda. If I could still love, I would love you," Vladimir cooed. "You are so like Mina."

Then, Murray smashed a holy water vial against his hand, nearly wilting it away. He shrieked and knocked her backward into the props. I watched as his hand grew back almost instantaneously. Then, he stomped up to Miranda, took one of the stakes from her hand, and plunged it into her stomach. She looked deep into the dark pools of his eyes, not believing what had happened.

"No!" I cried.

I ran through the line of vampires and activated the Coldseekers, and they began to beep as I threw them into the air. The three stakes separated into fifteen shards and nailed into the cold hearts of vampires they sought. Two shards managed to case Vladimir. He swatted the first away like a bothersome fly, but the second sunk into his other hand. He looked at me in awe of the weapon and then yanked the wood from his palm, tossing the smoking stick to the ground. I had nearly made my way up the steps when a certain vampire I had overlooked caught me unaware.

Who was it?

You guessed it!

The now grisly Jessica jumped me as I started up the steps after Murray and Dracula. I fell onto the steps with her at my back. As I turned around to fight her off, my other arm became trapped under the steps of the stage. I couldn't gain the advantage. As if it could grow any larger, she opened her great big mouth and came for my throat. Of course, nothing would have pleased her more than taking off my head. Then, out of nowhere, a handful of Holy Powder popped her right in the mouth! Jessica fell to the floor, gagging, smoking, struggling to spit out the rest of the powder.

Pete helped me up.

"Thank you, Pete!" I said.

"You're welcome, Vickie. Duck!" he said as one of the vampires flew over our heads barely missing us. "Now, go!"

Vladimir smiled like a smartass and faded into a fog that began to trail up the steps of the backstage area. I ran to Murray.

"Oh, no, oh, no, no, no…Miranda, please, wake up," I said to her as the blood flowed from her gut.

"Vickie, go. Don't worry about me," Murray said. "You have to kill him. Go!"

# BLESSED BE

That night, Pete Thorning became my hero in more ways than one. He watched me disappear up the stairs after Vladimir; then, he noticed something out of his peripheral vision. The bloody nun rose up next to him. Jessica reached to her mouth and scooped out the last of the soggy Holy Powder as she healed.

She laughed. In a flash, she attacked him, knocking him to the ground. He began to kick at her and she caught his foot. She forcefully twisted it to the left, fracturing his ankle. Pete screamed in pain and kicked her in the face with his other foot. She fell with a plop to the ground.

Pete got up and began to hobble away from her as fast as he could. She stood again and began to follow him. He made his way through the double doors of the swim team locker room, took a stake, and shoved it through the handles of the doors, locking them in place. She rattled the doors, peering at him through the small windowpane. He knew the piece of wood alone was not going to hold her long.

He limped through the lockers into the pool area that had been closed for cleaning. He knew if he could just make his way back to the supply closet, he could lock himself inside. The locker room doors burst open; she was inside. He made it to the far end of the large Olympic-sized pool and heard a *crack* as

209

his ankle completely broke. He screamed and toppled to the floor. There was no way he could go any farther. He began to crawl.

That was it. He just knew he was going to die, and at the hands of *Sister Mary Vampire!*

"Oh, Peter," Jessica said seductively from the other end of the room.

Pete stopped and turned around to see her standing at the other edge of the pool, facing the ceramic steps. "Uh, hey, there, Jess. Sorry about that, uh, powder in the mouth thing."

She took off her blood-soaked habit and tossed it to the ground. She looked at him with her pale skin and black eyes. Her flesh had already begun to wilt. She smiled a bloody smile and began unzip her costume.

"Pete," she muttered. "You know, I've always wanted you. And I know you've always wanted me." She let her costume fall to the floor, leaving her standing in only her bra and panties. "Well, I am ready. I'm ready to give myself to you."

Pete looked at her disgusted and said, "Uh, *ewww!*"

In true Jessica fashion, he said she placed a hand on her hip, cocked her head, and said, "Listen, idiot. I'm *still* hot. Anybody would want to get with this!"

She sank one foot into the pool and began to submerge herself into the blue water. Once completely under water, she swam toward where he lay immobilized. He could see her image morph into what appeared to be a massive black beast with the wings of a bat. The wings flapped in the water, propelling it along.

Well, poor Pete didn't know what to do. The thing would be at him in only moments. His heart pulverized his ribcage. At that moment, he could feel the cool gold of his father's crucifix around his neck. He reached down, touched the water, and tasted it. There was no chlorine added yet. It was just water, untreated and clean. He reached into his costume and pulled out the golden cross. Showing it to the water, he did the only thing he knew to do.

"I consecrate this water, Dear Lord," he said as she swam closer.

"May it be used for blessings."

She was only ten feet from him. She moved forward like a missile.

"Dear Lord, please take this creature into your heart and forgive her for her sins."

Five feet.

"I baptize you, Jessica Moores, in the name of the Father, the Son, and the Holy Spirit."

She erupted through the surface of the water directly in front of him, melting and screaming as her enormous wings flapped back and forth through the muck. She reached for him as she was immersed in the bubbling acid of the holy water he had created out of the entire pool. He caught one last glimpse of what used to be Jessica Moores as she disappeared into the slime. The pungent smoke from the water filled Pete's nose as he rolled over onto his back and tried to catch his breath.

"See!" he said throwing a hand into the air. "And they said seminary school would lead nowhere! Woo hoo!" He made a peace sign. "Hallelujah! God is good, y'all!"

# MEANING OF LIFE

While Pete caught his breath, I followed the trail of the fog to the roof of the school. Vladimir obviously wanted to lead me away from the safety of the large group of students. That was all right; *he* was the one who was going to need safety, not me. I had no fear inside, only anger fueled by the fire of determination. I felt as if someone else was with me, watching me, guiding me.

I slung open the door and stepped onto the gravel rooftop. There, standing with one foot on the ledge, staring into the night sky, was Vladimir. The moonlight shone through my angelic white wings. Looking like a pissed-off cupid, I drew an arrow and shot before I could even think about it. He caught it without even turning around.

"Stop!" he said. "Take a seat." He cracked the arrow in half and tossed it to the ground. "Let's talk."

I said, "I don't want to talk to—"

"Please! Insolent girl. I do wish you were more like Abraham." He turned back to the stars. "I miss him sometimes, you know. He was a very entertaining enemy. He and I used to talk for hours. We knew when to fight, and when to talk. When it was time to talk, we understood and respected that. Sit."

"I don't trust you," I said.

He said, "If there is anyone in this world whose word you can trust, it is mine, Victoria. Now, sit."

I huffed impatiently but was curious about what he had to say. How many times do you get to have an *interview with a vampire*? I believed he wasn't trying to trick me. I didn't know why I believed him, but I did all the same. Finding a somewhat comfortable place near a vent, I took a seat.

I was mad as hell, so I said, "Okay. So what do you want to talk about? You want to talk about how you've killed a bunch of my friends? Or do you want to talk about how you want to kill me too?"

"Oh, please, your friend will be fine. I hit no organs. She will recover in time," he said.

I said, "Okay, so what do you want?"

"I want to talk about life," he said.

I was stunned for a moment by the sincerity of his voice.

"What do you know about life?" I said.

He said, "I know I live, just as you live. Your necessity is no greater than mine. We are the same, you and I."

"But you take human life!" I said.

He laughed. "I take what? I take life! There is no *human* life. I grow so tired of hearing people talk about humans and their right to live! Your life is no greater than the life of the cattle you slaughter for your hamburgers or the fowl you kill for your *Kentucky* chicken!"

"Those are animals!" I said.

He said, "*You* are an animal, too, Victoria. Have you ever looked into the eyes of cattle and witnessed the humbleness, the wisdom? Do you ever stop to think about what crosses a bird's mind before you take its head? No, you don't. You humans think that because you have opposable thumbs and some type of limited intellect you are more important than other living things around you, but you are *not*. Your lives are no more precious than the worms that dig under your feet. To me, you are a talking cow, Victoria. I have knowledge and wisdom that spans thousands of lifetimes. Because I am smarter, does that make me better?"

I looked to him defiantly. "Smarter? You didn't even know what 'dude' meant! You'd like to *think* you're smarter, is all."

"No! No, I do *not* think so. Nevertheless, we have to live, you and I. Living is a loop. Just as you take the swine to the slaughter, I take you, the human.

Maybe if we all learned to respect life a little more, we would all be better organisms," he said.

You know, I hated to admit it, but it made sense, respectful sense. I had never stopped to think about how the hornet in my room felt when I crushed it that day, the day that seemed so long ago now, though it had just happened. What made my life any greater than that of a lamb?

"Why are you telling me this?" I asked.

"Because I want you to be more like Abraham, Victoria. Van Helsing had that respect, that honor. You, alas, do not, and it saddens me," he said.

"Did you respect Xavier before you killed him?" I asked.

"Yes! Yes, I did. He didn't feel a thing. I slowly took away his misery. I sat with him the entire time as he drifted on. His death was far gentler than the death anyone has attempted to bestow upon me," Vladimir shouted.

I looked away. "I can't let you do this, Vladimir."

"I know you cannot. Abraham could not either, you know. I am sure if a cow could shoot a rifle, humans would be more afraid of them than they are of me. Could you imagine…a big bovine with a double-barrel shotgun waiting on you?" He laughed.

I giggled unconsciously and stopped myself, feeling it inappropriate. You have to admit, Bessie sitting in the field with a shotgun does up the stakes, though.

I said, "Okay, so here's a wild thought. Why can't we learn to live together?"

"Well, because I need human blood, and I don't believe humans would allow themselves to be farmed. I mean, if you would, then we'd have a deal. Maybe I could have the degenerates, the criminals. Hmmm," he tapped his chin in thought.

The coolness of the night swept around my feet.

"You're strange," I said.

He laughed. "Tell me about it, *dude*." He listened to the crowd in the gymnasium. I could see the light from the Divine Light, the flashes of the Flares. "They are winning, you know, your friends. No matter. I shall make more."

"So, what do we do now?" I asked.

Vladimir turned around to me. "Well, in a moment, we are going to fight. You are going to think you have beaten me again, and then I am going to turn you and make you lead my army. That is the way I see it, anyway."

I smiled. "So, when do you want to start?"

Vladimir took a deep breath. "Well," he said standing to face me. "Let's begin now. Ready?"

I stood and pulled out the two hand swords I had taken from the truck. "*Let's…*"

We began.

I flipped, head over feet with the blades slicing through the air. Vladimir puffed into fog as I passed through him. He materialized too soon, resulting in a slice on his cheekbone. He reached up and touched the dark blood that ran down his cheek.

"My…where did you get those?" he asked.

"Are they not the coolest? Miranda had them," I replied.

I pulled a stake from my bag and hurled it at him. It barely missed him. Then, I pulled out a Flare and set it off. He deflected the flash as he morphed into mist again. Using a Coldseeker, I tried again. As it exploded into sections, he dodged every shard, deflecting the last one back to me. I flipped to my right, allowing it to barely miss me, grazing my arm, the red blood shining brightly in the white satin of my costume.

Vladimir closed his eyes and took in my scent. It made him grow more diabolical. He growled at me and charged. I tripped him, but he flew around me before hitting the ground and reappeared in front of me.

I took a stake and sliced at him, barely missing him as his claws ripped through one of my wings, sending feathers floating into the air. Then, we heard beating on the door. It was Rod.

"Vickie! Are you up here?" Rod yelled.

Vladimir smacked my face, snatched one of the swords from me, and threw it at the door, jamming the blade into the lock. There was no way Rod could open it. Then, as Vladimir turned, an arrow entered his shoulder. He cried out in pain. Then, another came, and another—I sailed them through the air as if I was firing them from the barrel of a gun. He began to look like a messed up pincushion.

He fell to his knees, the purity of the wood burning in his veins. I walked to where he rested, defeated and tired. I wouldn't make the same mistake I did at Simmons. This time he would be dead for certain, for *good*. I'd use the other hand sword to take his head.

"It's over, Vlad," I said.

"Yes," he sighed.

I pulled my last stake from my bag and held it along with the sword. I reared back.

"Is there anything you'd like to say?" I asked.

"Yes," he said, barely able to breathe.

"What?" I asked.

"*You look like an angel,*" he said in a tone that stopped me cold.

Then, his body began to transform. His skin became odd and bubbly looking, turning into *bugs,* insects of every creepy-crawly kind. His body seemed to be made of the things. The arrows that had impaled him slowly sank into the mass of bugs and fell to the ground. The buggy thing smiled at me as it shattered apart, throwing a horde of insects all over the rooftop. They crunched under my feet as I stomped them and squealed, but there was no way to kill them all. *Ewww!*

Was it over?

That would be a *no.* And I knew it wasn't over. He was there. It was just a question of where. I remained armed and searched all around me, my heart pounding in my ears, breath quickening. As I began to back against the wall, slowly and cautiously, I didn't see the insects piling up behind me, fusing back together, opening their mouth.

Vladimir sank his teeth deep into my neck. I reached behind me to try to stop him, but it was no use—I could feel the virus entering my body, taking over my blood. It burned like wildfire. He stepped away, letting me drop to the gravel. I screamed as the sickness ate at me. It ran in dark lines through the surface of my skin, filling my eyes with blackness. I was turning; he had won. At that moment, I let go; I allowed the fear to leave me. There was nothing else to do but accept it.

Then, I remembered Abraham's diary.

# October One Continued

"Well, shall we?" I asked as he gathered himself, realizing what had to follow.

Vladimir finished off the last of the whiskey.

"Let's..." he said.

He ran at me, kicking the coffin toward where I stood. I jumped over the casket with ease and loaded my bow while in the air. I shot two arrows at once, making sure I would not miss, and I did not. The first soared past Vladimir, but the second sank into his leg. He yanked it from his muscle and spun around, stabbing at me with it. I blocked his attack and throttled his ears with the palms of my hands. He grabbed his throbbing ears in pain.

As he swept me from my feet, I fell to the floor, tossing a stake into the air toward the dirt ceiling. Then, as we began to wrestle, the stake dropped downward, sinking into his back. He screeched, and I pushed him from me.

One of the vampires appeared from nowhere, and I impaled it with an arrow. Then, another advanced.

"No!" called Vladimir.

Another came from behind me and sank its fangs into my arm.

"I said no!"

And with that, Vladimir shoved his fists deep into the chests of the creatures, ripping their blackened hearts from the cavity, causing them to explode. This battle was to be between the two of us, and that was all. Vladimir considered unwarranted assistance dishonest, a cheater's game.

Gasping, I said, "I do believe you cheated, my good man."

Vladimir looked to me and wiped his bloody hands.

He said to me, "Abraham. I do apologize. I did not expect them to do this."

"No... do not worry. I understand. Thank you for stopping them," I replied

"Do not thank me yet, Abraham."

Then, the burning began. I fell to the ground at Vladimir's feet. He scooped me up in his arms and laid me atop one of the caskets.

"Shhh... do not fight it, Abraham. I hate that it happened this way, I do. I had wanted to do this myself. It would have been... easier. Now, relax and let it take you. We will be great friends—forever."

My eyes rolled into my skull and ran black as night as fangs lined my mouth. I growled ferociously. My fingers grew into long, clawed digits that dug into the wooden lid of the casket I was stretched upon.

"Vladimir..." I moaned.

"Yes, yes. It is almost done now. If that stupid beast had bit the neck, it would not be as painful," he consoled.

As I had planned, the virus began to subside. My left eye returned to normal. Out of my jacket rolled the steel syringe, my salvation, falling to the ground beside Vladimir's foot. I coughed and spat as the thick black virus of the bite began to seep from the wound and from my mouth. Vladimir backed away from me. He reached down and picked up the syringe.

"What?" he yelled.

I rolled from the casket and fell to the floor, breathing heavily and saying, "I am immune to your sickness, Count. I made certain of it long ago. True, the injections are quite painful, but they have safeguarded me from you."

Indeed, the drug addict was not an addict at all. The injections I had been giving myself were a solution of my own design mixed with vampire blood to make myself stronger against their virus, knowing eventually Vladimir would want me to join his faction.

Vladimir snapped my syringe in two. "You sly old fox."

I smiled and stood upright.

"Shall we continue?" Vladimir said.

"Certainly!" I replied.

Vladimir ran toward me as I shot an arrow into the earthy wall behind him.

"You missed! Are you sure you do not need a moment?" Vladimir said.

I motioned for him to continue. As he neared, I stabbed his neck with a stake and kicked him backward. The arrow I had purposely planted into the wall behind him erupted through his chest, nailing him there. Smoke poured from the wound as he howled in anguish. I walked up to him and shoved another stake through his chest. Grabbing his hand, I removed the golden ring from his finger, slipping it onto my own: my token. I turned my back on Vladimir and reached inside my coat to obtain the final stake.

"This is not over," he spat at me as the dark, foul blood dripped from his mouth.

"I know," I said. "Alas, it is about to be."

Though, when I turned around, I sunk the stake into an empty wall of earth that was now vacant of Vladimir's presence. The ring faded into darkness, telling me he was gone, but not forever.

I smiled.

# BLOOD MAGIC

As Abraham's story twirled through my head, I began to drift back into the light. At first, I didn't know how. The burning in my veins was beginning to fade away. Vladimir watched as my skin began to morph back to normal and my eyes transitioned to the sky blue they previously had been. He backed away from me, completely pissed. I nearly laughed aloud because I could tell the old bat was remembering.

"No…no! This is not happening again! What is it about you Van Helsings? Abraham took injections. He used the blood to keep himself safe. But you!"

I coughed and tried to stand. "How do you like that?"

"What is this magic?" he whispered to himself.

It wasn't magic at all. The injections Abraham administered to himself as protection against a vampire bite had become part of his genetic code. It all made sense. It was the same crap Mrs. Black went on and on about in class. What Abraham had done was create a solution that triggered his body's primary response to the vampire virus without causing the direct symptoms of infection.

A *vaccine.*

It was textbook. Without knowing it, Abraham had passed down his little gift through his children, his bloodline. He had given me the most special weapon of all.

*Immunity.*

And not only did my blood carry resistance to the vampire virus, it also carried a toxin, like *Vampire Raid!* I watched as Drac's skin began to bubble up with hives, as if he was having an allergic reaction to me. His eyes began to weep black tears as he gazed in wonder at his pale, patchy skin.

*"What is this magic!"* screamed the sickly Vladimir.

I stood up and looked him in the face. "Come on!"

He charged me with his mouth wide just as Rod broke through the door. If Vladimir couldn't turn me, he'd *kill* me. Reaching into my bag, I dodged to the right, allowing him to pass me.

"It's not magic," I answered.

As Vladimir turned, I could see that I'd managed to shove the last holy water vial into his big old mouth.

"It's called *naturally acquired passive immunity,* asshole!"

With that, I sent my final arrow sailing, shattering the glass and blowing Dracula's head into smithereens. His body flailed back and forth, searching for the head that was now gone, and then gradually drained into white sand on the ground, hands reaching for me, hoping to take me to the pits of death along with it. I fell to my knees, dropping the bow as Rod ran to me, grabbing me into his arms.

"I got a friggin' A on that quiz!" I sobbed into Rod's chest causing him to giggle a bit.

Now there was only a pile of dust where Vladimir once stood. Something glistened in the ash. Steadying myself, I walked to it and saw the ring laying there in the powder, reflecting the bright moonlight. The night air blew the particles around in a semi-whirlwind, leading me to the realization that what I felt was not relief or pride, but sadness. You're going to think I'm a freak, but there was something wonderful about Dracula—his wisdom, his philosophy. Eating people was the screwed-up part. The wind blew the last of his ashes into the night sky, and I watched them as they drifted into the abyss. The glowing stone within the bat's chest faded into black, and I picked up the ring and slipped it onto my thumb.

"Is it over?" Rod asked.

"Yeah, it's over," I said with a smile…and a tear.

# MY STORY

So, that's my story, and I'm sticking to it. You can bet that after the Halloween Ball, things changed for Kyle and me. We were no longer the outsiders looking in, the oddballs blending into the background. Kyle has turned into an even bigger doofus, but everyone likes his idiocy. I blossomed into a bright, semi-cute young woman who has an extra gift, an *ability*…and a junky butt.

There is a new sense of camaraderie among the student body at Rutgers. Those petty socialistic lines between attractive/unattractive, jock/nerd, and rich/poor simply faded away. That's what happens when someone saves your ass, of course. And we all saved many asses that night.

Kyle ended up with Lucinda, and they've been inseparable. They're so cute. Me? Oh, I got my prince, that's for sure. I think I kind of freak him out sometimes, though. A guy can only see his girlfriend kill so many vampires before it freaks him out. I didn't realize that.

Maybe I should include that in my valedictory lecture.

God, I despise public speaking. I'll add that to my *hate* list—stupid people, dead people, and *public speaking*. I've rewritten my speech so many times that I can recite it from memory. It goes:

*Good evening, senior class, faculty and friends. Here we are at the end of not only another school year, but also the end of our time at Rutgers High. Tonight we have come together to celebrate a turning point in our lives.*

*I could stand here for hours and try to give you the standard graduation pep talk about how we need to move forward into the future with hope and blah-blah-blah, but that would be mind numbing.*

*The scary part is that we can fill the future will all the hope we want, but it remains a future of uncertainty. Though I've been trapped at Rutgers with you dead beats for four years now, this year is the first year that I truly began to learn something: about you, and about me.*

*So, what did I learn?*

*Well, I'm no longer the old me, and that's good because the old me was silly. I could've gotten so much more accomplished if I could've just tapped the old me on the shoulder and clued her in to a few things.*

*I would have said, "Hello, Old Me. I want you to know some things about yourself. First, I want you know that, no matter what you think, you are pretty. You're not plain or ugly. I want you to know that you are smart. Most of all, I want you to know that you are special.*

*"I want you to know that you don't have to hide in the shadows. You're allowed to come into the light where you can be seen. You're allowed to fall in love with handsome princes who carry footballs. You're allowed to have friends. You're allowed to be loved.*

*"You're a fighter. You're a hero. You're Teresa Haffner. You're Lucinda Chandler. You're Missy Lynn. And, yes, you're even Jessica Moores. You're every young girl who has ever gone home and cried herself to sleep, every girl who has been afraid. Well, you don't have to be afraid anymore, Old Me."*

*Yeah—that's what I would've said to the old me. A very strange person I once knew taught me that the most important thing to life is simply—life. And no one life is greater than another. I think that's significant, because this year when things were their worst, we fought for each other's lives. And it didn't matter how much money someone had, or if they were popular, or if they were pretty—we were all together, on the same team. So, guys, above all else let's remember that. Let's remember each other. Never forget. None of us knows exactly what happened this year, but try to keep in mind how we all pulled together, and we did it regardless of our differences.*

*So, congratulations, everyone. I'll never forget you, and I hope you never forget me.*

Not bad, huh? I think it's okay as far as speeches go.

Tonight is going to be special. Not only because it's graduation, but also because there's a *full moon*. You see…I know they're out there, waiting to ruin my big moment and piss me off. They don't think I'm aware, but I have a big, furry idea.

I *feel* it.

That's the bad thing about being a Van Helsing…nothing creepy gets by you.

Dude, I hope Murray has some *silver bullets!*

# About The Author

A.J. Grea is an author and screenwriter living in East Tennessee with his husband of twenty years, three snarky cats, and a meddlesome squirrel who will not stay away from the windows. A lover of 80s horror, he began writing short stories at the age of nine.

One of his first stories, "The Monster Who Ate My Brother," resulted in a parent-teacher conference, during which his mother had to assure the concerned faculty that his siblings were fine.

When not spinning hair-raising yarns, A.J. spends time as most middle-aged comic book fans do--playing video games and collecting childhood toys that remind him of when his only responsibility was being home before streetlights began to glow.